Table of Contents

THE WHISPERING DEATH

By Sara Jayne Townsend

DEDICATION

For Michael McNulty
Friend, fellow LARPer and fan.
Thanks for leading the cheering squad.

ACKNOWLEDGEMENTS

This book was a great deal of fun to write, as I got to make reference to all my favourite nerd hobbies – D&D, LARP and *Resident Evil* – in one novel.

I need to go back to the beginning to say thank you – to Paul Froese, my first GM, when I joined my high school's D&D club in the tenth grade and first discovered the thrill of table top RPGs and how much fun it could be to escape to this interactive fantasy world.

Love and thanks to my husband, Chris Harlow, who's been my GM for over 25 years. Geeks who play together, stay together.

Thanks also to the boys and girls of the Heroquest Live Action Role Playing group, where I learned that there can be fun to be had running around the Forest of Dean lugging props and foam weapons about, especially if you are the group's only healer because then everyone wants to be your friend.

Thank you to Gary Couzens, Sarah Ellender, Laura Mauro and Damian O'Connor of the T Party Writers' Group for acting as my beta readers, and to Dave Gullen for suggesting the title.

And finally, I would like to acknowledge all those who've ever been called 'nerd' or 'geek' or 'dork'; who know the pain of rolling a 1 on a D20; who can recite every single line of dialogue in *Star Wars* episode 4 (in the right order); and who have named their pets (or even their kids) after RPG characters. You are my tribe, and without us the world would be a poorer place.

FOREWORD BY KENSINGTON GORE

We all play a role in life, partner, parent, sibling, friend.
There are some that role play. I for one have never dabbled.
Preferring instead to play my roles more on film, as a director
the creator of strange new worlds and lives and things that
scare and terrorise.

There are some that role play is a way of life, or to some
even death. *The Whispering Death* is about role playing and
unleashing evil. A mighty evil that can tear the world apart.
Just goes to show some games are very deadly indeed.

Sara Jayne Townsend is a very good writer, a female writer
that knows how to scare and connect with her reader. I for one
am so glad she connected with me and my publishing
company and I look forward to working closely with her and
publishing her books for many years to come.

Sara Jayne has a rather dark side, you have to understand
horror, but is a wonderful human being, and I am happy to
say a true friend.

CHAPTER 1

In the darkness of the forest, candlelight illuminated a group of six figures, their faces hidden beneath oversized brown hoods. A five pointed star was marked out on the scrubby ground with strips of white fabric, secured into the ground by metal spikes at each point. At each of these points, a shrouded figure knelt, holding a candle. Other candles marked out the perimeter, casting a flickering light that caused shadows to dance across the trees that encircled the forest clearing. The leader of the group, Cassius, stood in the centre of the pentagram, a candle in one hand and a sheet of aged parchment in the other. The words he read from the parchment were not in English, and though he occasionally stumbled over the unfamiliar language, he mostly read them clearly and unfaltering. When he finished reciting the words of the ritual he lowered the parchment and declared, "It is done."

The five figures that had been crouched around the pentagram got to their feet. "What now?" said Arlon, the chink of chainmail under his cloak revealing his warrior status.

"We head back to camp," Cassius said. "Our work here is done."

"Nothing's happening," said Ariadne, the party's healer.

"It will take time for the ritual to take effect. There's nothing else we can do tonight. We should head back to camp and get some rest. We'll know by morning whether or not it has worked." He moved around the pentagram, blowing out each candle one by one.

Holding battle candles to light the way, the six figures formed a straggling line as they headed through the woods. "We should be cautious," Cassius said. "The Minions of Darkness may be aware of what we've done. They might come seeking vengeance."

"But I thought we'd banished the demon?" said the group's scout, Pandora, with uncertainty. "Isn't that what the ritual did?"

"If we have indeed succeeded in banishing the demon, the magic user controlling it will know by now. He will undoubtedly send his minions out for revenge. Pandora, why don't you go scout? Let us know if anything's lying in wait for us."

Pandora nodded. Dousing the flame on her candle, she hurried silently up the path, slipping into the shadows and disappearing into the darkness.

"I don't like it, Cass," Arlon the warrior said. "We should have waited for daylight. In the dark, we're ripe for an ambush."

"As I've already explained Arlon, time is of the essence. The beast is gathering its full strength from the darkness.

If we'd have waited until morning, it would have been invincible.

By banishing it now, we only have to deal with the Minions of Darkness, not the demon itself."

Arlon peered into the darkness, unsheathing his sword. "There's someone out there."

"It's me," said Pandora, her disembodied voice coming out of the blackness.

"Did you see anything?" Cassius asked.

Pandora moved into the group and lowered her voice. "There's a group of four undead on the path up ahead. Two skeletons. One zombie. Another we haven't seen before. Looks more powerful. Maybe a ghoul?"

"Oh great," Arlon groaned. "Just when I was looking forward to a tankard of ale back at the camp."

"I told you our work wasn't done yet," said Cassius. He addressed the group one by one. "Okay, Valkyrie, you go for the zombie. They move slowly, you'll be fine. Koran, you've got a mace, go in for the skeletons. Only blunt weapons will defeat them.

Arlon and I will go for the other undead beastie; we've both got magic weapons and we might need them. Ariadne, if you can, try and get a hit on the skeletons with your mace too. But don't put yourself at risk; you're our only healer. And Pandora, keep to the shadows and try and find a chance to use that killer backstab of yours. Everybody ready?" Cassius looked around at his group.

The sound of a techno beat resounded in the darkness. "Fucking hell," Cassius muttered. "Who's that?"

The others pointed at the warrior Valkyrie, who was rummaging around in her pack. Her hood slipped off, and a mane of dyed blonde hair fell over her face.

"Chelsea, how many times do I have to tell you to leave your fucking phone back at camp?"

"Sorry, David." Chelsea pulled her iPhone from her pack and hastily hit the button to cancel the call.

David – also known as mage and party leader Cassius – threw his latex staff down on the ground.

"Who the hell's calling you at this time of night anyway?"

"I don't know," Chelsea said sheepishly. "I thought it was switched off."

"I don't know why the hell you've got it with you."

"I like to know what time it is."

"I keep telling you – no modern gadgets. If no one's allowed to carry watches, they sure as hell aren't allowed to carry mobile phones. If it rings again I'm going to toss it into the woods. Now you've really killed the mood. Just when I thought everyone was getting nice and spooked, your bloody phone rings."

"I'm really sorry. When we get back to camp I'll leave it with my stuff. Honest." Chelsea switched the phone off and stuffed it back into her pack.

David sighed. "Well, the monster crew know exactly where we are now, so we're not going to be able to surprise them. And if they heard that ring, I'll bet they're pissed off and ready to give us a hammering."

"They're between us and the camp," said the warrior Arlon, otherwise known as Mark. "Let's get this done so we can get back to the beer."

David picked up his latex staff and held it aloft. "Alright, crew. Let's go." Adopting a dramatic pose, he led his group of live action role players into battle.

CHAPTER 2

An hour or so later, Mark was feeling comfortably mellow in front of the camp fire. He drank Stella Artois from a pewter tankard and watched Elizabeth as she toasted some marshmallows. The weaponry he carried as Arlon, holy warrior and crusader, rested on the ground. He still wore his chainmail, heavy though it was. He'd learned from many years of live action roleplaying that you never took your armour off in camp. It took too long to get it on again and if you got ambushed you had to take the hits without the modification of armour, and that was a good way to die very quickly.

He had no idea what time it was, but he reckoned it had to be coming up to midnight. That last battle had been easier than he would have expected a final battle to be.

The zombies and the skeletons were fairly easy to despatch, but the ghoul had been tough.

Elizabeth's cleric was down on healing power too, so the party were now resting in camp, hoping that was it for the day. Mark had a feeling there'd be another battle though. They wouldn't be allowed to get off that easily. Not with one of David's games. They'd all have just enough time to sit around the fire getting cosy and pleasantly tipsy, before there'd be some Big Bad out in the forest that they'd have to go and deal with.

The fire was burning brightly, big orange flames licking the wooden logs that the site kept for these occasions. There had been no rain in Gloucester for six weeks and the wood was bone dry, making it just right for burning. The dry spell was about to end though – dark clouds had been gathering all day and the forecast had been threatening rain for a week.

They'd been lucky to have a dry weekend for this game. Mark cheerfully admitted to being a fair-weather LARPer – this was the first weekend of the year he'd ventured out onto a game.

Tromping about in the woods with foam swords and sleeping on bunks in wooden huts was all well and good when it was fair and dry, but it was a different story when it was wet and cold. As he watched the hypnotic flames from the camp fire, he felt the heat warming his face and hands and took another sip of his beer. It was evenings like this that he enjoyed the most when live action role playing. He and David had enjoyed many LARP weekends over the years, but it had been quite a while since David had been persuaded out – his medical studies took up much of his time nowadays. When he'd suggested to David that they have one more outing, before David got stuck into finals, he'd been surprised that David had agreed so readily.

He watched Elizabeth holding a long thin stick over the fire, a marshmallow speared to the end of it. Elizabeth had joined the game design company Mark worked for six months ago. Like him, she was a game designer.

Unlike him, she had a degree in software engineering.

Mark was just naturally talented when it came to understanding computers; Elizabeth had made it her passion. But a degree doesn't give you a high score in computer games – that came just as naturally to Elizabeth as it did to Mark. In fact, she was the keenest gamer Mark had ever met and in spite of several efforts he had made, he was yet to come anywhere near her score of total number of zombies slain in *Resident Evil*. Mark had fallen for Elizabeth the first time he met her. He had a thing for smart women. She was cute too, with her mane of auburn hair and her long eyelashes, enhanced by the glasses she generally wore.

She'd switched to contact lenses for the game, since running about in the woods was a good place to lose one's glasses, but he knew she didn't like wearing them and would take them out at the earliest opportunity.

First thing in the morning she would emerge from her bunk, squinting and marching straight to the toilet block with the little case she kept her contacts in.

Yes, there was no doubt that Mark had it bad for Elizabeth. The problem was he hadn't got around to telling her how he felt yet. He knew she was single and they chatted a lot at work about personal stuff as well as their jobs, but he was scared to take the plunge and ask her out.

Elizabeth held the stick over the fire, turning it around to toast the marshmallow on all sides. The long billowing sleeves of the blouse she wore as Ariadne dangled perilously near the fire.

"Watch yourself there, Ariadne," Mark said. "You don't want to set yourself on fire."

Elizabeth retrieved the stick from the fire and regarded the blackened marshmallow on the end of it. "Don't worry about me. I'm protected with a spell of fire resistance." She gingerly worked the marshmallow off the end of the stick.

"Spell of fire resistance?" Mark frowned at Elizabeth as she popped the gooey marshmallow into her mouth. "Don't I get a marshmallow?"

Elizabeth grinned at him as she chewed, pulling another marshmallow out of the bag on the floor and skewering it with her stick. "I liberally sprayed my costume with fire retardant. I am prepared for all occasions. And you can have this marshmallow." She returned the stick to the fire, turning it slowly to cook the marshmallow. "I called it a spell of fire resistance. I know David hates out of character talk."

"Not that those two are paying any attention." Mark looked across the fire to the other side, where Linus and Chelsea were sitting on a log together. Linus, aka Koran the fighting cleric, was Elizabeth's brother and had done LARPing before. Chelsea, however, had not. Linus appeared to have invited her along because he fancied her. Mark still couldn't figure out why Chelsea had agreed to come.

Being a newbie to LARPing, she'd been encouraged to play a warrior, as this was the easiest kind of character to play. However, it was clear from the start that she'd not been getting into the game.

She had half-heartedly swung her sword when it came to battle and she'd squealed and complained about being hurt whenever a member of the monster crew had landed a blow with a latex weapon anywhere on her person. She had complained constantly about getting leaves in her hair; or her trousers getting caught in brambles; or insect bites on her ankles; or feeling cold; or getting grass stains on her bum. In camp she complained about the uncomfortable bunk, the lack of toilet and shower facilities, not having anywhere to plug in her hair dryer, not having a decent sized mirror anywhere....it went on.

She had turned up enthusiastically enough, looking the part in sexy black leather trousers and a studded leather bustier, and initially she had responded fairly positively to Linus's flirting. But two days in the wilderness had clearly taken its toll and Mark thought that Chelsea had grown rather bored of Linus's attention.

Watching them now, the body language was clear enough. Linus was leaning in to Chelsea, whispering something he clearly thought was funny. She had her body turned away from him, arms folded, and her face was wearing a decidedly hostile expression.

"It's not looking like Linus is going to score tonight, is it?" Elizabeth said, following his gaze.

"Not at all," Mark said. "Of course, LARPing is a rather peculiar choice for a first date."

Elizabeth pulled the stick out of the fire to inspect the cooked marshmallow on the end of it. "And what would you recommend as a first date, then?"

"What?" Mark looked sharply at her. He could feel his face going red.

Elizabeth smiled. "Aw, did I embarrass you? Have a marshmallow. It will save you having to answer the question." She held the blackened marshmallow under Mark's nose enticingly.

The sweet, hot smell it emitted was wonderful. He pulled the marshmallow carefully from the stick.

"Not had toasted marshmallow since I was a kid," he said with his mouth full.

Chelsea got up abruptly from her log and crossed over to other side of the fire. From the disappointed expression on Linus's face, Mark reckoned he'd just asked a crucial question and been rejected.

"Liz, can I borrow your hand cream?" Chelsea asked. "Mine's got all grungy from falling on the ground earlier."

"Don't call me Liz," Elizabeth scowled.

"Oh, sorry. Ariadne, then. I know David – sorry, Cass – gets so mad when we use real names."

"It's character immersion, Valkyrie. Besides that though, I meant don't call me Liz. It's Elizabeth. I hate being called Liz."

"Really? Don't think I've ever met anyone who went by Elizabeth before. Can I borrow your hand cream, then? I'll get you some more when we get back home.

I just can't stand my hands all dry and cracked like this."

"Maybe you shouldn't have lugged it around with you on the overland, it wouldn't have got so dirty then," Elizabeth said. "Everything gets dirty on an overland. You should have figured that out by now."

"And have dry hands all day? Eww. Look, can I borrow it or not?"

Elizabeth sighed. "I suppose so. Come with me. I'll get it for you." She walked off to the sleeping hut and Chelsea followed.

Helen emerged from the toilet block and took Chelsea's place on the log beside Linus. He didn't acknowledge her. Linus and Helen had never met before this weekend. The only person in the group who had met Helen before, apart from David of course, was Mark. She'd been going out with David for about a year and Mark had met her at David's flat on a couple of occasions.

She was quiet and mousy – quite unlike the type of girl David normally fell for. Still, Mark reflected regretfully, he didn't really know David's tastes anymore. There had been a time when he and David had been soulmates, sharing everything and knowing more about each other than even their parents did. When they were in school, David spent so much time at their house that Mark's parents used to joke that they had an extra child. But neither of them were kids anymore and it was sad – if inevitable –that when people grow up, they grow apart from their friends. Mark sometimes wished he could go back to those simpler times, when David was such a big part of his life.

He saw David on the periphery of his vision, chatting animatedly with the referee who was leading the monster crew. After a cursory nod, David strode purposefully towards the fire. The other ref, decked out in cleric robes, followed in his wake. *Here it comes,* thought Mark.

He glanced down at the ground, locating where he had left his weapons when he put them down to enjoy his beer.

"It seems that our ritual was effective," David said in the clipped tones he adopted as his character Cassius. "The demon has been banished."

"So what's the problem then?" Linus asked. "Can't help but notice your friend there looks a bit anxious." He gestured at the monster ref.

"This is Meddoc, a cleric from the village on the other side of the forest," David said.

"His meditations have revealed a disturbance in the Dark Forces. It seems the Minions of Darkness are gearing up for a major attack."

"But why, if we killed the demon?" Helen asked.

"Clearly the evil magic user knows what we did and wants revenge. He's going to throw all he's got at us. If we attack now, we may get his minions before they reach full strength, and have a better chance of success.

I want everyone armoured up and ready to go in five minutes."

Mark drained the last of his beer and reluctantly set his tankard down on the ground. "Oh well, looks like relaxation time is over," he said. "Once more unto the breach we go." He picked up his sword and shield and reluctantly stood up, ready to go to battle once more.

CHAPTER 3

Trevor Carty sat slumped in front of the TV, the flickering light from the ancient set the only illumination in the room. The hand that clutched the can of lager in his lap was big and calloused, and trembled slightly.

The darkness in the shabby room camouflaged its disarray. It hid the mould growing on the remains of a pizza that had been sitting on the coffee table in its takeaway box for two days. It was hard to tell just how many empty lager cans were cluttered about. The spent whisky bottles that were left rolling around on the floor were hard to see. The stains on Trevor's torn vest and ripped jeans were not visible in the darkness, nor was the three-day-old stubble on his face. The fact that he hadn't washed his thin greasy hair in a while was also hard to tell.

The darkness could not mask the sour smell of unwashed flesh and rotting food, however.

Trevor Carty cared little about personal hygiene when he was in the grip of the demon that called out to him. He slumped in his arm chair, staring blankly at the football match on TV with vacant, red-rimmed eyes. He would eventually fall asleep in the chair, in a drunken stupor, as he had so many nights before. In the morning he would awake with a hangover, finally rousing himself from his chair in search of more alcohol to dull the pain. Painkillers just didn't work anymore and one day was just like another. Trevor didn't notice the passage of time. Apart from his neighbour, Sue, who would occasionally call round, nobody came to see Trevor. Nobody cared if he lived or died. Sue might have cared once; maybe once she'd worried about him. But lately the frequency of her visits had dropped off noticeably.

Trevor reckoned she only came round now to make sure he wasn't dead.

If he lay dead and rotting for weeks, undiscovered, the stench would probably bring down the price of Sue's house as it was attached to his.

The framed family photographs that were gathering dust on the bookshelf showed a version of Trevor Carty that was very different to the pallid, bloated, greasy-haired wreck that was slumped on the sofa. In the pictures he was handsome, rugged and smiling, his arm around the shoulders of a pretty blonde woman.

After Laura died, the life of her husband became pointed and groundless. He sought solace in alcohol, blind to the destruction it was wreaking on his own body. Or perhaps he was never blind – he just didn't care anymore. He became so wrapped up in his own grief he failed to notice how his son was suffering. There were no pictures of David Carty beyond the age of 12; the age he had been when his mother died. That day, family life in the Carty household had ceased.

When Trevor Carty fell into an alcoholic slumber, he always dreamed of his wife and the way she was before the cancer ravaged her body. He dreamed she was still young, pretty and full of life; her lovely blue eyes sparkling, her beautiful blonde hair loose and unkempt. He drank so he could see her again. And then he drank some more, to seek oblivion, because whenever he woke up and remembered Laura was dead, the reality was just too unbearable.

In the darkness of the room, the figure materialised unnoticed. Perhaps it was the sudden cold that accompanied it that made Trevor Carty open his eyes. Somewhere deep in his alcohol-fogged brain, an alarm began to tickle his consciousness.

The room was freezing. Trevor's breath was fogging in front of his face. The TV was no longer showing the game; the screen was full of snowy static. That feeling of unease in Trevor's brain was becoming more insistent.

He leaned forward to put the lager can on the coffee table. His hand was shaking so badly that he spilled it all over the scarred surface of the wooden table. The room was silent, apart from the soft hiss of the malfunctioning television. A flash of movement caught the periphery of his vision.

Trevor turned slowly. He had no idea what he was expecting to see – the small, logical part of his brain that hadn't been addled by years of alcohol abuse was insisting that there couldn't possibly be anything there.

A tall skeletal figure stood in front of him. Its face was mummified rubbery skin stretched over a skull. The eye sockets were empty and there was only a bony hole where the nose should be.

A tattered skull cap covered the crown of its head – the original colour was gold, but it had badly faded. Its desiccated body was adorned with a robe of a similar fabric. It hung in tatters, the mouldy fabric making the original colours – red and gold – almost indistinguishable.

The bottom of the robe and the area where the figure's feet should be disappeared into a haze of smoke.

The thing emanated a terrible smell – the stench of the grave and of long-dead flesh. Trevor's mouth hung open, his eyes widening. All the years he hadn't cared about life, wishing for the sweet release of death, disappeared in an instant. Suddenly he didn't want to die. Not like this. Not at the mercy of this unholy Thing. He wanted to scream but he couldn't; his insides felt like they'd turned to ice.

The thing advanced on him, raising its skeletal hands. As he got to see them closer, he could see they were mummified hands, the bones clearly visible beneath a thin layer of leathery discoloured flesh. Trevor froze in place as they touched his skin. Fear paralysed his body.

The thing was inches from him now.

It opened its mouth, a raw wound in the desiccated remains of its face, and in the wake of a blast of icy cold air that carried with it the stench of death, it rasped, "Fear me."

The thing laid its skeletal fingers on both sides of Trevor's face and enveloped him in the freezing blast of fear and death that it emanated. He opened his mouth but his vocal chords would not work. He was frozen with fear, his body cold all over apart from the warm mess in his trousers where his bowels had betrayed him.

As his life left him, Trevor Carty's last fleeting thought was that his worst fear of dying alone and undiscovered for weeks was about to come true.

CHAPTER 4

Mark stared at the lines of code on his computer screen. They made no more sense now than they had half an hour ago. Clearly he needed a break.

He left his cluttered desk, negotiating his way past the piles of papers that occupied the tiny dingy room he called an office, and crossed to the staff kitchen area. This room was also small – Avignon Games was not a big enough company to afford opulent premises – but it was functional, with a kettle, sink, dishwasher, microwave, and larder fridge. Tea and coffee were supplied by the company, and there was a soft drinks machine vending Coke and various other caffeinated drinks.

Some people stowed their lunch boxes in the fridge, but Mark generally bought his lunch from one of the many sandwich places around Tottenham Court Road.

He wasn't organised enough to make his lunch before leaving for work in the morning. Besides, the cluttered windowless premises of Avignon Games were a grim place to spend the day and it was nice to get out for an hour or so for some fresh air – or whatever passed for fresh air in Central London.

As he waited for the kettle to boil, he lined up two mugs with tea bags in, a spoonful of sugar in each. He smiled as he thought about Elizabeth's fondness of sugar. It was refreshing to meet a girl who wasn't constantly dieting and fretting about her weight, another thing he liked about Elizabeth. She had attractive curves, but for Mark what was on the inside was more important than what was on the outside. David had always gone for the buxom blondes, or at least he had when he was a teenager.

But while David had gone through a long line of short-lived, insecure and high-maintenance girlfriends in the last five years or so, Mark had always preferred women with more substance.

He thought once more of David's latest girlfriend Helen as he poured the boiling water into the mugs. Small and introverted, she was a departure from David's usual "type". Of course, quite a lot about David had changed since he started studying medicine. He used to be the life and soul of the party. Now he was much more inclined to go home early on a Friday night and study than he was to go out for a few beers with the guys.

With the tea ready, Mark snagged a few chocolate bourbons from the biscuit supply that was provided for the staff and stuck them on a plate. Carrying the two mugs of tea in one hand and the biscuit plate in the other, he headed for Elizabeth's desk.

She was hunched over her screen, frowning in concentration. Mark paused in the doorway for a moment, watching her as she pushed her glasses up her nose and moved her mouse in a circular pattern. The desk opposite Elizabeth's was piled high with papers, as was his own. When the company moved into the premises ten years earlier there had been twice as many people working for it, but difficult times had dictated that the company had cut back on the number of employees. There were now three games designers, not six; and each of them had a tiny office with a spare desk opposite. Mark couldn't imagine what it must have been like working in the small space with twice the number of people – it seemed cramped enough already. This meant that he had an office to himself with plenty of peace and quiet to get his work done, even though it was a bit lonesome sometimes. It also meant he was left alone, as the boss didn't believe in encroaching on his employees' freedoms.

So if someone wanted to check Facebook during their working day, or deal with personal calls, no one was going to say anything. Just as long as the work got done on time.

Elizabeth's office was next to his and Mark often paid a visit if he needed a break during the day. He found himself doing this more and more often as time went on. The third games designer, Stuart, was an OK guy but he kept to himself most of time and seemed uninterested in befriending any of his colleagues. He was also a smoker, so when he wanted a break he took himself outside for a cigarette. Mark and Elizabeth were not smokers –another reason why he liked her.

Mark entered Elizabeth's office and put the mug of tea down on the coaster on her cluttered desk. "Tea break time," he announced.

Elizabeth glanced at her watch. "Ten thirty on the nose. My, how punctual."

"I know you're a creature of habit. Biscuit?" He held out the plate of Bourbon creams.

"But of course. You know my sweet tooth, too." She took two biscuits, and picked up her tea. "You even used the right mug. I'm impressed." The IT Babe mug was one she had brought with her into the job, and he knew she was fond of it. He gathered it had been a leaving present from her former colleagues. "So what do you want?" Elizabeth asked as she leaned back to sip her tea.

Mark perched himself on the corner of the desk opposite Elizabeth's and helped himself to a biscuit. "Do I have to want anything to make you tea?"

"No. But my experience is that guys normally do, if they make tea without asking." Elizabeth crunched a biscuit.

"I just needed a break. I've been staring at the same line of code for half an hour and the more I stare at it, the less sense it makes. I think I'm probably suffering from post-game blues. It always takes a few days to get back to the real world after a gaming weekend."

"Yeah, I know what you mean. Somehow the commute into work seems a lot drearier this week. There was a particularly annoying chap who pushed in front of me on the Central Line this morning and forced his way into the last seat. Completely ignoring the very pregnant woman, who waddled on after him and stared pointedly at the seat. I asked him politely that perhaps he'd like to move so the lady could sit down. He told me to piss off. I thought about throwing a fireball at him. Then I remembered this was the real world and I couldn't." Elizabeth took a bite of her biscuit.

"So you enjoyed the game then? I know this was your first LARP experience."

"Well, it's a bit different from D&D, but the rules are similar enough, so I got the hang of it fairly quickly. Yes, I enjoyed it. It was good fun. It was rather nice escaping from the real world for a while, and leaving things like mobile phones and iPads behind."

"I don't think Chelsea shares the same sentiments."

Elizabeth shook her head. "I will never understand my brother's taste in women."

"I'm still surprised she came along, to be honest. She seemed so far out of her depth, it made me wonder what she was expecting."

"I expect Linus made it sound more glamorous than it actually is. The reality of sharing sleeping space with six sweaty adventurers, when shower facilities are few and far between, soon takes the gloss off. I did try to forewarn him that this wasn't an ideal scenario for a first date. I don't think he's given up on Chelsea, though. He's planning on calling her, trying to persuade her to go out with him on a proper date. And what about you?"

Mark nearly choked on his biscuit. "What about me?"

Elizabeth smiled sweetly. "What's your idea of a first date?"

"Oh, er...I'm not sure really. Dinner, I guess. A posh restaurant. Nice wine. A quiet romantic evening."

"You disappoint me."

"Well I suppose it depends on the person."

"That new zombie film comes out this weekend. The one in 3D." Elizabeth smiled coyly. "My idea of a dream date is going to see that. Then maybe out for pizza. Then back to his place for a session of *Resident Evil*, where he will vainly try to beat my score and we'll end up playing until late into the night."

Mark thought of his PlayStation 3 at home, still loaded with *Resident Evil 5* from the last time he'd been playing. Elizabeth was looking at him expectantly. He cleared his throat, and opened his mouth, but somehow his voice seemed to have disappeared.

"For heaven's sake, Mark, how many hints do you need? I've just given you the perfect opening."

"You want me to ask you out?"

Elizabeth rolled her eyes. "No shit, Sherlock. God, Mark, for an intelligent guy, you can be really dim sometimes."

"I was too scared."

"Why? Am I that scary?"

"I didn't know you liked me. I thought you'd turn me down."

Elizabeth sighed. "I thought I'd dropped enough hints. You guys don't do subtle, do you? Alright, forget the coy female approach. I'm asking you out. Friday night. *The Dead Walk*, followed by Pizza Express, followed by a session on your PS3. How's that?"

Mark found his voice. "That sounds great."

"Let's do the early show, so there's time to eat afterwards. There's a six pm showing at the Odeon in Leicester Square. I already checked the times."

"So all this time you were waiting for me to make the first move?"

Elizabeth smiled and sipped her tea. "Men like to pretend they're in charge. I thought you'd prefer it that way."

"Actually, I'm rather fond of forceful women. I like a woman who knows what she wants."

"I'll bear that in mind." Elizabeth put her mug on her desk and pushed back her chair. She stood up and crossed over to Mark. He could hear his heart pounding; it sounded like it was in his ears. He thought the whole world would be able to hear it.

Elizabeth was right up close to him now. He could smell her perfume – something light and floral. He could see her clear blue eyes and those fantastic lashes, magnified by her glasses. She was wearing a yellow cardigan that fell open over a white blouse; a respectable V-neck style that just hinted at cleavage. She put a hand on either side of his face and gently pulled him forward so that her lips met his.

The kiss was long, deep and passionate, and took Mark's breath away. His mind was full of static; he was aware of nothing but the moment, of her touch on his face, his lips.

He knew right then that he was helplessly and uncontrollably in love with this girl.

The sound of a cough startled them and broke them apart. Stuart, the third games designer, stood in the doorway, looking embarrassed. "The boss wants a meeting about progress on the new games designs," he said. "In his office, in five minutes." He turned and left hurriedly.

Mark felt his face growing red. He stared at Elizabeth, her face turning pink as well. Then they both started giggling. "We better not keep the boss waiting," Elizabeth said. "I'm going to splash water on my face."

Mark left Elizabeth's office and headed back to his desk to compose himself. He was aware that he was wearing a broad grin. He suspected he would be wearing it for the rest of the day. Possibly for the rest of his life.

CHAPTER 5

"Hey there," Mark said as David opened the door.

David scowled. "What are you doing here?"

Mark held up a plastic shopping bag. "I've got a bunch of DVDs and a couple of books you lent me a while back. Thought I'd return them before I completely forget they belong to you."

"There was no desperate hurry," David said. "It's not as if I get any time to watch DVDs these days."

"So are you going to let me in, or do I have to stand on the doorstep?"

David stepped to one side. "Sorry. Come in."

Mark followed him in, leaving the bag in the hallway. "Is something wrong, mate?"

David looked at him. "Like what?"

"I don't know. You tell me. You're not exactly making me feel welcome here."

"I just wasn't expecting you, that's all."

"I never used to need an invitation to drop round your place." Mark followed David into his small living room. Papers were scattered all over the coffee table and two thick medical text books lay open on the sofa.

"I was in the middle of some revision," David said.

"Oh." Mark settled himself into the armchair. "I guess I won't stay too long, then."

David swept the papers into a pile and balanced them on top of one of the text books. "I suppose a few minutes' break won't hurt."

"Pretty intensive, this studying kick you're on, isn't it?"

David scowled. "Being a surgeon involves a lot of hard work."

"But I thought you were a long way away from being a surgeon. From what you told me, you've got to get your medical degree, then a couple of years of foundation training, before you can even start training as a surgeon."

"But I already know that's what I want to do. You've got a far better chance of getting the specialty that you want if you do well at the med school exams. At least, that's the way I see it. It's not enough to pass. I have to pass with flying colours."

"Well, you know more about it than me," Mark said doubtfully. "Just don't work yourself to death. You're looking a bit under the weather."

"Thanks very much," David said darkly.

"I just mean… well you look a bit tired. Like maybe you haven't been getting enough sleep."

"Again, thanks. Nothing like the truth amongst friends. And you there, you're the picture of health." David stared at Mark suspiciously. "Actually, you are. What's going on? You've got this stupid grin on your face. Have you just had a shag or something?"

"Not quite," Mark said quickly. "But I have got a date."

David raised his eyebrows. "Oh yes? With who?"

"Elizabeth, of course. Who else?"

"Who else, indeed? Well I'm glad you finally grew a pair and took the plunge."

"Actually, she sort of asked me. Apparently she got tired of waiting for me to make the first move."

"So she's a lady who likes to be in control. Well, I hope you know what you're letting yourself in for."

"You don't like her?"

David scrabbled about amongst his papers, distracted. "It's not about whether or not I like her. You like her, that's the important thing."

"But you don't like her."

"I didn't say that." David shrugged. "She's just not my type, that's all."

"And Helen is?"

"Helen's alright."

"I'm not saying she isn't. She's a perfectly nice girl. But since you were sixteen you've gone out with a string of bolshie bottle blondes who wear at least a D cup, and suddenly you've taken up with this petite, timid, very sweet girl. A bit of a departure, that's all."

David was still scrabbling amongst his papers. "There comes a time in a man's life when it's time to grow up," he said. "I guess I've got to that stage."

"I guess," Mark said doubtfully. "As long as you're happy. You are, aren't you? You don't look very happy."

David looked up, startled. "Oh, I am. Or I will be soon. But I really ought to get back to studying."

"You're not going to offer me a cup of tea, then?"

David was staring at a bit of paper in his hand, looking like he hadn't even heard Mark.

"Are you sure you're alright, mate?" Mark said. "Tell me to mind my own business if you want, but you really don't look right."

David snapped his head round, his eyes wide. He seemed to be staring at a point in the wall, somewhere beyond Mark's shoulder. "Can I ask you something?" he said.

"Sure. You can ask me anything, you know that."

"What if you rubbed a magic lamp and a genie came out, and said you could wish for whatever you wanted? What would you wish for?"

"How many wishes do I get?"

David's mouth flicked into a smile. "You don't know how many wishes. So you have to assume it's just the one."

"Genies normally have three. That's what the stories say. If it was just one? Well, ask me that a week ago, I would have wished for the girl of my dreams to notice me. But I think she just has. Sometimes wishes come true anyway."

"You really have got it bad, haven't you?"

"I'm a hopeless romantic."

"Let's assume you've got the girl, then. Would you wish to win the lottery? If you had money, you could buy everything else you needed."

"I don't know. There's usually a price to pay for wishes like that," Mark said. "Don't you remember *The Monkey's Paw?*"

David frowned. "Year nine English class?"

"Year eight. Mrs Dawson. You must remember?"

"All I really remember about Mrs Dawson's English class was Becky Shaw."

"Ah, Becky Shaw. You spent all year trying to shag her. Didn't you finally succeed?"

"Not till Year nine," David said. "At Jason Clarke's famous party. And everyone else had already had her by then."

"Ah yes, the party. Jason was grounded for the rest of the year when his parents came home from holiday a day earlier than expected and he hadn't finished clearing up the mess. Happy days."

"It was a good party, though."

"I don't suppose Jason thought so afterwards. Wasn't there a year where we both fancied the same girl? Year 10 maybe?"

"I don't remember that," David said.

"Suzie Allen. Statuesque brunette."

"Ah yes. She led both of us on and then dumped us."

"I stopped speaking to you for weeks while that was going on."

"And all the time she was playing us."

"That was when you went off brunettes," Mark said. "After that, it was blondes all the way."

David rubbed his eyes wearily. "That was all a long time ago. I really have to get back to studying."

"OK," Mark said. "I can tell when I'm not wanted." He stood up and picked up his coat from the arm of the chair, where he'd carelessly slung it.

"I really came here because I wanted to tell you about Elizabeth. I was hoping you'd be happy for me. We used to talk to each other about things like that."

"Do you think it's true, about the price to pay?" David said abruptly.

"What?"

"The wishes. You said there's always a price to pay. Is that true?"

"I don't know, Dave. They're just stories."

"Yes. Of course." David stood up and followed Mark out into the corridor. "Look, I'm sorry I'm not in a mood to socialise, but I'm under a lot of pressure in the run up to my exams. I'm not going to be good company for a while. Maybe afterwards, we can hang out more."

"Sure," Mark said, finding himself speaking to empty air on the doorstep as David shut the door behind him.

CHAPTER 6

"That's the problem with modern zombies," Mark said. "They don't follow the usual conventions of zombies."

Across the table, Elizabeth picked up her wine glass and took a sip. "So how do you think zombies are supposed to behave, then?" They were sitting in Pizza Express, waiting for their order to arrive. The conversation had been revolving around the same topic since they left the cinema.

"For starters, zombies are meant to be slow and lumbering. This lot were moving far too quickly. That's the advantage that we should have over zombies – we can outrun them. If we can't do that, we're history."

"It means the characters have to find new ways to survive," Elizabeth said.

"And since when did zombies have brains? These ones figured out how to open locks. And they went hunting. Zombies don't hunt.

They burble around mindlessly, only get you if you're stupid enough to get in their way."

"What's wrong with finding innovative ways to make the genre more interesting?" Elizabeth swirled the wine around in the glass. "I'm as fond of an old-fashioned zombie film as the next geek, but you have to admit they've been done to death. This film was challenging the conventions of the genre. Just when you think you've figured out who all the stock characters are – who's the first to die, who's the one that survives, who's the one who'll get bitten and turned into a zombie – it spins all your expectations upside down."

"But there were no survivors." Mark picked up the wine bottle and topped up Elizabeth's glass. "How are they going to make a sequel?" He poured himself some more of the wine.

Elizabeth grinned playfully. "Who says there won't be a sequel? You clearly weren't paying attention. Did you notice that the film was careful to establish that none of the survivors had been in contact with anyone else outside California?

They all kept saying they wanted to head north; that the outbreak was contained and if they could get into the Northern States all would be well? But no one had spoken to anyone in the north."

"Sure, I picked up on that. So what? In zombie films the survivors are always trying to head somewhere else and somehow they never manage to get there, or they do and find the military base deserted. This lot never made it out of California."

"But didn't you notice the final shot, panning back and showing Earth from space? Right before the credits started to roll, all the lights across the globe started winking out, one by one. The outbreak's clearly gone global. The second film will deal with a group of survivors in some other part of the world. International zombies are the way to go. Look at *The Dead,* and *Resident Evil 5.* Both feature African zombies."

"You picked that up from the final shot? It must have been quick. I think I missed that one."

"You were trying to nibble my ear at the time."

"And you were swatting me away," Mark said in a hurt tone. "Nothing like making a man feel rejected."

"I was trying to watch the film."

Mark shook his head. "You're the first date I've had who's been more interested in watching the film than snogging in the back row."

"The amount you pay to get into the cinema these days, you need to watch the film to get your money's worth. There are far better places to snog than in the cinema."

Mark waggled his eyebrows. "You got plans for later, then?"

Elizabeth smiled coyly. "Depends on whether you can beat me at RE5."

"That's not fair. I've not managed to beat you yet."

"Well if you want to get your end away, you better start practising then."

"Does that mean you're not going to sleep with me until I can beat you at *Resident Evil*?" Mark said, appalled. "That means I'm going to be in for a lot of lonely nights."

Elizabeth smiled. "As I said, start practising."

"You drive a hard bargain."

"I just want you to know I'm not easy."

"I'm offended if you think I have ever made that assumption about you."

"Just as long as we know where we stand." Elizabeth winked at Mark.

"You're teasing me, aren't you?"

"Let's just see how things go. Ah, here's the food. Marvellous."

The waitress served their pizzas. Mark watched Elizabeth tuck into her Sloppy Giuseppe with gusto. "I love the way you enjoy your food so much," Mark said. "Too many girls refuse to eat anything more than lettuce leaves."

Elizabeth shrugged. "Life's too short to worry about what the diet fascists say. If I get fat, I get fat."

"You're not fat."

"I'm glad to hear you say so." Elizabeth grinned and sawed off another piece of pizza.

Mark groaned. "This conversation's going places I don't want to be going on a first date."

"Zombies are fair game for a first date then, are they?"

"If the lady's into zombies, then, why not?"

"Let's just see if you still think so when I whip your backside at RE5 later. I do hope you're not going to chicken out on me?"

"Of course not."

"I do, of course, have a bit of an unfair advantage when it comes to shooting games. I'm a crack shot, you know."

"What, with a proper gun?" Mark said, surprised.

Elizabeth smiled. "My dad was a farmer. He taught me how to handle a gun when I was ten.

I was going to the shooting range with him when I was sixteen. He said I had a natural talent for it – used to call me his Little Annie Oakley."

"I didn't know this about you. Do you still shoot?"

Elizabeth looked wistful. "I still belong to the gun club, but I don't go so much these days. Not since my parents died. It was never so much fun without my dad."

"But you have a licence to hold guns and things?"

"Oh yes," said Elizabeth. "I inherited my dad's shotgun and a couple of pistols."

"Are you going to tell me you keep them under your bed?"

"Of course not. There are strict rules about that. I keep them at the gun club. They have the regulation safes." She swirled the wine around in her glass. "Enough about me. Let's talk about you."

"Not much to say about me."

Elizabeth looked at Mark over the table. "I know there's something on your mind.

You've been distracted. I know you well enough to know that."

Mark sighed. "I don't know if it's appropriate to talk about it here."

Elizabeth raised her eyebrows. "If I don't know what it is, I don't know if it's appropriate or not. But now you've mentioned it, let's hear it."

"It's David."

"What about him?"

"We used to be best mates," Mark said.

"We'd tell each other everything. But the last few years he's become...distant. Detached somehow. He doesn't talk to me anymore. I miss him." He looked at Elizabeth. "I guess you think I'm being silly, don't you?"

Elizabeth put down her knife and fork and looked at Mark. "I don't think you're being silly. But I think it's the way of the world that people who were friends as children often grow apart as adults.

They develop different interests. They make new friends. It's just the way things go."

"But that's the problem. I haven't made new friends. David used to be my best friend. He was always my best friend. Now I feel like there's an empty space in my life where he used to be."

"You want to rekindle your friendship then? You have to spend more time with him in that case." Elizabeth picked up her cutlery and sawed off another piece of pizza. "Why don't you suggest we all go out for a drink? You, me, David and Helen. I'd like to get to know Helen anyway. I liked her, from what I saw of her at the LARP game. Unlike Chelsea, who was a pain in the backside."

"I guess that'll be a start. I'll ring him tomorrow."

"Maybe some time next week?" Elizabeth suggested. "I think I can do any night."

Mark nodded. "OK. Sounds good."

"Don't be too hard on yourself for feeling guilty about growing apart from David. It happens with friends. Especially when one person is in a relationship and the other one isn't."

"It was happening before Helen came along."

"I'm sure it was. But it probably got a bit worse at that time. Didn't you start to feel like a gooseberry when David wanted to spend time with Helen instead of hang out with you?"

"I guess so."

"So, another reason to start double dating then. We can all spend time together."

Mark grinned. "You're such a sensible person, you know that?"

"That's why you like me. Intelligent women are very sexy. Of course, you know that. That's why you don't really mind my whipping your arse at *Resident Evil*."

"It would be nice to win occasionally, you know."

"You need to try harder, then."

"Let's finish up dinner so we can get back to my place. Can't wait to get my hands on those zombies."

"As long as that's all you want to get your hands on." Elizabeth smiled coyly. "At least, for the time being. I don't put out on a first date."

"Unless I beat you."

"You won't. Trust me."

CHAPTER 7

Helen paused before knocking on the bedroom door, mug of tea in hand. David had disappeared in there over an hour ago with his text books, muttering that he needed to study, and he hadn't come out since.

She took a deep breath and inwardly chastised herself. Stressed or not, David was still the same man she'd fallen in love with a year ago. If he'd been studying for over an hour, he was long overdue a tea break. She knocked on the door and went in without waiting for an answer.

David was sitting on the bed with his books and papers sprawled over it. He looked up when she entered, and scowled. "I said I didn't want to be disturbed."

"I brought you a cup of tea." Helen put the mug down on the bedside table. "You need a break."

"I don't have time for a break. I've still got a lot of work to do and exams start in less than three weeks." David slapped one of the papers on the bed in frustration.

"You can't concentrate when you're dehydrated. Why don't you take a break for half an hour or so? Watch TV. Do something mindless. Then go back to it when you've given your brain a rest."

David glared at her. "I don't think you really understand how important these exams are."

"Of course I understand," Helen said in a wounded tone.

"My future career rests on my success in these exams. It's not like your English course, where you just had to write a few essays to end up with a degree that's actually completely irrelevant to what you do for a living."

"That's unfair. I worked hard to get my degree."

"But now you're an admin assistant for an insurance company. Working alongside people who left school at sixteen and have the collective IQ of a sponge."

"Sometimes you have to do what you can. I never said I enjoyed what I do for a living."

"My exams are different." David got up from the bed and started pacing, clutching sheets of paper in his hands. "I'm going to be a surgeon. It's not good enough just to pass the exams. I have to excel at them. Otherwise I'll never get the placing I'm after. Do you know how competitive this field is? Do you really know how important this is?"

"Of course I do," Helen snapped. "You've told me often enough."

"It's bad enough that I have to study in this shit hole of a flat, where I have to shut myself in the bedroom just to get some privacy. I need a proper study area."

"You've always been so proud of this place. Your first proper place."

"It's not enough anymore. What sort of doctor lives in a one-bedroom flat in Camden?"

David turned to look at her and she couldn't help but think how gaunt and haggard he looked. There were big dark circles under his eyes, and shadows along the hollows of his cheekbones. He'd lost weight in the last few weeks. His jeans hung on his hips and his larynx jutted too prominently from the tendons in his throat. His face sported several days' growth of beard.

"You're not a doctor yet, David. You're a trainee."

"I would be able to afford a new place now if that bastard gave up some of my inheritance," David ranted as he paced.

"What do you mean?"

"I mean my sodding father. He's got thousands in savings and what is he doing with it? Drinking it away. All he does is sit on his arse in front of the TV all day."

"I thought you hadn't spoken to him for years."

"That's beside the point!" David shouted, rounding on her.

"He never wanted me to go into medicine. Started going on about how much money it was going to cost. How I was betraying good old working class stock. What the fuck does he care about how much medical school costs? It's not as if he's paid me anything towards it. I was only able to go at all because I got a scholarship."

"Yes I know. You told me."

"Then you should try to understand how important these exams are. But your family have always been supportive. You don't know what it's like, trying to better yourself all on your own, when your family do nothing but bring you down."

"I'm trying to understand, David. Really, I am."

"If you did, then you'd leave me alone when I'm trying to study." David sat on the bed and put his head in his hands.

"I'm only trying to help," Helen said, her voice trembling.

David turned to face her. "Then leave me alone."

"If you're really worried about time constraints, perhaps you shouldn't have gone gallivanting around in the woods on that LRP game." Helen knew it was a snide comment, but she was feeling upset. David had no right to talk to her that way.

"You think I haven't thought of that? I let Mark talk me into running another game, over a late night drinking session. 'It's been ages', he said, 'and your games are the best. Won't you run another one?' I shouldn't have let him cajole me."

Helen stood up. "I think it's best if I go back to my own place tonight and leave you alone to study. I have to get up early for work tomorrow, anyway."

She looked back as she left the room but David ignored her, already collecting his papers and text books together. She closed the door behind her, gathered her things and left the flat, trying to blink back the tears in her eyes as she went.

Things will be better once the exams are over, she told herself as she headed for the tube station. *After he passes his exams, things will go back to the way they were before. They have to.*

CHAPTER 8

The first thing that Steve noticed when he and Debbie left the Green Man was how bloody cold it was. It was April – normally a time when flowers were blooming and you could walk down the street without a jacket. Tonight, it felt more like October.

He put his arm round Debbie as they staggered down the street together. They'd been out celebrating their one-month anniversary. The Green Man had live bands playing on Friday nights. Usually they were pretty decent, and the pub was the only place with any action in Lynley. People went on about what a nice quiet place Lynley was – how everyone felt safe, what a good place it was to raise a family – but in truth, it was bloody boring. The only reason Steve was still in this stuffy old place was because he couldn't afford to move out. One day, when he had enough money saved, he'd buy himself a decent flat in the city. Bristol, maybe.

Maybe Debbie would join him. Maybe, just maybe, if the two of them hooked up for the long haul and they could both find decent jobs; they could go all the way out to London. That's where the real action was.

Debbie had her hands underneath Steve's jacket. They were cold, but he didn't mind – that made it seem more exciting. He snaked his hand down her back and squeezed one of her buttocks. She giggled.

He leaned over and whispered into her ear. "Want to do it outside again?"

"What, tonight? Not likely – it's too bloody cold."

"Where's your sense of adventure, darlin'?"

"No way! It's frickin' freezing."

He pushed her gently against the wall of the nearest building, and said, "Just don't think I can wait until we get back to mine." He kissed her hungrily, passionately; his hands exploring her body.

As he found the edge of her jacket and then her top, he pushed up underneath it, to the soft flesh of her belly.

She yelped and pulled away. "Your hands are cold!"

"So are yours. You don't hear me complaining."

"Let's just get back to yours and get out of the cold."

"Oh, alright, if you insist. Let's make it quick then." Steve removed his hands from underneath Debbie's clothes and put his arm around her shoulders, hurrying her along.

The road was deserted as they made their way back to Steve's flat. It wasn't a long walk, but the side streets of Lynley were not well lit. They knew the way well enough – they visited the Green Man frequently – but they were both in a state of inebriation, and occasionally lost their footing and stumbled into the bushes as they staggered along. And of course, Steve was not really paying attention to the route. He let himself be distracted by nibbling on Debbie's ear, or massaging her buttocks.

They passed by St Stephen's, Lynley's oldest church, a charming structure that had been the hub of village life for nearly a thousand years. The graveyard traced the history of the village. It was still used for burials, and the more recent tombstones could be found in the far North West corner. Many of the older stones were so weathered that they were now illegible or had toppled over. These graves were so old; there were no longer any ancestors of the dead around to tend them.

Not that Steve was in a position to pay much attention to the church at present, or the low mist that shrouded the gravestones.

He leaned against the low stone wall that marked the church's boundary, and pulled Debbie to him. She giggled as he leaned in to kiss her, his hands finding their way up underneath her sweater.

"I told you, your hands are cold," she said, trying half-heartedly to swat him away.

"You're so hot, baby. They'll soon warm up."

In the graveyard behind them, something was stirring. In the far corner, the soil over one of the recent graves was churning. Beneath the mist that hung over the ground, a mound of earth appeared, as if a mole was burrowing its way to the surface. But what emerged from the ground was no mole. A decayed hand appeared; grey rotten flesh hanging off discoloured bones. The hand was followed by an arm. Then the soil boiled and churned, shortly before a head emerged and Samuel F Jones, dead of a heart attack and buried six months ago, climbed out of his grave.

He was not the only decedent to rise from the grave in that Lynley church yard that night. Four corpses, all buried within the last two years, emerged from the graveyard – leaving behind them empty coffins and the stench of decay. They stumbled on legs that were no longer able to support life; festering corpses, dropping body parts and bits of decayed flesh in their wake.

They moved slowly but steadily, incapable of rational thought but summoned to obey, and with the need to be somewhere.

When Steve finally broke off his embrace with Debbie, suddenly aware that something wasn't right, it wasn't the four corpses he noticed first. It felt suddenly much colder and he was aware of a keenly unpleasant smell surrounding them – the smell of death and decay. Then he heard a guttural, primeval groan. A sound made by something no longer human. It was followed by another, and then another, underscored by a dull shuffling noise in the silence of the Lynley night.

Steve looked up, beyond the church wall and into the graveyard. He could just make out the four shuffling figures moving steadily forward. For a moment, he did not trust his eyes.

The figures looked grotesque, like parodies of humanity; grey flesh hanging off discoloured bones; tattered clothing; empty eye sockets leaking a black viscous liquid as they staggered forward, their arms outstretched.

Debbie, growing frightened by the look on Steve's face, turned to see what he was staring at. Her scream was swallowed up by the foggy night. There was no one around to hear, and it was too late to run.

CHAPTER 9

Helen let herself into the flat. Encountering the silence, she felt relieved. She knew David was at work all day today. In the back of her mind, that was why she'd decided to come round. That made her feel guilty. She used to hate being in David's flat when he wasn't there as it felt so empty and sterile. But lately he'd become so difficult to deal with; so moody and unpredictable. Now she found herself craving the sanctuary. David's place was bigger than hers. She was looking forward to some quiet time before he came home. Whenever she thought about David now, an anxious feeling built up inside her, like a cherry stone lodged in her throat that she couldn't shift or breathe around. She knew it wasn't right to feel that way about the man she had been sure she loved. She kept telling herself it would be better once he'd passed his exams. But a small, insistent voice kept saying, "What if it isn't?"

Alone in his flat, she did a bit of tidying up and washed the dishes, before relaxing for a while in front of the TV. She'd just settled down with a cup of tea and a book when the phone rang. She'd spent enough time at David's flat that he was relaxed about her answering his phone, and quite often people rang for her there, so she picked up the call without thinking about it.

"Hello?"

"Could I speak to David Carty, please?" The voice on the phone was male; authoritative.

"He's at work at the moment. Can I take a message?"

"It is rather important. Could I reach him on his mobile?"

"He's at the hospital; he can't have his mobile switched on. I'd be happy to give him a message as soon as he gets home."

"It is rather important." There was a pause. "Excuse me if it sounds like a personal question, but may I ask if you are Mr Carty's wife?"

"I'm his girlfriend."

"I see. I do really need to speak to Mr Carty. I have some rather bad news, I'm afraid. This is PC Alan Harris calling from Manchester metropolitan police station. I'm sorry to say that Brian Carty has passed away."

Helen's heart leapt to her throat. "David's father? How?"

"It's currently under investigation. We'll hopefully know more when the results of the autopsy come through, but on the face of it, it appears to be a suspicious death. I really do need to speak to Mr Carty. Which hospital does he work in?"

"UCL. I've got the department number somewhere. Hold on, and I'll get it." With shaking hands, Helen fumbled for her bag, extracting her mobile phone and scrolling through the contacts until she came to the number marked as "David – work."

When she hung up the phone, she sat for several long minutes, her head spinning.

David mentioned he'd be in clinics most of the day and she knew he couldn't be disturbed – especially so close to exams, when he was trying so hard to retain all the knowledge he needed to pass. But his father was dead. Her instincts were to reach out to him, to try and get hold of him and offer comfort. But the police would have to pull him out of his clinics if they rang the hospital. A second disturbance would not be appreciated. Also, he may prefer to be alone. Maybe on hearing the news he'd come home early, in which case he might appreciate her being here for him.

Helen had been sitting there so long turning the news over in her head that her tea had gone cold.

She made herself a fresh cup and switched the TV back on, channel flicking blindly and not really knowing or caring what she was watching.

She was watching a rerun of an old sitcom when David arrived home about an hour and a half later.

He swept past her and barely glanced in her direction, before collapsing on the sofa and dumping his backpack on the floor. "I've had a bitch of a day," he said, lying back and closing his eyes.

"David, the police phoned," she said. "Did they get hold of you at the hospital?"

"Shall we get takeaway?" he said, without opening his eyes. "I can't be arsed to cook."

"David, are you listening to me? The police have been trying to get hold of you."

David opened his eyes. "Yes, I know. I spoke to them."

"So you know about your father?"

"Yes. I've already spoken to his solicitor."

"Solicitor? Whose solicitor?"

"My father's, of course. I'm the only surviving relative. As it turns out, he had a will."

Helen stared at David. "Your dad's dead, and all you can think about is getting your hands on his money?"

"It's not as if he gave me any when he was alive. The least he can do is give it to me now he's dead."

"But he's your dad!" Helen said, appalled. "Don't you feel any sadness that he's gone? Your flesh and blood? Now he's gone and you're an orphan. Doesn't that mean anything to you?"

David opened one eye. "And that means I'm supposed to care about the bastard, does it? What do you know about my father?"

"Nothing. You never talk about him."

"That's because he's not worth wasting time on. My father was an embittered drunk who thought the world owed him a living, and resented anyone who he thought was better off than him. Instead of being proud of my achievements, he was jealous of me. And all because I had the inclination to work hard for what I wanted instead of sitting back and expecting everything to be handed to me, like he did."

"He's still your father!"

"Only biologically. I stopped thinking about any connection he might have to me years ago." David got up abruptly. "I'm going to take a shower. Why don't you go over the road and get some fish and chips? We can eat when I'm done."

Helen remained frozen. A moment later, she heard the bathroom door slam shut, followed by the sound of the shower starting. It was then the tears started to flow, unbidden. Crying for a man she'd never met; crying the tears his son seemed incapable of shedding. She would grieve for Brian Carty, because he had no one else left to do so.

CHAPTER 10

"So maybe I should let you win." Elizabeth put down the PS3 controller.

"I wouldn't expect you to give me special treatment," Mark said.

"But I'll die of sexual frustration before you beat me."

"Aha." Mark picked up the wine bottle and sat on the sofa next to Elizabeth. "There is that, I guess."

Elizabeth offered her glass for a refill. "I suppose we could just relax the rules a bit. We both know I'm staying over tonight."

Mark grinned. "I could just let you seduce me."

"Where's the fun in that, when I've already got you ensnared? You're already following me around with your tongue hanging out. Men are so unsubtle."

Mark took Elizabeth's wine glass and placed it carefully alongside his on the coffee table.

"I'm sure we could still find ways of having fun." He took Elizabeth's spectacles off her face.

"You know I can't see a thing without those."

"But you're so cute when you squint like that." Mark traced a finger along Elizabeth's jaw line. She had a smattering of freckles over her nose, and frown lines between her eyes as she tried to see without her glasses. Her long wavy hair was loose, falling untidily over her shoulders. He moved his hands into her hair, luxuriating in its soft thickness. Then he moved his face closer to hers. She shifted position, anticipating the kiss, and he felt her hand stroke the back of his neck and move up to his hair.

Just as their lips met, the doorbell rang.

"Whoever that is, it's really lousy timing," Mark grumbled. "I've got a mind just to ignore it."

"It's nearly midnight. When the doorbell rings this time of night, it's generally important." As if to emphasise her point, the bell rang again.

"You're always so practical, you know that?" Mark scrambled off the sofa and straightened out his clothes. Elizabeth sat up and put her specs back on, smiling demurely.

Mark's mood darkened as he headed for his front door – if someone was ringing his doorbell at this time of night, it couldn't be good. He hoped it wasn't one of his neighbours having a late-night barney with their other half. He really didn't want to get involved.

He yanked the door open, ready to give whoever it was on his doorstep a piece of his mind. His mouth hung open as he saw Helen standing there. Her blonde hair was dishevelled, her eyes red, and her face pale. She looked like she'd been crying. "I'm sorry to intrude so late at night," she said. "But I really need to talk to you. Can I come in?"

Mark found his voice. "Of course." He stepped aside to let Helen enter.

She carried on talking as he shut the door and led her down the corridor into the lounge.

"I'm really sorry to come by so late, but I didn't know who else to talk to. I'm really worried about David. Oh, I'm really sorry. I've come at a bad time." Helen caught sight of Elizabeth getting up from the sofa as she rounded the corner.

"Don't worry about that. Just tell us what's wrong," said Elizabeth.

"It's David." Helen's eyes filled with tears as she sank down to the sofa.

Elizabeth reached for the box of tissues on the coffee table and handed it to Helen. "Did you two have a row?"

"Not exactly." Helen took a tissue and blew her nose. "He doesn't actually know I'm here."

Mark sat in the arm chair. "Tell us what happened, then maybe we can help."

Helen crumpled the tissue in her hands. "He was at work today, and I was in his flat. I took a phone call for him. It was some copper in Manchester, telling me that David's father had died.

I was so upset for him, wondering how I was going to break this news. But when he got home and I told him, he seemed to have no reaction. I know he didn't get on well with his dad, but still...he treated it like some mild inconvenience. This is still his dad, and it's as if he doesn't care. We had fish and chips, he drank a lot of beer, and then he went to bed. But it's not just that. He's...changing. So angry all the time. He used to be different. He used to be so charming, someone you could talk to. Now it's like he's a different person. I'm worried about him and there's no one else I can talk to. He's got no other friends from before."

"I'm not sure I would really classify myself as David's friend anymore," Mark said. "We don't hang out these days. It's almost as if he blanks me. I assumed he'd just moved on and found other friends."

"But he hasn't." Helen dabbed at her eyes with the tissue.

"There are people at the hospital he wants to get friendly with, but I don't think they really like him. He's isolated. He doesn't even talk to me much anymore. The only family he had was his dad, and now he's gone, he's alone. That's why I'm worried about his reaction. It just doesn't seem normal."

"Sometimes grief takes a while to hit," Elizabeth said. "And people react in different ways. Sometimes it takes the form of rage. Perhaps David's anger is a way of expressing his grief."

"But he was angry before he found out about his father."

"He's under a lot of stress for his exams," Mark said. "I'm sure that's the reason he's acting the way he is."

"I keep telling myself that but I think there's more to it." Helen looked at Mark.

"Do you know why David hates his father so much? You must have known him when you were children."

Mark sighed. "I used to hang around at David's house a lot when we were kids. His mum was always so nice and made me feel welcome.

Then she got cancer and was ill for years. It was rough. On everyone. David was twelve when she died, and it had been a slow and painful illness. His dad chose to escape reality by turning to drink. I think the only way he could deal with life was to drink himself into oblivion. I'd always gone to his house after school, but I hated going there once his mum was lying in bed, dying. The place smelled of death. And it was always a mess. She was the one who did the tidying up. Once she got too ill to do it, it just didn't get done. After his mum died I used to dread David asking me over. I told my mum that I didn't like going to David's house anymore. She sat me down and told me how alone David must feel now his mum was gone, and how much he needed me to be his friend, even if he couldn't tell me that. So I went. But I hated every minute. His dad was never there – he was generally propping up some bar somewhere – so we'd have to make ourselves beans on toast and we'd eat in front of the television. There were pizza boxes and beer cans everywhere, and coffee cups that had been there so long that they had mould growing inside them. And still there was that smell. Even though she was gone it smelled like David's mum was still upstairs, the cancer eating away at her insides. Things were never the same after that. David was distant. He grew to resent his dad, because he felt he'd abandoned him at the time he needed him most. Was it the alcohol that finally killed him?"

"I don't know," Helen said. "The chap on the phone was a bit cagey and said they're waiting on an autopsy, but he said there were 'suspicious circumstances'.

All David seemed interested in was how much he was going to inherit. Kept talking about his dad's savings. He didn't seem remotely bothered about his dad's death.

He went to bed and I paced around for a while, my head spinning. Eventually I had to get out of the flat. I couldn't think of where to go, so I ended up here, because you're the only person who really knows David."

"And I don't think even I know him anymore," said Mark.

CHAPTER 11

Elizabeth peered at the sizzling pan on the stove, pushing her glasses up on her nose. She wore nothing but an old blue flannel shirt of Mark's, which she pulled tighter about her. "I wondered what smelled so good."

"Good morning, sexy." Mark paused, spatula in hand, and kissed her. "I wanted to surprise you with breakfast. Bacon and eggs OK?"

"That sounds great. Shall I get plates?" Elizabeth began to poke about in the kitchen cupboards.

"Did you sleep OK?"

"I was lying awake for a while worrying about Helen."

"Yeah, me too." Mark took a plate off Elizabeth and set it down next to the stove. "I hope she got home OK. I felt bad putting her in a cab, but I'd had way too much to drink to drive her home."

"She sent me a text when she got home, thanking us for listening."

Mark levered the bacon from the pan to the plate. "I wish there was something we could do."

"What she does about David has to be her decision. She either stays with him and weathers it, or she leaves him. No one can make that decision for her."

"I suppose. But I'm a bit worried about him too." Mark cracked eggs into the hot fat in the frying pan. "He's putting too much pressure on himself to pass his exams."

"I think you're wasting energy worrying about him. David is a jerk." Elizabeth set another plate on the counter and forked half of the bacon on to it, as Mark added the fried eggs.

"Maybe he is at the moment. He's not always been that way though. He used to be a good laugh."

"I'll have to take your word on that because I don't see it. But you've known him longer than I have."

"The coffee's finished brewing," Mark said. "Why don't you pour us some and I'll take breakfast through to the other room?"

Mark was trying to find some decent Sunday morning TV to watch while they ate, when Elizabeth's phone trilled from the coffee table.

She picked it up and looked at the display. "Linus."

"My, aren't we popular this weekend?"

Elizabeth put the phone to her ear. "Good morning, brother dearest."

"And why do you sound so cheerful for a Sunday morning?" Linus said. "On second thoughts, I don't think I want to know. Are you at Mark's?"

"Yes."

"Then spare me the details. I need some female advice."

"Are you having women trouble, Linus?"

"Just one woman, actually."

"Who is she?"

"Chelsea, of course."

"Chelsea?" Elizabeth glanced at Mark, who rolled his eyes. "I thought you'd given up on her."

"My passions are not that fickle, sister dear. I still want to ask her out. I just need some advice on how to do it."

"I thought you asked her at the LARP game, and she made it clear that she wasn't interested?"

"I never actually got around to asking her. And it was more the general rustic atmosphere she wasn't keen on, rather than me. At least, that's how I'm choosing to see it. I rather hope that the prospect of a swish restaurant, without the taint of all that outdoors, might sway her."

"Why don't you just bite the bullet and ask her? Why the procrastinating?"

"Because I haven't seen her, that's the problem. She's not been at work the last couple of days. I guess she's sick."

"So what do you need my advice on?"

"I'm thinking about going around to her place."

"If she's sick, she might not want to socialise," Elizabeth said.

"But she might want some TLC. If I go over with a big bunch of flowers and offer to look after her when she's sick, she might warm to me."

Elizabeth sighed. "Most women don't want to be seen when they've got a red nose and streaming eyes. Especially by a potential date. I'm not sure it's a good idea."

"But if I see her at her worst and I'm not put off, won't that reassure her that I'm genuine?"

"It doesn't really work that way, Linus. And my bacon's getting cold."

"Mark made you breakfast? Wow, must be serious."

Elizabeth forked a piece of bacon. "Why don't you try phoning her, instead of going round?"

"I did. I've left a couple of messages. She hasn't rung me back."

"Maybe that's a hint."

"Or maybe she's not up to talking. Maybe she's got laryngitis and can't talk. Maybe she feels too weak to answer the phone. I think I'm going to go round. With flowers and chocolate."

"Linus, she's not interested."

"I'll tell her I'll wait on her hand and foot until she's better. Everyone likes being looked after when they're sick."

"Or maybe she's avoiding you. Why are you asking me for advice if you're not planning on taking it?"

"Because, I'm really keen on this girl."

"Well, don't come crying to me when your heart gets broken."

"Thanks a lot, sis. I don't give you advice on your love life."

"Linus, you asked for my opinion. I'm telling you that Chelsea's not the girl for you."

"And I think she is. She just doesn't know it yet."

"I've done my best. If you choose not to listen to me, that's not my fault. Can I get back to my breakfast now?"

"If you must. Thanks for the chat. Catch you later. Bye."

Elizabeth rang off and set down the phone. She stabbed at the bacon. "Linus is still chasing Chelsea."

"So I gather."

"It'll all end in tears." Elizabeth shoved a bacon slice in her mouth.

"What with Linus pursuing the unobtainable Chelsea and Helen doggedly sticking with the increasingly distant David, we don't have too many happy examples of romantic pairings in our social circle."

"Perhaps we have to be the exception to the rule," Elizabeth said. She smiled at Mark. "Let's show them how it should be done."

"I'll drink to that." Mark picked up his coffee cup. He and Elizabeth chinked mugs, before settling in to enjoy their bacon and eggs in front of VH1's Cheesiest 80s Videos.

CHAPTER 12

Chelsea lived in Clapham, in a large older house that had been split into four dwellings, each with their own front doors. A staircase and metal balcony allowed access to the top two maisonettes. Chelsea's was the one on the right.

Linus struggled up the steps with the roses. Finding a parking space nearby had been a problem, so he'd had to walk quite a long way. The thorns on the roses had snagged his sweater in several places and he had spiky leaves sticking to his jeans, not to mention a damp patch on them where the water in the flower bag had started to leak. He would be glad to get shot of them. He really hoped Chelsea appreciated the trouble he was going to.

After two minutes, he rang the doorbell a second time. Still no one answered. He knocked on the door, calling out, "Chelsea? It's me, Linus. Are you OK?"

He tried the door knob and was surprised when the door swung inwards. Linus stepped over the threshold cautiously, calling out again. The silence made him uneasy. Surely Chelsea wouldn't have gone out leaving her door unlocked; not in this area?

He had never been in Chelsea's home before – his only visit had been when he'd picked her up for the role playing game. On that occasion, she'd come out to him so he hadn't had to go inside. The layout of the place was quite odd – the house had been sliced into quarters when converted. A long narrow corridor ran down the length of the property, and all the rooms came off the right-hand side. The first door on the right was open, and Linus could glimpse what looked like the living room. He stepped through cautiously. "Hello? Anyone home?"

What had once been a large room had been divided by a breakfast bar, with a small living room on one side and an even smaller kitchen on the other.

The kitchen was modern; decked out in cheerful white and yellow. The living room was neat and tidy, but lacked any personality. The only books that were visible were some cook books stacked up on the breakfast bar. Linus's heart sank. He'd already suspected Chelsea was out of his league, but the fact she wasn't a reader was further evidence that she wasn't really interested in him. What did they have in common?

Everything looked neat and tidy, but there was a bad smell permeating from somewhere. Like the smell of rotting meat.

Opposite the living room door was a row of coat pegs hanging on the wall of the corridor. Beneath it, a shoe rack, with a dozen pairs of shoes all neatly laid out. There were also half a dozen coats hanging up, along with hats and scarves. He recognised most of them as coats he'd seen Chelsea wearing to work. What had first attracted him to her was her impeccable style. Elizabeth had always warned him that stylish women were high maintenance. Most classy women would never even give Linus the time of day.

The fact that Chelsea had done, was enough to make him think things were different this time.

Next to the coat rack was a small side table. He set the roses down carefully on the table and headed down the corridor.

The smell grew stronger, the further down he went. The hairs on the back of Linus's neck were prickling. Something was very wrong. Was Chelsea sick in bed? If so, he would have expected the place to be a little less tidy. And why was the front door unlocked?

The next room along was the bathroom. He opened the door and peered in. It was a tiny room, not even big enough for a bath tub – there was only a shower.

Again, it was all impeccably neat and tidy, with various toiletries, make-up and perfume bottles lined up on the counter. The room was dry – no evidence of anyone having had a shower recently.

Next to the bathroom was a small door that appeared to be an airing cupboard, and next to that, a final door that had to be the bedroom. The bad smell was strongest here. Linus paused outside the door, his heart hammering in his chest. He had a very bad feeling about all of this. Afraid of what he was going to find, he turned the knob and pushed the bedroom door open.

Chelsea lay on the bed, on a rumpled white bedspread that had been stained crimson with blood. The cream carpet bore a large red stain where the blood had dripped down from the bed. It had congealed underneath Chelsea's body, leaving her lying in a pool of gore. Blood covered her blonde hair, leaving it matted and discoloured. She lay on her back, her eyes wide open and her face smeared with blood, her mouth hanging open in a silent scream. Her long, shapely legs were also covered in blood; her toenails painted a delicate pink that looked so out of place in the pool of red her feet lay in.

Her head, legs and arms were the only parts that were still intact. The rest of her body was a pulped, bloody mess. The torso gaped open, revealing a hollow mass of red gristle and rib bones poking up, making her chest cavity look like the aftermath of a Sunday roast. What looked to be part of Chelsea's intestines snaked down in a trail from her abdominal cavity to the carpet, thick, purple and covered in goo.

Linus staggered back, a hand over his mouth. He could feel his stomach churning. He made it into the pristine bathroom just in time to vomit into the white porcelain toilet bowl.

CHAPTER 13

"I need to see my brother." Elizabeth scowled at the officer standing guard at the police cordon that was blocking access to the crime scene.

"I've already told you, we can't let anyone through. It's a crime scene," the police officer said.

"But he called me. He asked me to come." Elizabeth was losing patience. It had been difficult enough for her and Mark to get this far – with the street cordoned off, they'd had to walk from Clapham Junction station. It had been over an hour since Linus had called her, hysterically sobbing down the phone. All she'd managed to glean from him was that he'd turned up at Chelsea's place to discover her dead. The entire street was blocked off and in spite of there being three police cars and an ambulance present, she'd been unable to learn anything more.

Another police officer approached. Taller and stockier than his colleague, he looked Elizabeth up and down. "Are you Elizabeth Burns?" he asked.

"I am."

"The witness is asking for you. You'd better come through." The policeman lifted the yellow crime scene tape to allow Elizabeth access.

Elizabeth clutched Mark's hand. "This is my boyfriend. He has to come too."

"Fine." The first police officer scowled as his colleague let Elizabeth and Mark through.

Linus was sitting on the pavement in front of the building. The ambulance was in the middle of the street, as parked cars had blocked access to the curb. Its doors were open and one of the paramedics lingered outside, smoking a cigarette. His air of nonchalance gave away the fact there was clearly no rush to get this particular patient to the hospital.

Linus swivelled his head as Elizabeth approached, staring at her with red-rimmed eyes. He was wrapped in a foil blanket, clutching it about himself as if he were afraid of freezing to death. Elizabeth knelt and wrapped her arms around her brother. "Linus, I'm so sorry."

"So much blood," Linus mumbled. "So much blood."

Elizabeth sat on the ground beside Linus and continued to hold him, stroking his hair and rocking back and forth gently. She was four years younger than him and all of her life Linus had been the one to look after her, to look out for her. He'd always been her protector – even more so since their parents died. It seemed strange to her for the roles to be reversed.

The police officer who had let them through the barrier approached. "My name is DC Tim Lattimer. I understand this is your brother, is that right?" he said, indicating Linus.

"That's right," Elizabeth said.

DC Lattimer took out a note book and pen. "We've not been able to get much out of him.

All we know is that he came to visit Miss Brown, found her door open, and discovered her body in the flat."

"I don't know any more than that either. I spoke to Linus this morning and he said he was going to come round here to visit Chelsea."

Two paramedics came down the steps of the building carrying a stretcher between them. On the stretcher was a zipped-up body bag – clearly occupied. Elizabeth stared at it in horrified fascination.

Two other people followed the paramedics down the stairs – a pinched-looking man with a camera and a middle-aged woman with a briefcase. The two paused at the bottom of the steps and conversed with a couple more police officers who lingered there."

"Can you give me your brother's address?" DC Lattimer asked. "He's not been able to tell us himself. I'll also need your name and address."

"Can you tell us what happened?" Elizabeth asked.

DC Lattimer looked at her. "Miss Brown was murdered. In a bizarre and very violent manner. There'll be an investigation, and we might need to talk to you again."

"Is my brother a suspect?"

"Not at the moment, no. It's clear that Miss Brown had been dead for several days by the time your brother found her. But there are a lot of unexplained things about this case, and we're going to have to follow up every lead."

"When you say she died in a violent and bizarre manner, what do you mean, exactly?"

"I'm afraid I can't tell you that. We can't release information that might compromise the investigation."

"She was ripped open," Linus said quietly.

Elizabeth stared at her brother. "What?"

Linus rocked back and forth. "All of her insides had been ripped out. There was so much blood. And she had this look on her face. Like…complete terror. Complete and overwhelming terror."

Elizabeth wrapped her arms around Linus and held him tightly, but he continued to rock back and forth. "Can I take my brother home now, Officer? He's obviously in shock."

"We just need to get a few more details from you. I don't believe we have your name yet, sir." DC Lattimer looked at Mark.

Behind them, the ambulance carrying the remains of Chelsea Brown drove down the road and was let through the police cordon. There was no siren and no need for speed. Nothing could be done for Chelsea now. She was bound for the mortuary, not the hospital.

CHAPTER 14

The day of Chelsea's funeral was cold and grey. The weather was fitting. Mark had never been to a more depressing event. His only experience of funerals had been those of his grandparents, who had been old and ill, and a person grows up expecting to outlive their grandparents. But when someone young and healthy dies so violently and suddenly, everyone is left reeling, trying to make sense of it all as they deal with their grief.

The church was packed, mostly with young people sporting red eyes and streaky faces. Mark sat with Elizabeth and Linus in one of the rows near the back, amongst other people their age.

Chelsea's family were sitting at the front. Mark could identify her parents, the sad-faced couple in their fifties, in the front row.

Next to them sat two young men, undoubtedly Chelsea's brothers. On the other side sat a woman in her late twenties, with a tall dark-haired man and two little boys. These were aged about two and four and were dressed in matching miniature black suits. Probably Chelsea's sister and her family – there was a family resemblance. The two small boys had clearly been told to sit still and be quiet, and were making a valiant effort to do so. But the service was long and boring for such young children and every once in while they would start fidgeting, until one of their parents would lean over and hiss at them. At which point, the boys would freeze and sit up straight, their hands in their laps; a posture that looked artificial and undoubtedly uncomfortable.

Mark looked down at the order of service in his lap, an attractively laid-out document that looked like it had been produced on a high-quality printer.

On the cover was a lovely photo of Chelsea in a long pink dress, her skin sun-kissed and her blonde hair swept up in an elegant coiffure. It was a head and shoulders shot, but the hairstyle and pose of the shot made Mark think maybe it was a photo of Chelsea as a bridesmaid – perhaps at her sister's wedding. The photo had been cropped well but along the bottom there was a glimpse of the bouquet she was holding, and the far right edge of the picture held evidence that someone else had been cropped out. Perhaps this picture had been taken from a bigger one of the bride posing with her bridesmaids.

The service was about to start and people were filing in, although the church was already full. Mark, at the end of the aisle, looked up to see Helen pause at their pew. She was wearing a black coat over a fitted grey dress and had her hair pinned up, held in place with a black lacquered hair slide.

"I thought I was going to be late," she said.

"Not started yet," Mark said. He, Elizabeth and Linus all shuffled over to their left, to allow Helen to squeeze in at the end of the pew.

Helen looked around. "Isn't David here?"

"We thought he'd be coming with you," Elizabeth said.

"I didn't see him last night. We…had a bit of a row. But I spoke to him on the phone and told him he had to be here."

A hush fell over the assembled throng as the vicar stepped up and began to address the congregation.

The service was long and sober, with audible sobs being heard from various parts of the congregation. The vicar talked about Chelsea's beauty and energy; her zest for life; though it was clear to Mark that he hadn't known her.

However, the frequent references to Chelsea's parents being pillars of the community, and how the congregation was praying for God to help guide them through this tragedy, made Mark think that they were probably known to the vicar quite well.

Evidently Chelsea had not followed her parents' faith.

The service finished and the coffin was carried solemnly down the aisle by the pallbearers, two of which were Chelsea's brothers. Following the coffin's progress, Mark caught a glimpse of David standing at the back of the church and wondered when he had come in. He was leaning against the back wall, hands shoved deep into the pockets of a navy blue overcoat.

Elizabeth clutched Mark's hand and leaned to whisper in his ear. "It's so sad. She goes down the aisle in a coffin, not a wedding dress. No one deserves that."

Mark didn't know what to say to that, so he just squeezed Elizabeth's hand.

The congregation followed the coffin out of the church and Mark and the others caught up with David, who had stepped to one side to allow the procession to file out of the door.

Helen stood to one side.

The frostiness that passed between her and David was palpable; they exchanged a look but did not speak to each other.

"We should pay respects to Chelsea's parents," Elizabeth said, pointing out the sad couple who were standing by the church door, greeting people. She caught Mark's hand and pulled him over without waiting for a response.

"Mr and Mrs Brown? I'm Elizabeth Burns. I'm so sorry for your loss."

"Thank you for coming. Were you a friend of Chelsea's?" Mr Brown offered a hand to shake. His wife dabbed at her eyes with a well-worn hankie. Her face was hidden by a large black hat with a veil hanging off it.

"We all were," Elizabeth said. She introduced Mark, then Linus, David and Helen who were following behind.

"It means a lot to us that you came," Mr Brown said. "Perhaps you'll join us back at the house for the wake? The burial is family only, but you can go on ahead.

We'll be there after the service."

"Thank you."

"We were all planning on going to the wake, weren't we?" Linus said. "I want to be there."

"I'll go, but I'll need a lift," Helen said. "I came on the bus."

"I've got my car," David said. "You can come with me."

Mark, Elizabeth and Linus parted company with the others and headed back to Mark's car. Elizabeth said nothing, but she was speed-walking. Mark could tell that she was pissed off. The whole situation was depressing enough, but the fact that Elizabeth really didn't like David wasn't helping.

Mark unlocked the car. Linus and Elizabeth climbed in but no one spoke a word. Mark didn't break the silence as he got ready to drive off. Words seemed hopelessly inadequate.

CHAPTER 15

Helen sat in silence during the drive to the house. David programmed an apparently new GPS system with the address of Chelsea's parents and didn't utter a word to her as he drove. The expressionless electronic voice of the navigational system was the only sound breaking the silence.

Chelsea's parents lived in a semi-detached house in an affluent part of North London. The circular driveway was already full of cars when they arrived. Parking was a problem; they had to park the car in a side street several blocks away, and then walk back to the house.

Helen had no idea whom the woman was that answered the door, but she thought the family must still be at the burial service. They were ushered through to the living room – a room decked out in eggshell blue and tasteful polished oak.

Helen had never been to a wake before. It was strange to see a house full of people with drinks in their hands, a scenario that she usually associated with parties and celebrations. The sombre atmosphere permeated the house, as if the building itself was in a state of mourning. All the guests spoke to each other in hushed whispers, as though conversation was disrespectful. Helen made a beeline for Elizabeth, Mark and Linus, who were huddled in a corner.

"It feels so strange, so sad," Helen said. "What do you do in situations like this?"

"It's just about being there to pay your respects," Elizabeth said.

A young woman wearing a tailored black dress and black boots came around with a tray full of drinks – red and white wine, and glasses of orange juice. Everyone took a wine glass except Mark, who never drank alcohol when he was driving.

The girl's eyes were smudged with mascara, as if she'd been recently crying.

"Thanks for coming," she said quietly, before she departed.

They stood around for a while, not knowing what to say. Helen studied a painting on the wall. An impressionistic river sunset scene: all yellows, reds, greens and blues. It looked like a print, but it was carefully framed and gave the room a soothing, welcoming atmosphere. At least it would do, if the air of grief were not so oppressive.

"So," Mark said awkwardly, "has anyone heard if there's been any developments from the police?"

"About what?" David asked.

"About what happened to Chelsea."

"I think the investigation's still ongoing," Helen said.

"That means they haven't got a suspect." Elizabeth swirled barely-touched wine around in the glass she was holding.

"I hope they catch whoever did it soon. Poor Chelsea. I feel so sorry for Mr and Mrs Brown. I can't imagine what it must be like to bury your own child."

Helen was acutely aware that she was talking too loudly, but she couldn't help herself. After spending time with such an uncommunicative David and trying to squash down her grief at the funeral, she just had to talk to someone – anyone.

"I think they're back." Mark looked towards the open door. Out in the corridor there was a flurry of activity, then a blast of cold air as the door was open and closed. A glimpse of Mrs Brown's hat could be seen as she passed the door, the rest of her family following behind.

"I need some air," David said abruptly. "It's very oppressive in here." He stalked towards the front door. Helen impulsively went after him.

The family were heading into the kitchen. David slipped past them and out the front door, where he leaned against the front wall of the house, his hands shoved in his pockets. Helen followed him, pulling her coat tighter around herself. The chill in the air was noticeable after being inside the stuffy house.

"What's the matter?" she asked David.

"What do you mean?"

"Why are we standing outside?"

"I don't know why you're standing outside. I came out because I needed some fresh air."

"Everyone's sad. It's a funeral. But there's something else wrong. What is it?"

"I don't know what to say to anyone, what to do." David shoved his hands deeper into his pockets. "Death is...awkward."

"You're saying this as someone whose parents are both dead? I would have thought you were more familiar with death than anyone else."

"I didn't grieve for my dad. I didn't like him much. And my mother...that was too long ago. I don't remember."

"You must remember. It was a traumatic event and you were very young."

David shrugged. "I don't."

The front door opened, and Mark came out. "Hope you don't mind if I join you out here."

"Not at all," Helen said with relief. "Where's Elizabeth?"

"Passing condolences on to the family. She's much better at that kind of thing than I am. I felt like a third wheel."

"I think I'll do the same," said Helen, glad of an excuse to go back into the house.

CHAPTER 16

After Helen had gone back inside, silence fell. Mark rubbed his arms, feeling chilly in the fresh air, and leaned back against the wall. "We should go back inside," he said.

"Can't face it yet." David reached inside his jacket pocket, pulling out a packet of cigarettes.

"Since when have you been a smoker?"

David stuck a cigarette between his lips and put the packet back in his pocket. He grinned at Mark. "Don't you remember we used to sneak out to smoke together in school?"

"Yeah, but that was years ago. I didn't think either of us took it seriously. Besides, they were usually joints, not tobacco."

David fumbled with a packet of matches. As he held the book up to retrieve a match, Mark caught the name embossed in silver lettering on the white cover: Havering Heights Golf Club.

"I've been under a lot of pressure," David said. "With the exams and all. Suddenly I found myself craving nicotine. It seems to help with the stress." He lit the cigarette and leaned back, exhaling a long plume of smoke.

"Since when have you been hanging around golf clubs?" Mark asked. David looked puzzled. Mark pointed to the matches.

"Oh, that." David tucked the match book back into his inside pocket. "I used to mess about with it. I thought it was time to take it seriously. It's a good place to meet contacts, the golf course."

"You can afford to join the golf club?"

"I'm a doctor now." David took another drag on the cigarette. "At least I will be, when I pass my exams."

"Yeah. But have you suddenly found a job paying fifty grand?"

"What would you know about it?" David scowled. "Do you remember our business studies teacher in College? Mr Finch?"

"Yeah, sure, I remember him. Looked like Gordon Gekko. Complete with throwback eighties outfit. Red braces and skinny tie."

"He was amazing when it came to the right attitude for business though." David leaned back, looking thoughtful. "I remember when he was telling us about preparing for job interviews. The question of what to wear came up."

"I remember that. We were a class full of sixteen-year-old punks, in baggy ripped jeans and hoodies. None of us had ever had to go for an interview."

"Mr Finch was making a point about the right impression. So we discussed the fact that we should wear a suit to the interview. Some idiot suggested taking a shower and combing your hair, as if it was something he wouldn't do normally. But I remember what Mr Finch said. 'Don't dress for the job you're being interviewed for, dress for the job you want.' I always remembered that." David flicked ash carelessly on the driveway.

"I remember that. I wasn't sure what it meant at the time."

"I understand what it means now. It's not about whether you have the money. It's giving the impression that you do." David took a final drag from the cigarette and crushed it under the heel of his highly-polished loafer.

"Impressions are all well and good, but you still need the cash to pay for it."

"And I will. Just as soon as my inheritance comes through."

"But that could take months."

"It won't," David said.

"But it does. When my uncle died, it took a year and a half for his estate to get sorted out. There's so much to sort out, it's unbelievable. Your dad's been dead only a few weeks. It'll be months before you see that money."

David glanced over at Mark, and for just a moment, a chill ran through his soul. He thought he caught a glimpse of something behind David's eyes. Something that didn't belong there.

But then it was gone. "I need to get going," David said. "There's still time to get a cramming session in tonight. I'm feeling good about these exams now. I think I'm actually going to pass."

He disappeared back into the house, leaving Mark alone in the deepening twilight.

CHAPTER 17

David was shut away in his bedroom, studying. At least, on the face of it he was. His mind was in turmoil. That brooding presence was always there, at the back of his mind. It spoke to him. Not aloud, and not in English, but somehow in a form that his mind could understand. In his head, the words were in English. Brooding, persistent, and clear.

I CAN MAKE YOUR DREAMS COME TRUE, the presence said. JUST GIVE ME WHAT I WANT.

David threw his books down. "You keep saying that," he said aloud, "but I see no evidence of this."

YOU WISHED TO PASS YOUR EXAMS, the presence whispered.

"I haven't passed them yet. And Chelsea's dead. Is that the price I had to pay?"

PATIENCE. YOU NEED TO TRUST ME.

"That's what you said when I said I needed money. Now my father's died. I know I'll get the inheritance, but that will be months. Maybe years."

SOON. HAVE FAITH.

David put his hands to his head, then paced up and down the bedroom. "I still don't understand what you want."

POWER, OF COURSE. WHAT ELSE IS THERE?

"Why me? Why are you talking to me?"

YOU BROUGHT ME BACK FROM THE DEAD.

"It was that stupid ritual. I only used that because I thought it sounded good. I had no idea what it was going to do."

NEVERTHELESS, IT WAS RIGHT, AND I THANK YOU. NOW I AM CONNECTED TO YOU. I MUST CHANNEL POWER THROUGH YOU. I CAN GRANT YOU WHATEVER YOU WISH. THE MORE POWERFUL I GET, THE MORE I CAN GIVE TO YOU.

David sat down on the edge of the bed. "But these sacrifices you mentioned. You have to kill people to get the power, I get that. But why do they have to be people I know? Why can't you just go after some random stranger?"

THE GREATER THE SACRIFICE, THE MORE POTENT THE POWER. THIS IS THE PRICE. IS IT REALLY SO MUCH TO MAKE YOUR DREAMS COME TRUE?

An image came unbidden into David's mind. An elegant house on a hill with a cultivated lawn. A red Ferrari parked in the drive. A brand new Mercedes pulled up next to the Ferrari and David saw an older version of himself get out of the car – a version of himself that looked fit and toned. The dream version of himself opened the boot and took out a set of golf clubs. The door of the house opened and an elegant woman stood in the doorway.

She was slim and bronzed, dressed in designer gear with an expensive haircut and immaculately manicured nails. She smiled broadly, showing a set of perfect white teeth.

She came out to greet the dream-David, who leaned down to kiss her, rubbing her slender back with a broad, strong hand.

The vision clouded over and faded away, leaving David with an inexplicable sense of loss.

IT CAN BE YOURS, the brooding presence in his mind insisted. THE HOUSE. THE WOMAN. THE STATUS.

David looked up and stared apparently into nothing. "How?"

The laptop on the dressing table suddenly clicked into life. David stood up and went to it, moving as if in a dream. The screen displayed an estate agent's website. It showed a picture of a detached house in Hampstead with a white stucco finish and a large driveway. With a start, David realised it was the house in his vision. The price made his heart sink. "It's beautiful, but I can't afford this. Maybe on a consultant's salary, but not now."

WHY DO I HAVE TO KEEP TELLING YOU TO HAVE FAITH? WHATEVER YOU WISH, I CAN GRANT FOR YOU. AS LONG AS YOU ARE PREPARED TO PAY THE PRICE.

David stared at the house, his fingers touching the laptop screen. If that house was his, he could have dinner parties and invite all the people he wanted to make an impression on. They would come to the house and understand he was a man who was going places. The sort of man they wanted to know.

"I want it," he whispered.

THEN PAYMENT SHALL BE MADE.

A hesitant knock on the bedroom door made David start. The door opened a crack, and Helen poked her head around. The brooding presence in David's mind faded abruptly.

"You've been here for hours," Helen said. "Maybe you should take a break. I was about to sort out some dinner."

"Just leave me alone!" David roared. "How can I concentrate on studying when you keep interfering like this?"

Helen shrank back, a fearful look on her face. She retreated and closed the door behind her.

David turned to look at the laptop, still displaying the estate agent picture. The presence in his mind was gone. It had been with him so often of late, he had got used to it being there.

It was oppressive and malevolent, but it felt like it had become part of him. On the occasions it wasn't there, it almost felt like part of him was missing.

He went back to the laptop and stared at the picture of the magnificent house. Then he clicked on the 'contact us' link under the estate agent details.

CHAPTER 18

"I passed," David said to Helen when she picked up her office phone. "I've just had the results. I passed everything."
"I never doubted you," she said. "Congratulations."

"Let's celebrate tonight. Come round to mine after work. Pick up some Chinese on the way. I'll get a nice bottle of wine and we can have an evening in to celebrate my success."

"I've got a meeting later that's likely to over-run, but I'll get there as soon as I can. I'll see you later." *Maybe things will be back to normal now*, Helen thought as she hung up. *Now that David's passed, maybe he'll relax. Be less stressed. Get back to the way he was before.*

But some small part of her kept on with that nagging doubt. What if things didn't change?

The afternoon dragged interminably, but finally she was free. She didn't keep any clothes at David's, so she went home to pack an overnight bag before heading for his place.

Then she stopped at David's local Chinese takeaway to get some food.

Her heart sank when he opened the door to her. She was expecting him to look happier and more relaxed, but he didn't. He still had the dark shadows under his eyes and the sunken cheek bones. The scowl on his face. "I was expecting you ages ago," was the first thing he said to her.

She struggled over the threshold, her overnight bag in one hand, the takeaway bag in the other. "I had to go home first, to get some of my things," she said.

"You don't need to get your things. You can borrow mine," he said offhandedly.

She dumped her overnight bag in the hallway and carried the takeaway into the kitchen. "I needed some clothes. I don't have any here."

"I don't have room for your clothes here." He leaned in the kitchen doorway, glass of wine in hand. For the first time,

Helen noticed the bottle of Marquis de Risqual on the counter, open and half-empty. "I couldn't wait, so I started on the wine."

"So I noticed. I gather it's OK if I have some?" she said sarcastically, getting out plates for the takeaway.

He shrugged. "Of course, when I move, there'll be plenty of room for your clothes."

"You're moving?"

"I've got some money coming to me now that my father's dead. And I'm a doctor. I've got a certain image to maintain. It's time to get a bigger place. A nice house, in a nice part of London."

"So you've started looking then, have you?" Helen divided the food onto the two plates.

"I've found the house I want to live in. That's the most important thing."

"Surely the most important thing is what you can afford."

"I don't expect you to understand. I'll be moving in different circles now."

Helen got a glass from the cupboard and poured herself some of the wine. There wasn't much left in the bottle after she'd done that, but she figured David had a good head start on her already. "I just don't think it's a good idea to spend the money before you've got it. It might take a while to come through."

"Where's the problem? I'm the only surviving relative. It's pretty straightforward."

"Shall we eat?" Helen picked up her glass and one of the plates of food and went into the living room without waiting for an answer.

She was flicking channels on the TV, but when David joined her on the couch he took the remote from her without asking. He clicked on to a Bond film.

"Shall we toast your exam success?" She picked up her glass, asking the question to deflect from David's bad mood.

With every moment that passed this evening, she was becoming less inclined to spend time in his company.

David picked up his own glass and clinked it against Helen's. "The exams over, and I passed. Here's to a better future."

Better for whom? Helen thought darkly. She said nothing and started to eat her dinner, staring at the TV and trying to remember that she was with the man that she was supposed to love.

She didn't eat much of the takeaway – her appetite had left her. She noticed David didn't eat much either. He just stared fixedly at the TV and kept on drinking the wine. After the Rioja bottle was empty, he opened another one. He didn't offer to fill up her glass; he just kept refilling his own. The first glass of wine Helen had drunk now sat uncomfortably on the heavy knot on her stomach, so she didn't bother drinking any more.

When it became clear that neither of them were eating any more, Helen carried the plates and her empty wine glass into the kitchen, scraping off the leftover food and putting the crockery into the sink.

She peered around the corner into the living room. David was still apparently engrossed in the Bond film. She noticed he'd refilled his glass again. "I'm going to bed," she said. David nodded brusquely, not taking his eyes of the TV.

Although she'd slept in it many times, David's bed felt unwelcoming and cold. Helen lay awake for a long time, unhappy thoughts turning around in her head. She was physically and mentally exhausted, but sleep wouldn't come.

Eventually, just when she'd started to drift off, the light snapped on and jerked her into wakefulness once more.

David was coming to bed. The light dazzled her eyes, but she could just make out his shape as he took off his clothes and got into bed beside her.

She turned away and closed her eyes, pretending to be asleep. She didn't feel particularly passionate tonight. But his arms were reaching for her, coming up behind her and fondling her breasts. "No, David," she said sleepily. "Not tonight."

But his hands were more insistent, snaking up underneath her pyjama top. He pressed his body hard against hers; she could feel his erection pressing against her bottom, through the fabric of her pyjama bottoms. She started to wriggle out of his grasp. "Let's just sleep."

His hands moved down, feeling for the elastic of her pyjama bottoms and pulling it down. Helen felt uneasy. "David, no! Leave me alone." She wriggled some more but he yanked her bottoms down, and they became entangled in her feet. Her movement restricted in this way, it became difficult to move away from him.

He rolled her onto her back and straddled her, pinning her hips down between his thighs.

She opened her eyes. The light was still on and she blinked in the brightness. The look she saw in David's eyes made her feel afraid. "David, what are you doing?"

"What do you think I'm doing?" He leaned over and kissed her roughly, the unshaven stubble on his face harsh and raspy. The pressure on her body was making it difficult to breathe. She tried to tell him to stop, but he was forcing his tongue into her mouth and she couldn't speak. She struggled, but he was stronger.

He released one of her arms so that he could reach down, forcing his fingers into her, rubbing in and out. She slapped him on the back and turned her head to one side so she could breathe. "David, I mean it! Stop!"

"You don't want me to stop," he said. "I know you like this." He rubbed harder. So hard it was hurting, his fingernails carelessly catching the delicate flesh.

She yelped. "Please, David, stop! I mean it. You're hurting me."

She struggled to free herself, but he clamped his knees harder. Helen brought up her free hand to pummel him repeatedly on the back. "I mean it, David, you're scaring me. Stop!"

"You know you want it. But it really turns me on to hear you say you don't." David removed his hand and held her free arm down once more, putting his mouth over hers and kissing her roughly. Then he was inside her, thrusting and rocking. However much she struggled, it only seemed to make him thrust all the harder.

Finally he came and, grunting, rolled off her. Then he turned out the light. Helen turned away from him, trying to hold back the sobs in her throat and hoping that if she lay still long enough he would go to sleep. Her crotch throbbed painfully from violent and unwelcome sex, and her arms hurt from where he'd held her down.

Quietly, not wanting to awaken David, she scrabbled for her pyjama bottoms and pulled them up around her hips.

Then she curled herself into a foetal position as far away from him as possible. There she lay, crying silent tears; afraid to move, afraid to disturb him, afraid to sleep; until the morning dawned.

CHAPTER 19

Elizabeth was working on a particularly problematic line of code when her mobile phone rang. She dug it out of her bag and was surprised when she saw the display reading "Helen". She and Helen had swapped numbers since the game, but they'd never called each other.

"Hi Helen," Elizabeth said as she answered the phone.

"Hi. I'm sorry to ring you at work, but I wondered if you were free for lunch?"

"Mark and I normally go together, but we don't have anything special planned."

"Would he mind if it was just me and you today? I really need a girlie chat. I'm sorry if I'm causing problems, but it is quite important."

There was a quaver in Helen's voice that disturbed Elizabeth.

"It's not a problem to meet you. Mark can eat his sandwiches by himself for once." Elizabeth glanced at the clock. It was five past twelve. "When do you want to meet?"

"I'm round the corner from you right now, so any time is fine. When's good for you?"

"How come you're close by? Your office isn't near mine, is it?"

"No." Helen sniffed, the sob in her voice audible. "I took the day off sick."

"OK." Now Elizabeth really was worried. "There's a cafe called Mario's on Greek Street, round the corner from the tube station. Do you know it? I can meet you there in about ten minutes."

"That's fine. Thanks Elizabeth. I'll see you in a few minutes."

* * * *

Helen was sitting at a table at the back of the café with a cup of tea in front of her. As Elizabeth walked over to join her, she saw the misery on Helen's face; her face was red, blotchy, and streaked from tears.

"Helen, what on earth is the matter?"

Helen sniffed and blew her nose on a crumpled tissue. "I don't really know where to begin. I just needed someone to talk to."

A waitress came over to take their order. Elizabeth ordered an orange juice and a toasted cheese and ham sandwich. Helen said she wasn't hungry and didn't order anything.

As soon as the waitress was gone Helen said, "It's David."

"Well, I don't like the man, and you know that. But you're with him, so you must love him."

Helen looked up at Elizabeth, a sadness in her eyes that made Elizabeth's heart ache. "Last night he...well, he's getting violent. And I'm afraid."

Elizabeth reached across the table and took Helen's hand. "You need to leave him."

"I love him," Helen said, her voice filled with misery. "How can I leave him?"

"Because you deserve more respect. If he's treating you this way, he doesn't love you and you deserve someone better."

"Logically, I know that. But every time I think about leaving him, I remember the person he used to be. He used to be kind, gentle, and caring."

"Mark says he used to be a nice guy, too. I have trouble believing that. In the time that I've known him, I've only seen him being a jerk."

"He wasn't always that way. Something's happened to him, Elizabeth. It's not just the exams. It's since we played that LARP game. He's changed, somehow."

"People do change. A lot has happened to David. The exams. He's put a lot of pressure on himself to succeed. And his father's died.

87

Mark told us how hard it was for David as a kid and he's still probably dealing with that. People grieve in different ways."

"It's more than just that. I see him every day, and he's changed. It's almost as if overnight he's become a different person. I think it has something to do with that ritual."

"It was just a game, Helen."

Helen shook her head. "I know this is going to sound crazy to you, but I think he's…possessed. What if that ritual was real? What if it unleashed something?"

"I think you're making excuses for him."

"I know you think it's crazy, but I was brought up a Catholic. This stuff does happen. And I know he didn't make that ritual up – he found it on the Internet."

What David is doing to you is unacceptable. You don't need to put up with it. You have to leave him."

"Where would I go?"

"You can stay with me if you need to. But my place is a bit cramped – one of us would be sleeping on the sofa."

Helen smiled thinly. "Thanks for the offer. But it's not as if I live with him. I've still got my own place."

"How many women have gone on defending their man when he abuses them? Convinced themselves that somehow it's their fault? That they deserve it?" Elizabeth saw Helen's eyes fill with tears. "I don't mean to sound like a bitch, Helen. But it has to stop now. Next time David lashes out, you might end up in the hospital. Or in the mortuary. I don't want to see that happen."

"But what if it's not really David?"

"What do you mean?"

"What if there's something inside him, making him do these things? What if the real David's still trapped inside, wanting help?"

"You're back to the possession thing again. That's not possible."

"I was brought up to believe there are more things than those we can see and feel. Although I don't believe the Catholic doctrine I was brought up with anymore, I still think there are things out there that can't be explained. When I was a kid, our priest had to perform an exorcism. There was a lady in our village who'd been possessed. She'd been put in a mental institution because everyone thought she was crazy, but the priest was convinced she wasn't. There was something inside her, making her do these terrible things."

"I'm sorry, I can't share your viewpoint. Religion has been used too many times to let one group of people dominate another. You especially shouldn't be using it to explain David's behaviour."

"He needs help, Elizabeth. I can't just turn my back on him. Whatever's inside him, it's eating him up inside. I want the man I love back. I know he's still in there, somewhere. And I need to discover a way to let him find his way home. I need to be there for him."

Elizabeth sighed. "I'm sorry to hear that. I'm worried about you."

"I suppose it was too much to expect someone else to understand. It sounds nuts, doesn't it?"

"Listen to me." Elizabeth leaned across the table. "You deserve better. You are an intelligent, attractive woman, and you deserve someone who respects that. I'm begging you, please leave David before he wears you down completely."

"I appreciate your concern. Really, I do."

"But you're not going to listen to me, are you? At least spend some time away from David. Think about it for a while. And I want you to call me. Every day. At least once. Just so I can be reassured you're OK."

Helen smiled weakly. "I will. And thank you."

"For what? I haven't done anything."

"For listening. For caring." Helen got up from the table. "I better go."

"Go where?"

"I'm going to go home. I need to think about a few things."

"Promise me you won't see David? At least for today. Try and spend a few days away from him, if you can. It might help put things in perspective."

Helen hesitated for a moment and then said, "OK. I promise. Thanks, Elizabeth."

"Don't forget, ring me tomorrow. And every day after that."

"Thanks again. See you." Helen left the cafe without looking back.

Elizabeth watched her go with a growing sense of trepidation. She couldn't force Helen to stop seeing David.

Her appetite had left her. She pushed aside the remains of her lunch and got up to pay the bill. She wondered if it was worth getting Mark to go talk to David. After all, David and Mark were supposed to be best friends. Or they had been, once. Elizabeth recalled with sadness Mark's recent remarks about feeling estranged and distant from David.

If David was set upon a path of self-destruction, then no one could help him off it. But he didn't have the right to take anyone else with him. Somehow she had to find a way to help Helen.

CHAPTER 20

Mark rested the two cases of beer on the step and leaned on the doorbell. He shivered in the chill night, switching the carrier bag with the DVDs in it from under one arm to the other.

After a minute or so, the door swung open and David looked out at him. He tried to mask his shock. David looked thin and haggard, like he'd aged ten years in only a fortnight. He was wearing an old t-shirt and ripped jeans, with nothing on his feet. His hair was tousled and uncombed, and he looked like he hadn't shaved in at least a couple of days.

He stared out at Mark expectantly. "So can I come in?" asked Mark, when David didn't speak.

"Yeah. Sure." David turned abruptly and disappeared off into the flat. Mark picked up the beer and crossed the threshold, using his foot to push the door shut behind him.

He went straight to the kitchen and put the beer down on the counter, next to an open bottle of red wine that was nearly empty. "Starting without me, eh?" Mark attempted to put an air of joviality in his tone.

David shrugged and picked up the half-empty wine glass on the side. "I've had a rough day. Actually, a rough week."

"Sorry to hear that. I hope you don't mind if I start on the beer?" Mark pulled a bottle of Kronenberg from the pack and stowed the rest in the fridge, then followed David into the living room. "I brought some DVDs along," he said. "I thought we could make it a boy's night."

"Has Helen been spending any time with Elizabeth?" David sat on the sofa.

"Why do you ask?"

"Because she hasn't been spending it with me. If she's not been with Elizabeth, then she must be seeing someone else. I just thought I'd check."

"She hasn't got someone else."

"You've seen her then?"

Mark hesitated. He had no desire to dig a deeper hole for himself. "Not exactly. But Elizabeth's talked to her. In fact, they've talked a few times." He knew that, in fact, Elizabeth had spoken to Helen every evening since the day they had met for lunch.

"So why the hell is she avoiding me?"

This was getting into dangerous territory. "I think she's a bit upset, mate."

"That time of the month, is it? Well I can't be doing with women's moods, but I wish she'd mention it. Then I'd understand why I'm not getting any."

Mark stalled by taking a swig of his beer and pretending to look through the DVDs. "Look, what goes on between you and Helen is none of my business, but don't you think maybe you've been behaving unreasonably?"

David slammed his wine glass down on to the coffee table.

"You're right. It's none of your business. But whatever that bitch has been telling Elizabeth, it's all lies."

"Hey, take it easy! I thought we were having a chill-out night. Why are you so wound up?"

David stared at Mark, his eyes hard. "You have no idea what goes on in my life. You don't know what you're talking about."

"Then tell me. We used to be mates, David. We used to talk. What's happened to you? We all thought it was exam stress, but the exams are over now and you did OK, so why are you still acting this way?"

"The exams are just the beginning. You have no idea what pressure I'm under. I'm a doctor now. I have an image to maintain."

"Since when are you worried about image?"

"Things are different now." David picked up the wine glass and drained it. "It's not enough just to be a good doctor, you know. To be successful, it's all about the image.

Who you know. The circles you move in. The hobbies. Having the right postcode."

"So are you taking up playing golf or something?" Mark said. David threw him a sharp look. "Oh, man, you are playing golf. You told me about joining the golf club at Chelsea's funeral. You always said it was an old man's sport."

"It's a rich man's sport."

"You're not a rich man, either."

"Not yet. But I will be." David put the wine glass back on the table. "I'm moving, too. I need the right postcode." He went off into the kitchen, returning a moment later with the bottle of wine.

"So where are you moving to?"

"I've put in an offer on a place in Hampstead." David poured the remains of the wine into his glass.

Mark nearly choked on his beer. "How the hell can you afford a place in Hampstead?"

"I'm the sole beneficiary of my father's inheritance."

"But that's going to take ages to come through, surely?"

David shrugged. "It's academic. It's all in cyberspace anyway. I've got lawyer's paperwork that verifies the money is coming to me. The property sale will take ages to sort, and by the time it's all done and dusted I'll have my inheritance."

"I can't believe you're going to inherit enough to buy a place in Hampstead."

"I only need enough for a deposit," David said, as if talking to a very stupid child. "I can still get a mortgage."

"But mate. You'll be in debt till retirement."

"Once I have the image and the contacts, the salary will follow. I'll soon start earning enough to pay the mortgage."

"And what about Helen?"

"What about her? Do you want another beer?"

"No, thanks, I'm good. I think she's a bit confused about where she stands. Does she actually feature in this grand plan of yours?"

David took a long gulp of wine. "I think she'll conform to the appropriate image of 'doctor's wife', should she choose to do so. That's up to her."

"Is that all she is to you? Part of the image?"

"That's assuming she wants to stick around. Since I've not seen her for a week, it would seem she's decided, for no apparent reason whatsoever, she's had enough of me."

"No apparent reason?" Mark stared at David. "You've got to be joking?"

"What, you know something I don't?"

"She told Elizabeth what you did to her."

"She's lying. Or Elizabeth is. You know she doesn't like me."

"Elizabeth doesn't tell lies," Mark snapped. "And I don't think Helen does, either."

"What business is it of yours, in any case, what happens between Helen and me?"

"Because I'm worried about you."

"Why should you be worried about me? I'm doing fine."

"Something's wrong, David. The way you're behaving. You've changed."

David drained the wine glass and slammed it down on the table. "Yes. Maybe I have changed. I'm becoming successful and you can't deal with that."

"That's a low blow, David. And it's not true."

"Isn't it?"

"Of course it's not. Things have been wrong since the game."

"Maybe I just realised the games are childish."

"You've always loved the games. Even more than I have."

"And maybe I've suddenly grown up. I'm a doctor now. I'm moving in higher class circles with higher class people. I'm about to start earning a shit load of money and I no longer have time for stupid games and geeks who refuse to grow up. Maybe I've just seen the light."

Mark sprang to his feet, his fist clenched. "And maybe you're just full of shit."

"It's a harsh reality, but you have to face the fact I've outgrown you."

Mark stood still, focusing on his breathing and trying to keep himself under control. Hitting David now would not solve anything, tempting though it may be. "I think maybe it's time I left."

"I think that's a good idea." David flicked on the TV and did not look around as Mark stormed out of the room.

As an afterthought, Mark retrieved the beer from the fridge. He was tempted to take it home and drink all of it alone; wallowing in his anger, but the sensible part of him insisted that wasn't a good idea.

Standing in the middle of the pavement, the beer on the ground beside him, he pulled out his mobile phone and dialled Elizabeth's number.

He was in dire need of sensible and sympathetic company tonight, and there was no one who fit the bill better.

CHAPTER 21

Helen knew exactly where David's LRP kit was – it was still in the bottom of the cupboard in the hallway, where he had dumped it when they had come back from the game. He hadn't touched it since.

She was still holding on to the vain hope that now that David had passed his exams, things would go back to the way they were. But he remained distant. He hadn't been violent with her again, not since that night, but she couldn't bring herself to stay the night and she was finding excuses not to have sex. She wasn't feeling well; she had a stomach upset and might have thrown up her Pill; she had a heavy day at work tomorrow.

David hadn't tried to force her again, but he hadn't really been speaking much to her either. The time at his place was mostly spent sat on the sofa, not touching, drinking wine, and staring at the TV.

It saddened her. But some small part of her still wanted to get to the bottom of why David was acting the way he was. If she could work out what made him change, maybe she could even fix it. She couldn't bring herself to accept that the relationship might be over. She thought what they had was worth salvaging and she wasn't prepared to give up on it yet.

On her next day off, when David was at work, she went round to his place without mentioning she would be doing so. He'd never asked her for his key back, so she still had it.

The flat was silent, unwelcoming and empty. Absurdly, she found herself creeping around.

Sure enough, the LRP kit was still in the bottom of the closet. The cloak and tunic smelled musty – nothing had been washed since the game. Even the boots hadn't been cleaned; the mud was dried and caked, flaking away to leave a dirty patch on the floor of the cupboard.

Helen pushed aside the costume bits and pulled out the big kit bag that David kept all his gear in.

She was counting on the fact that he would have tossed all of his referee notes in here too. At the end of a game, when he was packing up in a hurry, everything got thrown together and shoved in one place. She was willing to bet he hadn't moved it since then.

She dumped the bag on the floor of the hallway and unzipped it, dropping dirt and fragments of leaves and twigs from the Forest of Dean in the process. She began pulling things out haphazardly. Belt pouches. Potion bottles. Studded leather greaves. Medallions and talismans. Finally, near the bottom of the bag, she found the leather document holder she'd been looking for – the bag that held David's game documents. She remembered him buying the case from Camden market. Made from rigid leather with straps and clasps, it was just the right size to hold A4 papers and David had decided it was ideal as an in-character document holder for his ref's notes.

Sitting on the floor, she opened the holder. She flipped through the pages of game notes, typed on the PC and printed out. Notes about the world, the plot, the NPCs. Most of the pages had handwritten annotations scribbled on them; many were crumpled, bearing evidence of spending many hours in the forest. She came across a page entitled 'Big Bad' and paused. The paper was covered with scribbled handwritten notes, but in the middle of the page was what looked, at first glance, like a poem. She recognised it as the ritual that they had read out, allegedly to stop the summoning of the Big Bad in the game. Underneath the printed words was a web address, written in red pen and circled.

This is what she was looking for. Helen folded the piece of paper up and stuck it into the back pocket of her jeans. She was just closing the clasps of the leather folder when she heard the front door slam and her heart leapt into her mouth.

She gathered up all the gear in one swoop and stuffed it haphazardly back into the bag. "David?"

After a pause, David called out, "Helen? What are you doing here?"

"I had the day off." She frantically tried to shove the bag back into the hall closet. She was just closing the doors when David came around the corner.

"What are you doing?"

"I lost an earring. I thought it might be here." She stood up and brushed her hands, aware of the dried mud on the hallway floor.

"It won't be in there," David said, indicating the cupboard. "Nothing but junk in there."

"I think I lost it at the game. I was hoping it would have ended up in the kit bag."

"It's probably lost in the woods somewhere, then." David said dismissively, sweeping past her to get to the bedroom.

"Why are you home so early?"

"It was quiet, so I thought I'd take the afternoon off. Besides, I'm celebrating."

Helen peered round the door to see David toss his work trousers on the bed and pull on a pair of jeans. She was shocked to see how thin he was. He used to take such pride in his toned body. Now each rib was painfully visible through the translucent skin of his torso. "What are we celebrating?" she asked.

David picked up a t-shirt and pulled it over his head. "I put down an offer on the house. The one I saw yesterday. It's perfect."

"Has it been accepted?"

David smirked. "Of course. Subject to contract and the usual bullshit, of course."

"You didn't tell me about this house."

"Why should I? David pushed past her on his way to the kitchen. "It's my house, not yours."

"I see," she said, wondering if he'd already pre-empted her decision to end the relationship.

In the kitchen, David was pouring himself a glass of wine from the open bottle in the fridge. There was always an open bottle of wine in the fridge these days, she noticed. It was usually good stuff, too. He didn't offer her any. She thought about helping herself but something held her back. "So is this flat on the market, then?"

"I talked to an estate agent today. But it doesn't matter whether or not it sells. I'm moving anyway."

"Where are you getting the money?"

"My inheritance will be enough for the deposit and a mortgage will cover the rest."

"But that money might take ages to come through."

David slammed the glass down on the kitchen counter, making Helen jump. "Why does everyone keep saying that? It's my goddamned money. My father's will was clear."

"It's just that these things take a long time to sort out. There's usually a lot of red tape."

"Not this time there won't be. So are you staying for dinner, or did you just come over to rifle through my stuff?"

"I-I wasn't rifling through your stuff," Helen stammered, inwardly cursing her lifelong inability to lie well.

David grabbed her arm. "Don't give me that bullshit. I caught you at it. You were pawing through the stuff in the cupboard."

"I told you I was looking for an earring."

"And I don't believe you. If you'd have lost an earring at the game, you would have mentioned it before now. What were you looking for?" He shook her.

"David, let go, you're hurting me!"

"Why are you sneaking around behind my back, looking through my stuff?"

"Let go! Please!"

He suddenly, violently, threw her against the wall.

The side of her face slammed into the kitchen wall and she collapsed to the floor, tears flowing down her cheeks.

The side of her face throbbed.

She climbed to her feet shakily. David stared down at her. "I'm going home now," she said.

David held his hand out. "Key."

"Wh-what?"

"Give me back the key to my flat."

She blinked at him through the tears. "You're finishing with me?"

"Correction. You're finishing with me. Why else would you be snooping around my flat without telling me? You're the one who's always said trust is everything. If you're going to use my keys to go through my stuff, I can't trust you anymore. Hence, you must be breaking up with me. Give me my key."

Helen fumbled in her pocket and found the key to David's flat that was on the cartoon dog key ring that was also his. Such a fun design seemed so inappropriate now. It was hard to believe he'd ever been a man to find joy in a cute key ring.

Sniffing loudly, she dropped the key into David's outstretched palm. He pocketed the key and turned away from her, picking up his wine glass from the counter.

"Goodbye David. You seem to be set on a path I can't follow. I hope it brings you happiness."

He paused for a moment, but then carried on into the living room, without speaking, without looking back.

Helen held her sobs back until she'd let herself out of the flat and gone halfway down the street. Then the floodgates opened. She collapsed by the side of the road and bawled, all the pent-up anxieties and doubts over the last few weeks erupting in a seemingly unending stream of tears.

CHAPTER 22

"I've left him," Helen sobbed as Elizabeth opened the door. The tears were still flowing freely. She'd been crying all the way over; she just couldn't stop. She'd managed to hold it together long enough to phone Elizabeth's mobile and discover she was at Mark's, but she hadn't been able to keep the distress out of her voice. Elizabeth hadn't said anything, but the look of concern she wore on her face showed she had a good idea of what was going on. She hadn't said anything about Helen's black eye either; but the way her face was throbbing, Helen knew it must be visible.

Elizabeth hugged Helen, there on the doorstep. "It's OK. Come on in." She ushered Helen inside, resting a hand on her back. Helen dug in to her pocket and pulled out a crumpled tissue, using it to blow her nose.

Mark appeared at the end of the corridor. "I've left David," Helen blurted.

"Come on in, love. Sit down. Have a nice cup of tea." Elizabeth ushered Helen into the living room.

"I'll go put the kettle on," Mark said, disappearing into the kitchen.

Mark's living room was in disarray. The coffee table was in the middle of the room. A cardboard screen adorned with drawings of elves and monsters was propped up on it, masking a pile of papers. There was a small pile of coloured dice on the table that were in various geometrical shapes. More papers were piled up on the floor, along with some hardback books – one entitled 'Players' Guide'; one entitled 'Games Master Guide'; another entitled 'Monster Manual'.

"We were just playing a little D&D," Elizabeth said apologetically. She swept aside some of the papers from the couch and indicated Helen should sit down. Helen glanced at the top paper – it was headed 'character sheet'.

Covered with figures and annotations, the most striking element of the paper was a rather lovely pencil drawing of an elven woman. She had long hair and robes dramatically windblown, and was holding a towering staff aloft.

"I'm sorry if I'm interrupting something." Helen sat down and blew her nose again.

"Oh gosh, don't worry. I knew something was wrong when you phoned."

"I was over at his place. He's just been so aggressive, so violent. I guess I knew it was over a long time ago but I didn't want to accept it. He came home and got angry to see me there. He pushed me and I fell." Helen gingerly touched her swollen face, where it had hit the wall. "Then he asked for his key back. And I left. I guess it really is over."

Elizabeth enveloped Helen in a hug. "Oh, love, I'm so sorry. I know it hurts now, but you'll soon find someone who appreciates you. You deserve better."

Helen sniffed. "But I still love him. Or I love the man he used to be. He's changed."

Mark appeared, carrying three mugs of steaming liquid. Elizabeth took one from him, and he handed another to Helen. "Milk, no sugar, yes?" Mark asked.

"Yes. Thanks." Helen sipped the tea. Warm and comforting, it went some way to soothing her soul.

"People do change sometimes," Elizabeth said. "There's nothing you can do."

"But I know that somewhere in there is the man that I fell in love with."

Elizabeth sighed. "Helen, he's started hitting you. He might kill you. Don't be one of those women who ends up being a statistic."

"He changed after that role playing game." Helen perched her tea on the coffee table and fumbled in her pocket for the piece of paper she'd taken from David's flat. "Mark, you must see that. You know him better than anyone."

"I used to," Mark said sadly. "He seems to have decided I'm not good enough for him anymore. He seemed to start changing around the time he sat his exams. I thought maybe it was the pressure. Then his dad died. His reaction was a bit weird, but people grieve in different ways."

Helen smoothed out the piece of paper. "Something happened at the game. I'm sure of it. Have you got your laptop handy?"

Mark looked surprised. "I can get it. Why?"

"I want to check out this website."

Elizabeth peered at the piece of paper. "What is it?"

"David's notes on the role playing game. He referred to this website when he did his research for the Big Bad. I'd like to take a look."

"I'll go get the laptop." Mark stood and left the room.

Elizabeth picked up the piece of paper. "Where did you get this?"

"David's kit bag. I admit it, I was snooping. I knew he did some research on the Internet for the ritual and I was looking for his notes. Then he came home and caught me. That's when it all kicked off."

Mark returned with the laptop. Elizabeth cleared a space for it on the coffee table while Mark booted it up.

"I'd just like to know what he'd been researching," Helen said.

"Let's take a look, shall we?" Elizabeth peered at the piece of paper and typed the URL address into the internet browser. She peered at the screen, a frown appearing on her face, and pushed her glasses further up her nose. "Huh?"

"What is it?" Helen asked.

"It seems to be a website all about a magic user in eleventh century England," Elizabeth said. "Ragnor the Black."

"What, like a character in a novel?" Mark asked.

"The way this site is presented, it's like a piece of research. Listen to this.

'The young Ragnor knew early in life he had a gift. But he was viewed with suspicion and hostility by his peers. He was eager to learn how he could use his gift to enhance his own life, and that of his fellows. But in those days, what he was learning was considered to be the work of the Devil. Any form of magic was considered to be unnatural and evil. It was all grouped under the phrase The Black Arts. Hence, he became known as Ragnor the Black.'"

"And this is where David found the ritual for the game," Helen said.

"There's some stuff here about what happened to Ragnor," said Elizabeth. "He practised his magic and became really powerful. Everyone around him got to be afraid of him. They thought he was in league with the devil, and so on. It says here he began to fear for his life. Worried that he was going to be killed by an angry mob, he began looking into ways of coming back from the dead." Elizabeth swivelled the laptop around so the others could see. "Take a look at this."

Mark and Helen leaned in closer to see. Helen could make out the phrases displayed on the screen, set out like a poem. "This is the ritual we used in the game. The one to dispel the demon," she said.

"That's not what it does according to this," Elizabeth said.

Mark was still reading the screen. "It says this is the spell that Ragnor left with his followers to bring himself back from the dead. He left detailed instructions that when he was killed they were to retrieve his body within twelve hours of death. They were to remove his organs and store them safely, so that he could retrieve them when he came back to life. They had to bury him in a shallow grave, and when it was safe for him to raise again, they needed to recite the words of this ritual."

Helen's eyes were wide. "I was starting to suspect that David had been possessed by a demon. Nobody believes in that sort of stuff anymore but I was brought up to believe it exists. And I've seen it happen. This Ragnor was into dark magic. It was David that recited the ritual. It brought Ragnor back, and now he's possessing David."

"There's something familiar about this." Elizabeth picked up the Monster Manual and began flipping through the pages. She laid the book on the carpet in front of Mark and Helen. "Take a look at this."

"What is it?" The picture in the book showed a drawing of a hideous corpse-like creature, dressed in tattered wizard's robes. Helen didn't understand what she was looking at.

"It's a lich," said Elizabeth.

Helen frowned. "A what?"

"Essentially a re-animated wizard," Mark said. "A bit like a zombie – but a creature with intelligence and the ability to use magic. One of the most powerful D&D monsters around."

"But surely it was made up for the game," Helen said. "Wasn't it?"

"The word wasn't," Elizabeth said. "Lich is an old Anglo Saxon word meaning 'corpse'. It's why church gates are called lich gates – it's where they carried the coffin to during funerals."

"Most of the monsters used in D&D are inspired by myths and legends," Mark said. "There's often more truth to them than you'd think. Where was this Ragnor chap buried?"

Elizabeth spun the laptop around again and peered at the screen. "It says something about ancient woods near the town of Lynley. A place rumoured to have connections to ancient powers."

"Maybe we should research where that is in on a modern map," Mark said.

Elizabeth stared at him. "You don't really think David released a lich, do you? That's just....ludicrous."

"Most people think possession is ludicrous," Helen said. "But there are plenty of documented cases in the past.

And I've seen one myself – the woman from my church, when I was young, that I told Elizabeth about. Evil exists, and it manifests itself in ways that most of us can't comprehend."

Mark looked grim. "Most of my brain is screaming at me that this is not possible or logical, and I shouldn't be entertaining such a stupid superstitious thought. But maybe it's the geek in me – there's a small alarm bell ringing loudly enough that I think we should do some more research. After all, what have we lost if we're wrong?"

"We're on a wild goose chase and everyone thinks we're nuts," Elizabeth said.

Mark shrugged. "They all think we're nuts anyway. We spend our weekends running around in the woods in strange costumes, waving foam swords around. I think we should find out more about this Ragnor character."

CHAPTER 23

It was well past midnight and Helen had to get up for work in the morning. Even so, she was unable to tear herself away from her computer. Her little flat was shrouded in darkness; the only light was emanating from her desk lamp. Several empty mugs containing tea dregs littered the desk. A note book sat beside the keyboard.

She'd been researching liches. To be honest, she hadn't got very far. Liches weren't really mentioned much outside Dungeons & Dragons and Warhammer sites. But the basic concept behind a lich – a reanimated corpse possessing intelligence and the ability to use magic – was mentioned on many mythology sites. A couple of them had even made reference to Ragnor the Black. The more she learned about him, the more she thought this was not someone she'd want to cross.

She was reading about Ragnor's Phylactery. In order for the resurrection ritual to work, according to one website, the body had to be mummified. Then the organs needed to be removed, preserved and placed in a container.

Container of organs = *phylactery*, Helen wrote on her notepad. *Source of Ragnor's power. Must be buried at a source of power. Close to body. Ancient woods? Druidic power?*

She leaned back in her chair, rubbing her eyes wearily. She didn't know what she was accomplishing. Surely this was just a wild goose chase, as Elizabeth had said? She didn't really think David had been possessed by an ancient creature, did she? It sounded ludicrous. More likely he'd always been a jerk and she'd just never seen it before. She ought to give this up and go to bed. She was losing the ability to think clearly.

She closed the website and shut down the PC, gathering up her notes and tidying them away into a folder before tossing them onto the shelf next to the computer.

She stood up and picked up the dirty mugs, turning around to take them into the kitchen before going to bed.

Then she stopped dead. The mugs slipped out of her hands, the dregs in the bottom staining the cream carpet under her feet. She opened her mouth to scream at the horrific sight in front of her, but her vocal chords were paralyzed, unable to make a sound.

A figure stood in the doorway. It was tall and dressed in tattered robes; a bizarre and grim imitation of a human form. Leather-like skin stretched taut over discoloured bones.

The face was little more than a skull; hollowed out sockets instead of eyes and a lower jaw that was hanging slack in a grotesque parody of a grin. It made not a sound, and the bottom of its robes hovered six inches from the floor.

An odour of putrefying flesh and old graves emanated from it in waves. Helen stood frozen in place. The thing floated closer, and the stench washed over her.

Had she been able to move, it would have made her gag. The temperature of the room seemed to drop ten degrees. The thing opened its grotesque mouth and rasped, "Fear me."

Helen's mind was screaming: *Run! Run!* But she was unable to obey. The thing kept moving towards her, reaching out with skeletal hands. The last conscious thought that flooded her mind was that they were right after all; this was the thing that David had summoned. Then a wave of agony washed over her as the thing's bony hands penetrated her flesh.

* * * *

"Hi, this is Helen. I can't answer the phone right now, but please leave me a message."

"Helen, it's Elizabeth. Give me a call, please. We've not heard from you in two days and want to check you're OK. Call me. Please." Elizabeth clicked off her mobile. "She's not answering at home, either," she said to Mark. "I'm worried about her."

Mark was playing *Resident Evil 4*, negotiating Leon down a creepy dungeon corridor. "Did you try her at work today?"

"Yes. They said she didn't come in. I assumed she was sick, but she should be at home if that's the case."

A mummy-like creature lumbered into view on the screen, accompanied by ominous music. Mark fired ineffectually at the creature and muttered curses under his breath.

"You know you've got to use the infra-red scope on the rifle on those," Elizabeth said. "It's a regenerator."

"I hate these damn things." Mark switched to the weapons screen. "Too hard to kill."

"Maybe you should be practising RE5, not RE4, so you can beat me next time we play."

"I actually think this is a better game. And it's a solo game so I can get practise in alone. Besides, I like the nostalgia factor in having to hook up the PS2 again."

Elizabeth peered at the screen. "Makes you realise how far graphics have come in just a few years, though."

"Can't argue with you there."

"I think I'm going to go over there. I just have a bad feeling."

"Do you want me to come with you?"

"No, you stay here in case she phones." Elizabeth plucked her bag from the hallway and found her coat.

"Give me a call when you get there?" Mark called out from the living room. He descended into more cursing as a barrage of gunfire came from the game.

"I'm sure I'm fretting for nothing, but I'd rather make sure she's OK." Elizabeth laced up her trainers, picked up her house keys, and went out the front door.

* * * *

Standing in front of Helen's front door, Elizabeth couldn't shake off the growing sense of unease. Helen's flat was on the ground floor, with all the windows clearly visible from where Elizabeth stood. The curtains were closed and a soft light glowed from the bedroom.

But Elizabeth's repeated knocking went unanswered.

She tried ringing Helen's land line number. The phone rang until the answer phone kicked in; the ringing echoed inside the building and was just audible from Elizabeth's vantage point outside. Then she tried ringing Helen's mobile number. The voice mail kicked in before the phone even rang once. The phone had to be switched off. Or out of power. If Helen was out, why didn't she have her phone switched on? If she was at home, why wasn't she answering? Elizabeth couldn't shake off the feeling of dread inside her that was insisting something was wrong. She tried the door handle. To her surprise, the door swung open.

She stepped over the threshold, the hairs on the back of her neck prickling. She walked down the corridor and the sense that something was wrong became stronger. There was a faint unpleasant smell, a bit like meat that had been left out and gone off. Suddenly Elizabeth wished she'd taken Mark up on his offer to accompany her.

The flat had a corridor running all the way down, ending in the kitchen at the back. All the other rooms came off the corridor – bedroom and bathroom on the left, a long living/dining room on the right; something Elizabeth knew from previous visits to Helen's place. The bedroom was the first door on the left. Knowing that this was where the light was on, Elizabeth paused outside the door. It was ajar. The smell seemed to be stronger here. Suddenly afraid of what she might find, Elizabeth dug her phone out of her bag and clutched it in her hand, for easy access.

Cautiously she pushed the bedroom door open. She saw the bed in the middle of the room, neatly made.

An array of cheerful stuffed toys adorned the bed. As Elizabeth stepped into the room, she heard a buzzing noise, and the smell became overwhelming.

The bedroom contained a chest of drawers and a wardrobe, both of which were closed.

Everything was neatly in its place.

Unlike Elizabeth, Helen was a neat freak. She never threw her clothes on the floor or tossed them over chairs.

It took a moment for Elizabeth to comprehend what was wrong. Beyond the bed, a computer desk with a desktop PC and an office chair occupied the alcove by the window. The desk lamp was on – this was the light source visible from the street. The computer was off. And then Elizabeth noticed it.

The computer screen was moving. Flies crawled all over it concentrating on the thin band of red fluid that spattered the screen in a diagonal line. Elizabeth's hand went to her throat. She called up Mark's number on her mobile and pressed 'dial'.

As she took a couple of steps closer to the edge of the bed, a swarm of flies rose up from the space between the other side of the bed and the computer desk. Elizabeth squealed as they flew towards her, batting them out of her hair and ducking as they swarmed out of the open door into the corridor. At that moment, Mark answered the phone.

"It's me," Elizabeth said. "I'm at Helen's place. Something very bad has happened."

"Is Helen there? Is she OK?" Mark asked.

Elizabeth could not speak. Having cleared the edge of the bed, she could now see what it was that the flies were finding so interesting. A body lay face up on the floor, between the bed and the computer desk. It looked like the body of an old woman. The hair was pure white, the skin dry and withered.

The eyes were open, staring sightlessly; the mouth frozen open in a silent scream. There was a big hole in the chest around where the heart should be.

A pool of blood was coagulating beneath it, saturating the carpet and the edge of the duvet on the bed. A thick spray of blood covered the computer chair and then ran up the computer, culminating in the streak against the monitor that Elizabeth had noticed first.

"Elizabeth?" Mark said. "Are you OK? What's happened?"

Elizabeth's muscles turned to water. The phone slipped out of her hand, and her legs gave out from under her.

CHAPTER 24

The emergency services had already arrived when Mark arrived at Helen's place. He pushed past everything – the ambulance, the police car, and the paramedics in luminous jackets rushing past; the police officers talking in the radio – to look for Elizabeth.

He found her wrapped in a blanket, perched on the back of the ambulance. The doors were open and there was no sign of the paramedics. Mark folded Elizabeth into his arms. She was shaking like a leaf.

"Are you OK?" Even as he said it, he knew it was a stupid question. Of course she wasn't. Helen was dead, and Elizabeth had been the one to find her.

"It's David," she said. "It has to be. Or whatever the thing is that David has become. He must have known she was getting close."

A forty-something man in a rumpled suit and thinning brown hair approached. He had the air of someone used to being in charge. Detective Inspector, Mark guessed, just as the man said, "I'm Detective Inspector Fred Thierry. I'm in charge of this investigation. We'll need to take your statement, Miss Burns, if you can kindly come down to the station. My Detective Sergeant over there can organise a lift." He pointed to a tall, slim woman in a trouser suit who was coming out of the property with a frown on her face.

"Do we have to do this now?" Mark said. "She's in shock. She should be going to hospital."

Elizabeth laid a hand on his arm. "Mark, I'm fine. The paramedic's already checked me out."

The DI swivelled his gaze towards Mark. "And you are?"

"Mark Lawrence. I'm Elizabeth's boyfriend." Inappropriate though it was at this point in time, he still felt a swelling sense of pride in speaking those words aloud."

"And do you mind telling me what you're doing here?"

"I'm here for Elizabeth. She phoned me. After…after she found Helen."

"Fine," the Detective Inspector said gruffly. "You can come to the station as well."

The tall woman approached. "Forensics are here, guv," she said.

"Jolly good. Can you get one of the uniforms to give Miss Burns and her boyfriend here a lift to the station? She's willing to give her statement now."

The woman pulled a small notebook out of her voluminous shoulder bag. "We'll need to take names and addresses," she said. "And do you happen to know the details of Helen Thomas's next of kin?"

"I don't know her parents," Elizabeth said. "They don't live around here and I don't think she was very close to them. But she'd recently broken up with her boyfriend, and I think you should talk to him."

The Detective Sergeant paused in her note writing. "Oh? Why do you say that?"

"He'd been getting increasingly violent. And I don't think he was happy about the break-up."

"OK. What's his name and where do we find him?"

"David Carty. He's recently qualified as a doctor. Works at UCLH."

"Have you got contact details?"

"I have." Mark pulled out his mobile phone and called up David's entry. He passed the phone to the Detective Sergeant. She nodded and made a note.

"Right Jane, we need to find out what the forensics boys have found out," the Detective Inspector said brusquely.

His partner nodded. "I'll be right with you, guv. I'll just get these two in a car to the station."

* * * *

It was after one o'clock by the time Mark and Elizabeth were free to leave.

They were driven back to Mark's place in a patrol car. Mark insisted that Elizabeth stayed over at his that night, and she put up no resistance. Neither of them wanted to be alone.

Although it was late and it had been a traumatic day, neither of them could sleep. Eventually they brought the duvet into the living room and curled up on the sofa together, channel flicking through old movies.

"I can't believe she's gone," Elizabeth said, the first words she'd spoken since they'd got back to Mark's place. "Why did we let her go home alone?"

Mark squeezed Elizabeth gently. "We had no idea what was going to happen."

"It was me that encouraged her to leave David. I thought he was going to kill her. So she takes my advice and leaves him, and she ends up dead anyway."

"Don't say that. It's not your fault. And we don't know who killed her."

Elizabeth looked at Mark sadly. "There's a pattern. Don't you see? First David's father, then Chelsea, now Helen. And you didn't see the body. Something happened. Her hair…it had gone white. It didn't look like Helen. She saw something…whatever it was scared her to death. Maybe literally."

"I heard the paramedics talking. They said her heart had been ripped out."

"But the look on her face…" Elizabeth shuddered. "What was it she saw just before she died?"

"I can't believe it was David. I know he's changed, but he's not capable of murder."

"Maybe he's not David. Maybe he has been possessed, like Helen thought."

Mark frowned, shifting to look at Elizabeth. "You think there's something in this ritual business?"

"This guy, Ragnor, was into some seriously powerful magic. What if the ritual is a way to bring his spirit back into someone else? What if David's possessed by some evil wizard?"

"Because it sounds ridiculous. We're talking magic. In twenty-first century London."

"Just because we can't see and hear a thing doesn't mean it doesn't exist, you know. We're all too quick these days to dismiss the irrational explanations. The things we can't explain. We choose not to believe in magic anymore. That doesn't mean it isn't there."

"This is some pretty hard core stuff, Elizabeth. You're talking about black magic."

"And if it's true, we're all in a lot of trouble." Elizabeth sighed and rested her head against Mark's chest. He put his arm around her and saw the tears gathering in her eyes. Again. She'd only just stopped crying.

"Maybe we should let the police investigate," Mark said gently.

"But what if they don't know what they're looking for? You remember that website we found? The one with the ritual on it? What if Helen went off to research it? What if she found out some more incriminating information? What if David – or the thing that's wearing David's body – killed her because she was getting close to the truth?"

Mark's mobile phone began ringing suddenly, startling them both into a sitting position. "It's four in the morning," Mark said. "Who the hell's ringing me at this time?" He disentangled himself from the duvet and retrieved his phone from the table where he'd left it.

The display number was an unfamiliar 0207 number. "Hello?"

"Mark, thank God you're answering," David said. "I need you to do me a huge favour."

"David? Helen…"

"I know. I've been arrested for her murder. I've only got one phone call and I can't get hold of my solicitor. In fact you're the only person who's answered."

"I'm here with Elizabeth," Mark said. "She found Helen..."

"Listen, Mark, I really need your help. I need you to make some calls for me."

"David, it's four in the morning."

"Yes I know. And I'm going to be in a cell for the next twenty-four hours. Can you please phone my solicitor? He'll be at his desk by eight. I also need you to phone my boss and let him know I won't be at work. But please don't tell him I've been arrested. Tell him...I don't know what the hell to tell him. Just tell him I need to take a couple of days off, and I'll be in touch when I can. I'm going to give you the names and numbers of the people you need to call. Have you got a pen and paper?"

Mark reached for a sheet of paper from the A4 notepad amongst the D&D books that were still piled up in the living room, and the HB pencil he used to make notes on character sheets. "Erm...sure. Go ahead."

He glanced over at Elizabeth, still huddled on the couch. He tried to reassure her with his smile that everything would be OK, as he waited for David to recite the phone numbers. She just stared at him, her eyes full of sorrow.

CHAPTER 25

There was nothing that could be done until business hours, so after David's call, Mark and Elizabeth went to bed.

After a little while, Elizabeth seemed to sleep, but Mark's head just kept turning over all the terrible things that had happened. Chelsea was dead. Helen was dead. Both had been killed in the same horrible manner. The police clearly thought David killed Helen. Was he responsible for Chelsea's death too? What motive could he possibly have for killing her? And what about his father? David had been many miles away the night his father died – surely he couldn't have had anything to do with that one?

At six, Mark gave up trying to sleep. He got up and put some coffee on, drinking two cups as he stared out the window at the sunrise. He had a pounding headache developing in his temple.

He went to shower and dress, swallowed a couple of paracetamols, and sat down at the kitchen table with his laptop to surf the net. The silence in the flat was getting to him, so he switched on the little radio he kept in the kitchen, just for some background noise.

At seven, he was on his fourth cup of coffee and some toast when Elizabeth appeared, looking pale and bleary-eyed. Mark didn't even ask her how she was feeling – it was a stupid question. Instead, he kissed her gently. "Do you want some toast?"

"I'm not sure I can keep anything down. My stomach's churning."

"You need to eat."

Elizabeth sat down at the kitchen table. "I could really use a cup of tea." She glanced back at the radio, which was broadcasting the seven o'clock news. "Hey, what was that? Turn it up."

Mark turned up the volume on the radio just as the newsreader was saying, "The two bodies, found in woodlands a mile from Reading service station, were badly decomposed and missing body parts. Police say the bodies may have been lying exposed for several days, and looked like they had been eaten by wildlife. Similarities to two other murders in the last month – a body found in a similar state in Swindon, and two bodies found in woodlands near the Gloucestershire town of Lynley, have been noted. Police say it's too early to draw any conclusions though. Cause of death has yet to be established. Police claim they are not looking for a serial killer."

"That's a bit weird, don't you think?" Elizabeth said. "Bodies being found looking like they've been eaten? Nothing human can do that."

"You don't think it's connected to Chelsea and Helen? Chelsea was ripped apart. She wasn't gnawed on."

"And Helen looked like she'd been scared to death." Elizabeth slumped forward on the table, head in her hands. "It's all so messed up. What the hell is going on?"

Mark stroked Elizabeth's hair. "Shall I run a bath for you? A good soak might help you relax a bit."

Elizabeth smiled weakly. "Yes, OK. What are you going to do?"

Mark checked the time on his mobile. "I promised David I'd phone his solicitor. He said the guy gets to his desk at eight, so I'll just hang around until then.

"Has David been languishing in a cell all this time? Why didn't he go for the duty solicitor?"

"He's insisting on this guy, apparently – says he's used him before and he's good. But he wasn't contactable last night, which is why I have to do it. I also promised to phone his boss.

Not sure what I'm going to tell him, though. David doesn't want his employers to know he's been arrested."

"Why's he hiding it? It's going to come out sooner or later."

"Only if he's guilty, I guess."

"And you think he isn't?"

"I don't know what to think. In spite of all the recent shit he's put me through, David's been my friend a long time. He asked me to do him a favour. I feel like I should do it."

"I hope he appreciates what you're doing for him, Mark."

Mark shrugged. "He's my friend. That's what friends do. I'll go run your bath." He walked out of the kitchen.

* * * *

At eight o'clock precisely, Mark phoned the solicitor. It was a brief conversation. The guy was professional and to the point, and said he would go see David at the police station right away.

Then Mark phoned the mobile number David had given him for his boss. A far more difficult conversation, but the phone rang straight through to voicemail.

In some ways Mark was relieved – leaving a message was the easy way out. It might make things more awkward for David in the long run though. "Hello, my name is Mark Lawrence. I'm phoning for David Carty. I'm sorry to have to leave a message, but David's got a personal problem to sort out and he can't get to a phone right now. He asked me to let you know he won't be in work. He'll phone you himself with more information as soon as he can."

After that, he phoned his own boss. Jack was already at his desk – he usually got in early. "Hi Jack, it's Mark."

"Hey, Mark. How are you?"

"I've been better. I won't be in work today."

"Oh hey, are you sick?"

"Not exactly." Mark paused. "A friend of ours was killed last night. Elizabeth found her."

"Oh God, how terrible. Is Elizabeth alright?"

"She's shocked, as you can imagine. She won't be in today, either. The thing is we don't know if Helen has any family around, and we've got to talk to the police, and so on."

"Do they have any idea who did it?"

"I'm not sure. They think it might be her boyfriend, but he's a friend of mine too."

"Oh, God, that's rough. Take all the time you need."

"Thanks, Jack. I hope we'll both be back tomorrow."

Mark rang off and contemplated putting another pot of coffee on. But he'd already had four cups, and on top of the lack of sleep, his brain was fizzing. Maybe it wasn't such a good idea.

As he was putting his cup in the kitchen sink, the door buzzer went. He went to answer, wondering who was visiting so early in the morning.

It was Linus. He came in looking pale and unshaven; his hair uncombed and clothing rumpled.

"I just got Elizabeth's message about Helen," he said shakily. "It was on my mobile when I switched it on this morning. I guess she's here, is she? I hope she's here. She shouldn't be on her own."

"She's here. She's taking a bath. Come on in." Linus followed Mark down the corridor.

"Terrible news," Linus said. "First Chelsea, now Helen. Could there be a connection?"

"I think there's most definitely a connection. They were both killed in the same way. Do you want coffee or tea?"

"Coffee would be great, thanks." Linus sank into a chair.

Mark rinsed out the coffee machine and put in fresh grounds. "The thing is, David's been arrested."

"David?"

"Elizabeth and I have been worried about Helen for a while. David's been getting increasingly violent. And Helen just finished with him, a few days ago. He didn't take it well." Mark put water in the coffee machine and switched it on.

Elizabeth came into the kitchen wearing a pink fluffy bathrobe, her wet hair wrapped up in a towel. "I thought I heard Linus's voice."

"I came as soon as I got your message." Linus pulled his sister into an embrace. "I'm so sorry. Whatever I can do, let me know."

"Don't you have to go to work?"

"I phoned in sick."

Elizabeth threw a look at Mark. "I phoned Jack," Mark said. "I explained what had happened and told him neither of us would be in today. He was very understanding."

Elizabeth sat wearily. "I'm not sure if there's anything any of us can do. I don't have contact details for Helen's family. The police will have to deal with it."

Mark filled the kettle to make Elizabeth a cup of tea as the coffee machine gurgled away. She looked so miserable that his heart ached, and he wished he could wave a magic wand and make everything alright again.

But of course that was impossible. Chelsea was dead, Helen was dead, and nothing was going to change that.

CHAPTER 26

Elizabeth spent the day with Mark at his flat. Linus stayed for a couple of hours, then left. Mark found it hard to concentrate on anything, and every time he and Elizabeth talked about Helen, she started crying. So they spent most of the day playing computer games, as a distraction more than anything else.

They were just thinking about what to do for dinner when the buzzer went. Wondering who it was, Mark went to answer. "Hello?" he said into the speaker.

"Mark, it's David. Can I come in for a minute?"

When Mark opened the door to the flat, David stood on the threshold looking pale and dishevelled; the hollows of his cheekbones clearly visible beneath the thick shadow of his unshaven chin. His hair was tousled; the jeans and sweater he wore, rumpled. "Hi. Sorry for dropping in unannounced. I won't stay long. Can I come in?"

"Sure." Mark held the door open and stepped aside to allow David passage. The odour that accompanied him made it clear that David hadn't showered in a while.

Mark shut the door and led David into the living room. Elizabeth looked up from the couch. The expression on her face clearly indicated that David was not someone she was pleased to see.

"I'm sorry if I'm disturbing you," David said. "I just wanted to say thanks for your help this morning, with the phone calls and so on. I really appreciate it. I know I dropped you in it, asking you to phone my boss."

"I had to leave a message in the end, I couldn't get through," Mark said. "It was all a bit awkward."

David sat heavily on one of the armchairs and wearily ran a hand through his hair. "I shouldn't have asked. I was just so stunned when the police turned up."

"Evidently they released you," Elizabeth said.

"They said Helen was killed sometime on Sunday night. I was on the late shift, working all night. Lots of people at the hospital could verify I was there. My colleagues, my supervisor – even the patients. I'd not been home long when the police turned up. They just started questioning me about Helen and how we recently broke up. I guess I got angry. They decided to take that as a sign that I was guilty, and arrested me. But when they went to the hospital today and talked to a load of people who could verify I was at work at the time, they had to let me go."

"So your boss knows anyway," Mark said.

"Very awkward, but the police came asking questions so it was hard to avoid." David rubbed his head absent-mindedly, leaving his untidy hair standing up on his head in peaks. "It's very embarrassing, and God knows what it'll do to my career. I spoke to my boss earlier and he seems to be understanding. I'll just have to see what happens when I go to work tomorrow."

Elizabeth stared at David. "I don't believe you. Helen's dead, and all you can think about is how it'll affect your career?"

David glared at her. "Of course I'm upset Helen's dead. But moping isn't going to bring her back, is it? I didn't kill her. Life has to go on and there's a lot of shit going on in my life at the moment."

"If you had put Helen before all that shit in your life, maybe she'd still be alive," Elizabeth snapped.

"Helen made her choice. She was the one who wanted out of the relationship."

"And you don't think beating her up and raping her had an impact on that?"

"Elizabeth, maybe now's not the time to get into that," Mark said.

"I have to go." Elizabeth stood up abruptly.

Mark followed her as she stormed to the door. "I thought you were staying tonight."

"I've got stuff to do before work tomorrow. Laundry and so on. Besides, it's too crowded here at the moment. I'll see you in work tomorrow." She kissed Mark, collected her bag and coat, then left.

Mark sighed and headed back to the living room. David still sat on the chair, staring listlessly into space. "She might have a point," Mark said gently.

David frowned. "About what?"

"About your being so focussed on work, after what's happened."

David looked at him. "This is the most crucial stage of my career. Any screw-ups now and my future as a surgeon is finished before it begins. It's terrible news about Helen, but I have to compartmentalise. Keep my private life private. No one's going to hire a surgeon who can't keep cool under pressure."

Mark sat on the sofa. "The police were asking about Helen's family. I know nothing about them."

David shrugged. "Her mother died years ago. She's got a brother but I think he lives in Australia. Her father remarried. Lives up North somewhere. I've never met them. She didn't talk much about her family."

"Who's arranging the funeral?"

"The police are trying to track down her father. They said they found her mobile phone, and they're holding it as evidence. No doubt they'll get her dad's number from there."

"She spoke to Elizabeth a lot."

"So I gather," David said. "Elizabeth knew she was leaving me before I did."

"Are you really surprised, after the way you'd been treating her? You've been getting violent. What's that all about? You never used to be that way."

"I keep telling you, I'm under pressure."

"So is everyone. It doesn't mean we have to lash out at everyone. But of course, I can't possibly understand what you're going through. I'm beneath you now. As you've reminded me."

"I just meant you've got the sort of job where you can walk away at the end of the day. And if you've had enough, you can leave and walk straight into another. Computer programmers are in demand."

"And doctors aren't?"

"It's more complicated than that. You have to consider what you want to be specialising in, the facilities at the hospital, what the teaching is like. And then there's the years of studying for exams. If you're not in that world, you really can't understand what it's like."

"So you keep saying. If it's that much hell, why put yourself through it?"

"Being a surgeon has been my dream since I was a kid. You must know that. I talked about it in school. And everyone said, 'Don't be silly, boy. People from your kind of background don't become doctors.' But I'm on the way there. I'm going to prove them all wrong."

"I know you feel you have something to prove," Mark said. "But don't lose sight of what else is important in your life. What about your friends?"

"I have friends. Really influential friends. I'm starting to go places now."

"I don't mean your new golf club friends. What about us? Those of us who were with you at the beginning? Those of us you role play with – or you used to. Are you beyond such childish pursuits now?"

David shrugged. "People change. Life moves on. What can I say?"

"I just think you're losing sight of what's important. Follow your dream by all means, but don't stomp on those of us at the bottom as you make your way to the top."

"I have to go." David stood up. "Lots to do. I only came by to say thank you for helping me out this morning. I thought I should show my gratitude."

"Yes, and that's appreciated. Just don't lose sight of the people who count."

David sighed. "So much to do. Not just in work, but now for the move as well."

"What move?"

"There was one piece of good news today. The mortgage company called me to say my mortgage has been approved. My purchase of that house in Hampstead is going through. Thanks again, Mark. See you soon."

"Yeah. See you." The door slammed behind David, leaving Mark alone in his flat.

CHAPTER 27

"Are you sure you want to do this?" Mark said. "It feels wrong."

"It's a small price to pay to get to the bottom of what's going on," Elizabeth replied.

Mark stared at the yellow police tape that covered the front door of Helen's flat. "I think it's that tape. Maybe I've watched too many crime dramas. They all say you shouldn't disturb the tape."

Elizabeth began pulling off the tape and inserted the key in the door. "The police gave the go-ahead to Helen's dad and said that he could start clearing out her stuff. Only he's asked us to do it, because he can't face it. And I promised we would. First, it's the least we can do for Helen; second, maybe we can find out why she was killed."

"The police couldn't." Mark resolutely followed Elizabeth over the threshold.

"The police aren't looking for a supernatural beastie."

Mark found himself moving quietly and speaking in hushed whispers for some inexplicable reason. The place was empty; they were disturbing no one. He thought how strange it was that once you knew someone had gone, their home reverted to being nothing more than bricks and mortar; as if it was the soul of a person that seeped into the brickwork and made a home – and once that had departed, it was nothing more than an empty building.

Only Helen's place wasn't empty. It was still full of stuff. He realised he'd never been in Helen's home before, and that saddened him. Helen hadn't had many friends, by all accounts. Why hadn't he taken the time to get to know her better?

Elizabeth stopped in the middle of the living room, a look of sorrow evident on her face.

Her eyes were full of tears. "I thought I could do this," she said. "It's going to be harder than I thought. But I made a promise."

Mark folded her in his arms. "Let's start with looking for what we want to find. We can always come back and sort the rest of the stuff out later."

Elizabeth sniffed sorrowfully. "She was doing some more research on the ritual. Maybe that's why she was killed."

"That's a good point, but something else has occurred to me," Mark said.

"What's that?"

Mark led Elizabeth to the couch and sat her down on it, taking both her hands in his. "We found out this ritual unleashes some kind of supernatural magical creature, yes? And we've been assuming this creature possesses David. But David isn't behind the killings – he has an alibi for all of them."

"Maybe it's controlling him."

"The day after Helen was killed, when he came round to see us. You left before the end of the conversation. He told me he's had his mortgage approved for this fancy new house he wants to buy."

"So what?"

"When Chelsea was killed, he passed his exams. When his dad died, he came into money."

Elizabeth frowned. "He came into money because his dad left it to him. What's your point?"

"Good things keep happening to David, while people keep dying."

"You think David's making this happen, somehow?"

"I think we need to investigate it. We need to look at Helen's computer, to find out what she learned."

"The computer's in the bedroom. That's where she was found."

"Which suggests she was working on it when...it happened."

"No one's cleaned up yet. I don't know if I can face it."

"I'll go in there if you like," Mark said. "You can stay here."

Elizabeth sighed. "No. I don't want to be alone in this place. You're right. We have to go see."

Hand in hand they made their way cautiously into the bedroom, gingerly skirting the bed to the computer station on the other side. Mark had told himself not to look, but his eyes were drawn to the stains. The unpleasant coppery smell of blood still hung in the air. He felt Elizabeth's hand tighten around his.

The trail of blood carried on up the computer monitor. But the spot where the computer had sat was conspicuously empty. "It's gone," Mark said. "The police must have taken it away for evidence."

"We don't need it." Elizabeth released his hand, crossed to the computer desk and started hunting through the papers on the shelf by the desk.

"Helen always printed everything off. She never trusted computers enough to have everything only backed up electronically. She always had hard copies." Elizabeth picked up a blue file folder from the top of the pile. "And the things she worked on most recently were always the closest to hand. This is it." She moved away from the desk quickly, as it if it were a living, hostile thing, then crossed to the other side of the bed – as far away from the blood as possible.

"Are you sure?" Mark asked.

Elizabeth put the folder down on the bed and pulled out the first couple of pages. "These are from her notes. 'Container of organs equals phylactery. Source of Ragnor's power'. This is what we need."

"And what about sorting out the flat?"

Elizabeth sighed. "I made a promise, and I can't go back on it. But I can't face it tonight. Let's go back to your place and pore over these notes. Tomorrow we'll come back and go through the place.

I've got tonight to psyche myself up. There's just one more thing we need to do tonight before I'm able to face it."

Mark followed Elizabeth out into the corridor. "What might that be?"

"Get very drunk," Elizabeth said.

CHAPTER 28

For the next couple of weeks, Mark went through his life feeling like he was sleepwalking. Sorting out Helen's flat with Elizabeth; meeting Helen's distraught father; the funeral. It all felt like a bizarre nightmare that he was desperately hoping to wake up from. And yet it went on, and on.

At the request of Helen's father, her body was shipped up North to be buried in the family plot. None of Helen's London friends were able to make the trip. Mark and Elizabeth were able to swing having the same day off work, thanks to their sympathetic boss. The funeral was on a Friday. They planned to travel up to Leeds by train after work on Thursday, stay in a B&B for two nights, and return to London Saturday morning.

They had talked about staying the weekend and doing some sightseeing, but neither of them was of the right mind-set for something that seemed so frivolous.

Especially after the funeral. Helen's father and stepmother were Catholic. The service was long and depressing, with the church full of weeping elderly aunts and an army of distant cousins that probably hadn't seen Helen in years. Mark sat in the cold church, Elizabeth's arm laced through his. A plump middle-aged lady in unrelieved black, down to the feather in her ridiculously elaborate hat, squashed on the other side of the pew. He wore his best job interview suit – the only black suit he owned; the trousers felt scratchy and uncomfortable, the constricting tie around his neck felt like it was strangling him.

As the elderly priest went on about a young life being called to Heaven, he thought about how little he knew about Helen's family.

It was clear that the priest didn't know Helen at all – if it wasn't for the university graduation photo on the front of the order of service he clutched, now crumpled and smudged in his sweaty hand, he might have thought he'd walked into the wrong funeral. The priest was talking about a completely different girl to the one he'd known. Helen wouldn't have cared for the pompous expression of being called to God, or all that stuff about her soul being in Heaven, sitting on the right hand side of Jesus. How can you go to Heaven when you don't believe it exists? Helen wasn't in some other-worldly paradise, free of all pain for eternity. She was lying cold and stiff in the coffin that squatted before the altar. As Mark stared at the coffin, an image of Helen lying in it came unbidden to his mind. Skin pale and spongy. Eyes open and staring. Her lovely hair spread out over silk pillows. Was that right? Did coffins have silk pillows? What use did the dead have for pillows? She was probably clad in a dress, even though Mark had never seen Helen wearing anything but jeans and combat pants. Why did people get buried in their best clothes? He could understand it in America, where funerals involved open caskets – allegedly so people could say goodbye to the deceased person. But here in the UK, caskets were sealed. What did it matter if it was lined with silk, or the person was dressed up to the nines and covered in make-up to make their face look more life-like? Nobody was going to see them again. If you were buried in the ground you were food for the worms, lying there bloated and rotting away until nothing remained but bones. You may as well be buried naked in a cardboard box.

I want to be cremated, Mark thought suddenly. He wondered if Helen would have wanted to be buried in the ground to rot away like that. The burial was her father's wish, not hers. She probably hadn't even thought about it.

He realised his eyes were filled with tears. The priest was talking about the full life Helen had led.

She was twenty-four, Mark thought bitterly. What chance had she had to live any kind of life? She'd had so much potential, but her life had barely started. And now it was over – cut short, brutally and suddenly.

Beside him, Elizabeth took his hand in hers and squeezed it. He looked over at her and saw that she was crying too, silent tears rolling down her cheeks.

Her mascara was smudged underneath her glasses. Mark squeezed back.

When the seemingly unending service was over, the coffin was borne out of the church by six young men – cousins or other family members presumably, although none of them bore any resemblance to Helen. The mourners solemnly followed the coffin out.

By the door of the church, Helen's father and stepmother greeted the guests, as each one dutifully lined up to shake their hands and bow in deference.

Mark took Elizabeth's hand and stood in line, acutely aware of the fact that the two of them didn't know another soul at the service. When they got to the head of the queue, Helen's folks thanked them, not only for coming to the funeral but all the help they'd given in clearing out Helen's flat. "It's so difficult for us to get away and go all the way down there," Helen's stepmother murmured.

"You're welcome to come to the house," her husband added. "For the wake. You know."

"Thank you very much, but we really need to be going," Elizabeth said. "We're getting the train back to London."

Helen's father smiled sadly and turned away, his attention on the next person in the queue.

Elizabeth had a firm grip on Mark's hand and she pulled him down the path and out of the church yard. "I thought we were staying another night," he said as soon as they were out of earshot.

"I don't think I can face a house full of strangers, can you?" Elizabeth said. "None of these people knew Helen. They probably hadn't seen her in years. They should have had the funeral in London. Then her friends would have been able to come. The people that really knew her. The people that loved her."

"This is what her father wanted," Mark said. "We knew we'd be the only London people here. We wanted to be here."

"Yes." Elizabeth stared back at the church and at the sea of people emerging in a wave of black. "To abide by her family's wishes and pay our respects. But we've done that, and I can't bear to be in this place any longer. Let's go back to the B&B, pack our stuff, and go home."

CHAPTER 29

It was about a week after the funeral when Elizabeth told Mark that she'd made arrangements for him to go to the shooting club.

"To do what?" he asked in disbelief.

"To practise shooting, of course." She looked at him, an amused expression on her face. "What else?"

"I don't know anything about shooting a gun."

"So you've said. And that's why we're going. So you can learn something."

"That all sounds a bit intense. I don't have a gun."

"It'll be fine. I've booked you in as my guest. There are plenty of guns there you can use."

And so, one Thursday evening after work, on an unusually cold and frosty evening in July, Mark found himself accompanying Elizabeth to a remote part of North London where her gun club was held.

The club resided in a converted warehouse on an industrial estate. Somehow Mark had been expecting a farmhouse in the middle of nowhere.

Elizabeth checked them in and was handed a key, which she explained was for the locker that safely stored her guns. The door she opened contained a pump-action shotgun and two automatic pistols. She retrieved the two pistols, and some ammunition.

"All these are yours?" Mark asked.

"They were my dad's."

The gun club instructor gave Mark a patient lesson on how to load, aim and fire a gun, emphasising the need for safety. Equipped with safety goggles and ear protectors, he was eventually allowed down to the shooting range with Elizabeth.

Somehow, Mark was surprised not to be shooting at cans on some farm.

From his position behind the waist-high concrete barrier, he stared at the target that seemed to be impossibly far away on the other side of the room. Around them, others were firing at their targets; the noise was deafening. The set-up reminded Mark vaguely of a bowling alley, except that everyone was shooting pistols instead of rolling balls down the alley. He glanced at Elizabeth and gestured that she should go first. She had already forewarned him of the futility of trying to have a conversation in the target area; the noise made it impossible to hear each other.

Elizabeth took her turn first, firing off five bullets. When the target was reeled in, he was impressed at just how good a shot she was – three of her five bullets were within the centre of the bull's eye, and the other two were pretty close.

He took his own turn, trying to heed what the instructor had told him about focus and aim. However, when he reeled the target in and inspected it, he realised he was a rubbish shot.

Only one of his bullets had actually hit the target, and it was in the far left corner of it – nowhere near the bull's eye. "No wonder you kick my butt at *Resident Evil*" he said to Elizabeth.

At the end of the session, the guns were carefully locked away again and the two of them made their way back to the tube station hand in hand."

"So what do you think?" Elizabeth asked. "Did you enjoy it?"

"It's never an enjoyable experience to realise you're so rubbish at something." Mark said.

"Everyone's got to start somewhere. I've been shooting since I was a kid. The only way to improve is to keep at it. So shall we do it again soon?"

It was a fairly long walk back to the tube station, and the area they had to go through was mostly residential. Much of it was old and well-established.

The church they were passing looked like it had been standing for several centuries; the gravestones in the churchyard were blackened and weather-beaten, many of them leaning to one side. It was an unusually cold night; a frosty fog hung over the ground.

"There's something not right here," Elizabeth said suddenly.

Mark slowed. "What's wrong?"

"Can't you sense it? A feeling of...wrongness." She looked over towards the churchyard. "There's someone there."

Mark followed Elizabeth's gaze. He could make out a shadowy figure hunched over one of the gravestones. Something about it seemed wrong.

The figure stood up slowly and began to move towards them with an awkward, shuffling gait. Its head was skewed at a strange angle, and one arm seemed longer than the other.

For the first time, Mark noticed the smell that was wafting from the figure's direction.

A smell of decay and rot, and it was getting stronger by the minute. "Let's get out of here," he said, and urged Elizabeth forward.

A few steps later, he stopped dead. Two more figures were ahead of them. They moved slowly, but they were less than thirty feet away. With every shuffling step they took, the smell got stronger. They looked like they had been human once, but now they were nothing more than grotesque parodies. Their faces were distorted; jaws held askew. Strips of rotten flesh hung from their faces and viscous fluid dripped from their mouths. Their eyes bulged from their sockets. They let out a guttural groan, raising their arms as they shuffled forward.

Elizabeth gripped Mark's hand. "Look," she said, pointing back towards the graveyard. The shuffling figure they had first spotted had been joined by companions. Half a dozen of them were now moving forwards in slow but determined progress. The smell was overwhelming.

Mark had to fight back the urge to retch.

"What the hell are they?" he said. "They look like..."

"Zombies?" Elizabeth supplied.

"That's impossible. It can't be."

"I really don't want to stay and argue existential theory with these things. Let's get the hell out of here. But we can't go that way."

"Come on." Clutching Elizabeth's hand, Mark took an abrupt left, crossing the road and heading directly away from the church.

The figures began to follow them, grouping together and lurching across the road, their low groans forming a dissonant cacophony. They moved slowly but determinedly.

Mark and Elizabeth cut down a side street, breaking into a run. There were houses here, but they all looked dark and empty. Nobody was out in the street – no one at all. In retrospect, Mark thought, they should have realised there was something odd about that.

"Should we ask for help at one of these houses?" Elizabeth said breathlessly, hurrying to keep up with Mark.

"If no one answers we waste time. Somehow I think none of these people want to get involved. These things aren't moving quickly. We can outrun them."

"A bit ironic we left the guns behind. We could really use them right about now."

The two of them ran down the street and in a rough circle, approaching the tube station from the other direction. There was no sign of the zombies when they got there.

The tube station was deserted. They passed through the barriers and ran down the escalators, stopping to catch their breath when they reached the station platform. There was no one on the platform, which again seemed odd.

"We should tell someone about this," Elizabeth said when she got her breath back.

"Tell them what? Zombies are rampaging in North London?"

"Someone might get hurt. They could be on the attack."

The train pulled up to the platform. As they boarded, Mark let out a breath he had been unaware of holding. He had been almost convinced that the train would not come, and that they would be trapped underground at the mercy of hordes of zombies.

There were a few people in the carriage; mostly wearing headphones and oblivious to everything but their music. No sign of any zombies, thankfully, and for a moment Mark allowed himself to think that they might actually have imagined it.

"Let's go home," Mark said. "And see if there's anything on the news. We need to find out what the hell's going on."

CHAPTER 30

Once they were on the underground, there was no further sign of the zombie horde, and they arrived home without further incident. There was nothing on the news about zombie sightings in London or anywhere else in the country either. Mark watched the news closely over the next few weeks, but there was nothing about unexplained attacks or strange, undead creatures. However, there was a story about a missing person or a violent death at least once a week – a body that had been discovered that looked like it had been ripped apart by something with inhuman strength. Perhaps these stories had been on the news before and he'd never noticed them, but perhaps they hadn't.

In the aftermath of Helen's death, things had become a lot more difficult. Although he did his best to pick up normal life, Mark often felt like he was just going through the motions.

Elizabeth's presence made everything so much more bearable. She spent much of her time at his flat, staying overnight and travelling to work with him in the morning. Everyone at work knew by now that they were an item. There was some good-natured teasing, but they did their best to try and keep it professional in the office and nobody seemed to mind their inter-office romance.

Occasionally Elizabeth went home to spend the odd night in her own flat or bring in some different clothes to keep at Mark's. When she did, he found that he missed her immensely. He'd so quickly got used to Elizabeth sharing his bed that when she wasn't there, it felt empty and lonesome. He started to wonder if he should introduce the subject of them moving in together.

They would probably have to get a bigger place – his little flat wasn't really big enough for two people. But was it too soon to bring this up?

They'd only been seeing each other for four months. Maybe Elizabeth valued her own space, and she liked the nights that she spent alone in her own flat? Maybe he was moving too quickly? After all, he really had no clear idea how she really felt about that sort of commitment.

And then he got to worrying. He was sure that what he felt for Elizabeth was love, proper love, and he'd never felt this way about anyone before. What if she didn't love him? What if she saw their relationship as a bit of fun? What if she were to get scared off if he started to come on too heavy? What if she were to leave him? The concept of his life without Elizabeth in it was too depressing to bear, and that was an even more worrying thought.

He tried not to dwell on it. It was Friday night and he and Elizabeth had a quiet weekend ahead. She was in his kitchen, as she'd promised to cook him dinner. The delicious smell of chilli cooking wafted into the living room, where Mark was sitting with his laptop.

Best not to think about the heavy subject of commitment. He should just enjoy Elizabeth's company.

To distract himself, he logged onto Facebook, idly checking his friends' statuses for interesting updates. He'd heard nothing from David since he had turned up at the flat after being released from jail six weeks ago, in spite of the fact that he'd left several messages for him – at work, at home, on his mobile. Increasingly worried about his friend's wellbeing, Mark's messages to David had become more and more urgent. But David just wasn't phoning him back.

Mark couldn't help but think that David was avoiding him, and that hurt. Not too long ago David had been his best friend. Why was he keeping his distance? Mark clicked on David's profile, curious as to what was keeping his friend so busy. It was clear from David's statuses that he had recently moved into his new house.

That all seemed to go through very quickly, Mark thought.

There were several photos of the house on David's profile page. It was a white stone detached place, looking quite old and refined.

It had a big black-painted front door, a stone porch with an elaborate awning, and a massive driveway.

The most recent posting on David's wall was from someone calling himself "Doctor Bob". "Looking forward to tomorrow night, mate," it said. The comment was linked to an event. Curious, Mark clicked on the event.

Elizabeth poked her head around the door. "Dinner's nearly ready, babe. Could you come and pour the wine?"

Mark stared at the computer screen. "Uh, yeah, sure." After a moment he got up from the couch and followed Elizabeth into the kitchen.

Elizabeth was spooning chilli and rice into bowls. The smell was heavenly. "Did you know David's moved into his new house?" Mark said.

"That was fast," Elizabeth said.

Mark opened a bottle of South African merlot. "He's having a house warming party tomorrow night."

Elizabeth put the empty chilli pan in the sink and filled it with water. "Oh really?"

"It's on Facebook. Looks like it's a big event. He's invited loads of people. But not us, apparently."

"His loss, then."

"But why haven't we been invited?"

"I don't think he likes me very much."

"That's not the point." Mark set the bottle down and slammed the cupboard doors as he got wine glasses. "He used to be my best friend. We've known each other most of our lives. He's invited me to every big party in his life. Except this one. And this house move – this is a big deal for him.

On Facebook he's going on about how important it is; about how this marks the start of his life as a doctor; how he's now a proper grown-up; ya da, ya da.

And he's purposefully excluded me."

Elizabeth laid a hand on Mark's arm. "If it's that important to you, why don't you call him?"

"What am I going to say to him? 'Hey David, why haven't you invited me to your party?' I'd sound like a petulant five year old."

"And of course, sitting here sulking is so much more mature."

Mark scowled and picked up the wine bottle. "You're very irritating when you're logical, you know that?"

"You and David haven't seen eye to eye for a while, you know that? But you blokes are so keen on keeping your feelings bottled up that things fester. Maybe David doesn't realise how much it's upsetting you to have him shut you out."

"I've tried calling him. Several times, actually," Mark said as he filled the wine glasses. "By not returning my calls, he's made it pretty clear he doesn't want to talk to me. I'm not resorting to grovelling. I do have some pride left."

"Then why don't you go and see him? Talk things through like grown-ups. Tell him how much you miss not spending time with him."

"That's not the manly way."

"If men expressed their feelings more, there'd be fewer wars. If women ran the world, how different things would be."

"Yeah, yeah." Mark sighed. "Maybe you're right. Maybe I'll go see him."

"Why don't you take him a housewarming gift? Let him know that you don't hold a grudge about not being invited to the party?"

"But I am holding a grudge."

"If you forgive him, he'll feel guilty and be more willing to talk to you."

"There you go, being all logical again."

"That's why you like me." Elizabeth picked up her bowl of chilli and a wine glass.

"Now I suggest we stop talking about David and get down to watching that *Alien* movie marathon we promised ourselves tonight."

"Sounds good to me." Mark picked up his own food and wine and followed Elizabeth back to the living room. "You think we can get through all four tonight?"

"I'm game if you are."

"If you fall asleep before me, I get to pick the films for our next movie night," Mark said.

"You're on," Elizabeth said. "But don't expect to win."

CHAPTER 31

Mark drove slowly down the street, looking for David's house. The street was full of large modern homes; semi-detached and detached two storey houses with shiny front doors, well-tended lawns and large driveways. BMWs and Jaguars occupied most of those driveways. At the house just ahead on the right, a woman with blonde highlights, an out-of-the-bottle tan, and designer jeans was unloading Waitrose shopping bags from the boot of a shiny black four wheel drive that had clearly never seen off-road action. A little girl, aged about seven, emerged from the back seat of the car as Mark passed by. The school uniform she wore consisted of a grey woollen skirt, smart green blazer and straw boater with a matching green band.

A few houses later, Mark spotted number 32 – a tasteful detached home with an adjoining garage.

He recognised the house from the Facebook photo. The exterior walls were adorned with white stucco, and the window frames were painted with a shiny black gloss. A two-foot high brick wall encircled the property, with a pair of stone lions topping the two posts that marked the entrance way. A three-year-old black Jaguar X-type sat in the driveway in front of the double garage. Mark parked his shabby ancient Audi next to it, feeling acutely self-conscious.

He gave the car a reassuring pat on the roof as he locked it. "Stay strong, old girl. I know we're a bit out of place here, but I'd appreciate it if you didn't self-destruct out of shame while I'm gone."

He crossed the paved driveway to the front door of the house. The centrepiece was a tree with rounded shiny leaves, growing out of a stone base.

The tree looked neat and well-tended – no stray leaves littering the ground around it. Mark knew nothing about foliage. He didn't think David did, either.

The doorbell echoed hollowly within the house. Mark waited for such a long time that he started to think that maybe David wasn't home, in spite of the car in the drive. But then the door opened and David was standing there, blinking in the light.

Mark couldn't suppress the gasp of shock that escaped him when he saw his friend. David looked like a walking corpse. His face was thin, the contours of his skull clearly visible beneath the thin grey skin. His eyes looked bulbous in his face, emphasised by the dark shadows underneath them. His face sported at least three days' worth of stubble. He'd lost weight and his jeans hung loose around his bony hips. His arms emerged stick-like from beneath the sleeves of his filthy t-shirt. "Mark," he said, frowning. "What are you doing here?"

Mark forced a grin. "Hi mate. I thought I'd bring you a little house warming gift." He held up the bottle of champagne.

David blinked at Mark. "Oh. Thanks."

"Have I caught you at a bad time?"

David seemed to recover himself. "No. Come on in." He stepped back from the doorway.

Mark followed him in, closing the door behind him. "Sorry to drop by unannounced. I left a few messages for you, but you never phoned back."

"Sorry about that. I've just been a bit busy." David led Mark down a corridor that was tasteful but sparse – cream walls, a parquet floor. No furniture, no pictures on the walls. "Um, do you mind taking your shoes off? The carpet's new, and I'm trying to keep it clean."

When Mark entered the living room, he understood the rule about no shoes. Everything was white and clean. The carpet was cream, thick and lush and felt wonderful underfoot.

It was so new that fibre clumps were still gathering by the edges. The walls were painted white.

The three piece suite was cream leather.

The rows of CDs and DVDs in the silver and glass wall unit that also housed the stereo added the only colour to the room. A 47 inch flat screen TV playing the BBC 24 hour news channel took up most of the back wall. The other walls were blank – no pictures in here either. The room was tasteful, but soulless.

David sank into the leather sofa. Mark perched in the armchair across from him. "Things are a bit hectic at work at the moment," David said. "I think I must have nodded off. I woke up when you rang the doorbell."

"I guess you've been keeping busy then." Mark put the champagne bottle down on the glass coffee table.

"There's a job opened up in the Trust I want to apply for," David said. "It's the perfect job. But the competition will be stiff. I've been putting in extra hours to prove myself."

In the silence that followed Mark blurted out, "The house is really nice. And I see you got a new car, too."

"Yeah."

"I noticed you had a house warming party. I saw it on Facebook. I wondered why I wasn't invited."

David gave a weary smile. "I told you, I'm angling for this job. It's all about who you know. So I invited certain select people to the party."

"So you're embarrassed by me now? Is that it?"

"Not exactly. But you wouldn't really fit in with the people I work with."

"Why not?"

David sighed. "We've had this conversation before. It's all about image. I knew you wouldn't understand."

"I just don't understand what's going on with you, David. You've got this fancy house you can't really afford and you're mingling with people you don't want me to meet. You know, when you try to pretend to be something you're not, it all goes wrong in the end."

"That's why we're growing apart. You don't know me anymore. It happens.

When people are friends as kids, they become different people when they get to be adults."

"You've only become a different person in the last few months," Mark said. "Why can't we get together the way we used to? Come over to mine some time. Drink beer and eat take-away and watch DVDs with me and Elizabeth."

"Elizabeth doesn't like me. I think it's great that you both have got it together, and she's obviously making you happy, but I know she doesn't like me. She doesn't want to put up with me hanging around your place."

Mark opened his mouth to protest, and then closed it again. He couldn't deny the truth of David's words. "OK then, why don't me and you go out? Let's have a pub night. We'll drink beer and talk about the old days. Like we used to."

"Because things have changed. We can't go back to the old days. We're living different lives now."

"You're living a different life. I'm still the same. Is this really the life you want, David? You look terrible."

David scowled. "Thanks very much."

"I mean it. You've lost weight. Too much weight. You look like you haven't slept in a while. Is everything alright?"

"I told you, everything's fine. I've just been working very hard and I'm a bit tired, that's all. Everything's working out exactly the way I want it to."

Mark shook his head sadly. "If that's true, then I hope it brings you happiness."

"You've chosen your path. I've chosen mine. It's leading us in separate directions. That's why things can't be the same again."

"So you keep saying," Mark said. "I just hope yours is taking you somewhere you want to go."

CHAPTER 32

"What bothers me most," Mark said, "is that he doesn't seem to see it."

"What's that?" Elizabeth said absently. Sitting in bed next to Mark, she was engrossed in her laptop. They were having a lazy Sunday morning in bed. Mark was allegedly reading, but his science fiction paperback lay on the covers. He hadn't got more than a couple of paragraphs in.

"David," Mark said. "He doesn't seem to realise what's happened to him. Everyone else can see it. Why can't he?"

Elizabeth looked at him. "Are you still stressing over that? David's made it clear he doesn't want to spend time with you anymore. Maybe you should let it go, baby."

Mark sighed and rubbed his temples wearily. "I can't let it go. He's my best friend. The thing is, I keep thinking, this isn't him. Helen was convinced he'd been possessed by something.

Crazy as it sounds, I'm starting to wonder if she had a point. I couldn't believe this lich idea when we first came across it. But the more I think about it, the more it makes sense. We've got to find a way to banish this thing. Maybe then, David will be back to his old self."

"What do you think I've been researching?"

"Have you found a solution?"

Elizabeth frowned and tapped a couple of keys. "I have found something interesting here, connected to Ragnor the Black, and this ritual." She peered closer at the screen, squinting behind her glasses. "Allegedly, these are the instructions Ragnor left behind to his servants about how he wanted to be buried."

"What does it say?"

"I think this is a rough translation. It says that after death his body must be preserved. Emptied of all fluids and all organs removed, then wrapped in bandages, to stop the moisture getting in."

"He's talking about mummification, then."

"A variation, yes. Then it says his body must be placed in the earth, no more than six feet down, in the enchanted woods. It specifies he must not be sealed in a casket, for he needs to find his way out again."

"Creepy," Mark said. "So does it mention where these enchanted woods are?"

"It just says in the magickal clearing, five miles North West of the town of Lynley."

"Magical?"

"Magickal. With a 'k'".

"Does that make a difference?"

"It does to him, I think. He evidently believed in all this stuff.

"So that was it? He's buried somewhere in the woods?"

"All these were specific instructions to make sure he could come back. There are also instructions about how to perform the ritual, and when, and where."

"Okay…so what does it say about where?"

"It has to be within this magickal circle. But the circle's a pretty big one. Two hundred feet radius. As long as both his burial place and the ritual site are within this circle, he'll come back from the dead. Or so it says here."

Mark sat up straighter and looked over at Elizabeth. "And what does it say about when?"

"It says within five days of the full moon. 'Near the witching hour'"

"What does that mean, near the witching hour?"

Elizabeth pushed her glasses up her nose. "The witching hour is traditionally midnight. I don't know if they had the same means of measuring time in those days, but there are annotations on this web page, and the general opinion seems to be within an hour of midnight."

Mark was silent for a moment, lost in thought.

Then he said, "So when we performed that ritual during the game, do you know what time it was."

"I remember sneaking a look at my watch when we got back to camp, and by that point it was quarter to twelve."

"So we did perform this ritual within an hour of midnight. We weren't within five days of the full moon, were we?"

"I remember thinking on that night that the moon was very bright. So I looked it up. That night we did the ritual was a full moon."

"So the time was right, and the day was right. It still seems a bit far-fetched. How could the location be right? We don't even know where this place is. Those woods are probably not even there anymore, even if we could pinpoint the location."

"I found this map of Gloucester and the Forest of Dean in the 1500s," Elizabeth said, turning the laptop around so Mark could see the screen. "Here's the town of Wicksford. Five miles north west would be about here." She stabbed her finger at a spot amidst vast forest land. "Now then. Here's a map of modern day Gloucester."

Elizabeth called up a second map, and reduced the two images so that they were side by side on the screen. "The town of Wicksford isn't there anymore, but I think it would be roughly here. Between these other two towns." She pointed at the map. "Can you work out where our role playing site is?"

Mark studied the forest area on the map. "Well, here's the nearest village to the camp site. And there's the road that leads up to it. So we'd be about there." He pointed at the map.

He looked at the ancient map, and then back at the modern one. "Which means we performed this ritual right on top of Ragnor's burial site. Bugger me."

"Quite," Elizabeth said. "Right time, right place, right day. If the ritual was going to work, it would have worked when we performed it."

"Did David plan it all along? Did he know what was going to happen?"

"I could be generous and give him the benefit of the doubt. It may have been a bizarre coincidence. But the fact remains, he was the one that recited the ritual, and he was the one that released Ragnor."

"So what else does it say? What does releasing Ragnor do, exactly?"

"It just says that whoever performed the ritual would grant Ragnor eternal life, and they would be rewarded with whatever their heart desired."

"But there's a price to pay?"

"Of course there's a price to pay. There's always a price, with that kind of power. Reading between the lines, I think the gist is that Ragnor will grant you whatever you wish for, but he requires a blood sacrifice. This resurrected form of his needs constant replenishment. With life blood."

"So whatever David wishes for, someone has to die for him to get it. He wanted money and his dad died. He wanted to pass his exams and Chelsea died."

"He wanted his dream house and Helen died."

"We've got to stop this thing, Elizabeth. Any clues as to how?"

"The only hint here is about the phylactery."

"The what?"

"It's what they used to do with the organs they removed from bodies prior to mummification," Elizabeth said. "In ancient Egypt, they put them in jars and buried them in the tombs, so the pharaohs would have them for the afterlife. They knew that the body wouldn't stay preserved with the organs inside, so they removed them and preserved them, storing them in jars."

"Nice," Mark said.

"It was all quite high-tech, when you think about it. For an ancient race, the Egyptians had a very advanced knowledge of anatomy."

"So what's this about Ragnor's organs?"

Elizabeth clicked back to the website she'd been reading from. "It just says Ragnor's organs needed to be removed from his body and stored in a phylactery, to be buried separate from his body but still within the magic circle. It seems to suggest that the phylactery is the source of his power."

"Perhaps if it's the source of his power, that's the way to take it away," Mark said.

"I thought so too, but I can't find any more references. There's only so much info on the web about this."

"We need to find out more about this Ragnor dude."

"Perhaps we should take a trip to Gloucester?" Elizabeth suggested. "Go to one of these modern towns that swallowed up Wicksford. Maybe the local library will have something on local legends."

"A long way to go on a whim, though."

"That's why we research first. I'll see if I can look up local libraries. I can always give them a call and ask if they have anything on this sort of thing."

Mark groaned and swung his legs out of bed. "Somehow the urge for a lazy Sunday has left me. I no longer feel relaxed. Time to get up."

"Yes, I suppose you're right." Elizabeth closed the laptop and set it to one side. "Any plans for today?"

"Nothing I had in mind. What about you?"

"I'd like to drop in and see Linus."

"What, just drop in? Is he expecting you?"

"Well, I hope so. I've left several messages saying we wanted to drop in, but he hasn't called me back. So in the end I just left one saying we'd be by on Sunday, and to call if that's a problem."

"Maybe he's got a new girlfriend, and that's why he's been distracted."

"If there is someone new in his life, he hasn't mentioned it to me."

"Brothers don't tell their sisters everything, you know. He might be seeing a complete nympho. We could go over and drop into an embarrassing scene."

Elizabeth frowned. "Linus? Somehow I don't think so."

"You never know, if he meets the right woman." Mark found a pair of jeans from the pile on the floor and pulled them on. "He might suddenly transform into a complete stud."

"Maybe I will try calling first."

"If you want first dibs on the shower, I'll make us some brunch," Mark said.

"Brunch? How sophisticated." Elizabeth pulled on Mark's bathrobe and tied it around herself. It was the only thing she was wearing and it was way too big, but somehow she still managed to make it look sexy.

"Only bacon and eggs. Don't get excited."

"Still sounds good to me. I never turn down a man who'll cook for me." Elizabeth gave Mark a kiss, and sashayed off to the bathroom.

He grinned and headed off to the kitchen.

CHAPTER 33

"Hi, this is Linus. I can't come to the phone right now, but please leave your name and number and I'll get back to you." Elizabeth rolled her eyes at the phone. "Hi, Linus, this is your dear sister. I can't help feeling you're avoiding me. Give me a call." She put the phone down on the kitchen table, where Mark was busy with his laptop.

"So I guess he's still not answering then?" Mark said.

"It's just not like Linus." Elizabeth filled the kettle. "Do you want another cup of tea?"

"That'd be great, thanks. Like I said before, he's probably got a new girlfriend."

"It just seems a bit strange he hasn't mentioned it to me."

"There are some things guys just don't tell their sisters."

Elizabeth switched on the kettle. "Yes, but we normally talk about most things."

"I bet you don't tell him about everything we do."

Elizabeth grinned. "Some things are private, obviously. But Linus knew all about how I felt about you from the beginning. He knew I liked you before you did, because I kept talking about you."

"Maybe Linus has met someone he doesn't want to tell everyone about. Maybe she's married."

Elizabeth rinsed out the two mugs they were using earlier and put tea bags in them. "Doesn't seem his style, somehow. You know Linus. He's got a peculiarly old-fashioned sense of chivalry."

"Sometimes you have no control over your heart. Stop worrying. I'm sure Linus is fine. When he's ready to talk, he'll ring."

"I suppose you're right. So what are our plans for today? Shall we have another go at RE5?"

"Sounds good in theory, but I keep getting depressed that I still can't beat your kill count."

"So practise some more. That's the key, you know." The boiling kettle clicked off, and Elizabeth filled the mugs with water. You got through RE4."

"You have me licked on accuracy, though. Too bad that one's not a two-player game. I just think you've got a natural talent. My girlfriend, Ace Zombie Slayer. I'll never be as good as you."

"Some of us have just got it. Better get practising though, because we haven't even started *Resident Evil 6*." Elizabeth finished off the tea, and carried both mugs over to the kitchen table. "So what are you doing on that laptop that's got you so engrossed?"

"Just checking the news."

"Are you still looking for some mention of zombie attacks?"

"Well, it was very strange, don't you think? We see a bunch of zombies lurching down the street and there's no mention of it anywhere? I'm starting to think we imagined it."

"I'm pretty sure we didn't. But you're right; it's strange no one else has seen anything weird."

"There's frequent mention of violent and unexplained deaths, but no conclusive evidence on what attacked the victims. Hang on a minute." Mark peered at the screen. "There's something here."

"What?"

"A story about some people in London claiming to be attacked by strange creatures. They say they were walking home from the pub, and they encountered 'something out of a horror movie' – creatures they describe as looking like mummies and skeletons, emitting a terrible smell."

"What happened?"

"They ran like hell. The story seems to be emphasising how drunk they were at the time. There's not much more than that."

Elizabeth wrapped both hands around her mug. "But they lived to tell the tale. I wonder how many of those people who have gone missing or turned up dead were victims of regular killers, and how many were killed by these strange things?"

"Do you really think there are zombies in London?"

Elizabeth shrugged. "What we saw looked like zombies to me. But what raised them, and where were they going? They weren't moving randomly. They were in a group. They looked like they were going somewhere. They didn't come after us when we ran the other way. They've got to have something to do with the lich. I can't believe it's a random coincidence that all these undead creatures have appeared at the same time. I mean, listen to us. We're talking about zombies and liches. In the real world. Who could have imagined that would happen?"

"Do you think the zombies are connected to David, then?"

"I don't know. Maybe the lich is controlling them, and David is controlling the lich."

"More like it's controlling him," said Mark. "That would explain his personality transplant. The only way I get to know what he's doing is by checking his Facebook statuses. I keep expecting him to un-friend me, but I guess he's not got around to it yet. He's got a new job, apparently.

He's crowing about it all over Facebook. Going on about how this was his dream job, and he applied for it thinking he wouldn't get it, but he did. Keeps saying how everything is perfect now."

Elizabeth sank into the kitchen chair. Suddenly she was having trouble breathing. Spots danced before her eyes.

Mark frowned, scraping his chair back as he hurried over to her. "Elizabeth, what's wrong? Are you feeling OK? You've gone pale."

Elizabeth found her voice. "I think we need to go see Linus. Right now."

* * * *

Linus lived in a modest maisonette on the outskirts of Orpington. The drive took nearly an hour. It was one of the reasons she didn't visit more often, Elizabeth thought with regret. She didn't have a car and before dating Mark, it had been difficult to get there. Linus didn't have a spare bed either, so she couldn't stay over. They had always found it more convenient to meet somewhere in Town. Even now she had Mark, and his car, Linus came over to see them far more often than they went to see him.

The street was quiet and everything seemed ordinary. Still, Elizabeth could not shake the sense of dread. "The curtains are closed," she said.

"What?" Mark switched the car engine off and looked up at the house.

"Why are the curtains still closed at this time of day?"

"Maybe he's away."

"I still think he would have let me know if he was going away."

"So maybe he's still in bed."

"At three in the afternoon?"

"It's Sunday. Remember my theory about the new woman?"

Elizabeth stared at the house. "Something's wrong. I just know it." She got out of the car, clutching her bag tightly. She couldn't shake that uneasy feeling. She waited for Mark to lock up the car, and the two of them approached the front door together.

The sound of the doorbell resounded loudly through the house. They waited. Elizabeth rang again.

"There's no question of not being able to hear that bell," Mark said. "He's clearly not home."

Elizabeth fumbled in her bag and found Linus's spare key, which he always left with her. "I think we should go in and see," she said.

As she put the key in the lock, she was overcome with an overwhelming feeling of nausea. She staggered back.

Mark was behind her. "What's the matter?"

"I have a very bad feeling," Elizabeth murmured. "Can you go in and have a look around? I don't think I can do it."

"You don't want to go in?"

"I can't explain it. But I'm getting a panic attack just thinking about stepping inside."

"Okay," Mark said uncertainly. He gripped the key and turned it in the lock, pushing the door open cautiously. "Hello?" he called into the house. There was silence. He cast a worried look at Elizabeth, and stepped over the threshold.

Elizabeth leaned against the wall, taking slow deep breaths until her heart rate returned to normal. She just couldn't shake the feeling that something terrible had happened. She'd been the one to find Helen. That had been awful enough. If something had happened to Linus, she didn't want to see.

A minute or so later, Mark appeared in the doorway. His face was ashen, and when he looked at her, she knew that somehow her instincts had been right.

"Call the police," he said shakily. Then he doubled over and threw up all over the pavement.

CHAPTER 34

When Elizabeth was four and Linus was eight, she used to
follow him around everywhere. He seemed to find this a
burden most of the time, especially since their mother kept
insisting Linus take his sister when he went out – no doubt
because it got Elizabeth out of her hair. Linus always made
out that this was a huge inconvenience, but she had a memory
of going out with Linus and his friends when they were
playing football. One of his friends poked her, calling her a
baby. It hurt, and she started to cry. Then all the other boys
started joining in and laughing at her. Linus got quite cross
and told them to stop. When they wouldn't he took
Elizabeth's hand and they walked away. "I didn't want to
play football anyway," he said. "Why don't we go play on the
swings?" And so they went to the park, just the two of them.
That was the way Elizabeth remembered her childhood with
Linus. Sometimes he'd made out she was a pain in the neck,
but when it came down to it, he'd always stood up for her,
always been there for her. And when their parents had died,
Linus had been the rock – the one that had helped her hold it
together and get through the grief. Now he was gone, and she
was all alone. She sat on the kerb outside the house, as the
police and then the ambulance arrived. The cold seeped in
through her bones, but somehow it didn't seem to matter. She
would never be warm again. Linus was gone. No more
Christmases together; she and Linus, sharing a turkey and
watching the Queen with silly paper hats on. Never again
would she be listening to Linus on the phone, mooning over
some girl he'd set his sights on who wouldn't give him the
time of day. Linus always seemed to go for unobtainable
women.

Elizabeth had formed a theory that he was so afraid of being hurt in love that he was unable to let himself love anyone he might actually have a chance of forming a relationship with. So instead he became fixated on women who were way out of his league. Women who went for good-looking, arrogant men with good jobs, flash cars and expensive watches. Women who would never be interested in sweet but nerdy admin workers. Women like Chelsea.

And Chelsea had ended up dead, at the hands of whatever unnatural thing David had summoned in the woods that day. And then Helen. And now Linus. Who would be next?

"Why don't you get in the car? It's warmer." Elizabeth became aware that Mark was crouching down next to her. He put his arms around her. The winter coat she was wearing seemed insubstantial; she was shivering. She allowed herself to be guided into a standing position and steered towards the car.

She was still waiting for the tears to come. She had shed lots of tears for Helen, and even for Chelsea. But none had come for Linus. She felt numb; empty inside.

Mark sat her in the passenger seat and fastened her seat belt. He switched on the engine, and turned the heating up. "The police want to talk to me, and then we can go home," he said.

"We have to stop him, Mark," Elizabeth said. "David. Or whatever evil thing he's become. You know he did this. We've got to stop him. Whatever it takes."

Mark didn't look at her. "I know."

Elizabeth watched Mark through the car window as he walked over to the police officer standing in the doorway of Linus's home. The heating was on full blast, but she was still shivering. She couldn't get warm.

She watched one of the two paramedics close the ambulance doors. The gurney with Linus had been brought out earlier.

She couldn't see anything of him; he'd been shrouded in a blanket. She'd asked to see, but Mark had told her it hadn't been a good idea. Now he had to talk to the police because he'd been the one to find Linus. They'd wanted to talk to her, too, but Mark had taken them aside and spoken to them in low voices. The police officers had nodded and cast sympathetic glances in her direction, then left her alone after that.

She overheard one of the paramedics puzzling over the fact that Linus had been found with pure white hair, in spite of being only in his twenties. Helen's hair had been white when she was found, too.

Out of the six of players in the LRP game, only she and Mark were left. And David. He'd been the one to summon the lich, or whatever it was. Had it possessed him? Was it controlling him? Elizabeth didn't know, and she didn't really care. All she knew was that David had to be stopped. He had to pay for taking Linus away from her.

"Linus is dead," she said aloud, just to see if she could. The words echoed hollowly around the car. "Linus is dead." They were meaningless, empty words. And yet, when she spoke them, the tears started to flow. They rolled down her cheeks. A great sob welled up in her throat, so huge she couldn't breathe, until finally it broke fee and she began to cry bitterly. Once she started, she thought she wouldn't be able to stop.

* * * *

Elizabeth had cried in the car all the way back to London, but had not spoken a word. Mark had brought her back to his flat, afraid to leave her alone. Eventually she stopped crying but she still said nothing – just sat around looking like a zombie. Mark made her countless cups of tea, which she hadn't drunk; he cooked dinner for her which she hadn't eaten; and then he ran a bath for her which she'd lain in for over an hour.

When he eventually went in to check on her, worried that she might have fallen asleep, he'd found her lying in water that had gone cold, staring at the ceiling.

Eventually they went to bed. They were both sitting up reading, but Mark was willing to bet that Elizabeth was still staring at the same page she had been on half an hour ago, as he was. Now she lay her book down and spoke, for the first time since leaving Linus's. She said, "We have to stop it."

Mark didn't have to ask her what she meant. He lay his own paperback down on the bedclothes. "I thought we didn't have enough information yet to stop it? You wanted to do some more research?"

Elizabeth swivelled her head to stare at him so intently it made him uncomfortable. "We know enough. We have to destroy the phylactery. We know it has to be buried near the body. They both have to be in the same general area where we did the ritual. That's enough. We go there, we find it, we destroy the phylactery. That will destroy the lich."

"We don't know yet whether it will destroy David."

"It doesn't matter."

Mark paused, trying to find the right way to phrase what he wanted to say. "I know you're grieving. I know you want revenge. I can't imagine how you must be feeling. What happened to Chelsea and Helen was terrible enough, but to have it happen to your brother, I … I won't pretend I can know how you feel. But if David's been possessed by the lich, by destroying it we might kill him. Don't you think there's been enough killing?"

Elizabeth stared at Mark for a long time and said nothing, but then something in her face softened. "If we don't stop him, someone else will die. And out of the gaming group, it's only me and you left, apart from David. If someone else dies it will be one of us. We've got to stop him before that happens. Destroying the lich might kill him. Or it might release him. We don't know. But we can't wait any longer."

Mark looked at Elizabeth. She was wrapped up in fleece pyjamas, her eyes large and soulful behind her glasses and her freckles standing out in stark relief against her pale face. It broke his heart to see the grief etched on her face, knowing there was nothing he could do to save her from it. He wished so much he could protect her from all the bad things in the world, but he knew that some things he couldn't protect her from. And there was nothing he could do to bring her brother back. That was a grief she was going to have to work through herself. All he could do was look after her when she wanted him to. Provide a shoulder to cry on when she needed one. Put his arms around her to show how much she meant to him. He found himself doing this now; he couldn't help himself.

Elizabeth sighed and settled into the embrace, leaning her head against his chest. Her hair felt soft and smelled of coconut shampoo, the unruly curls tickling his chin. "Let's drive down there tomorrow," she said. "We'll take the notes and the laptop. We'll check into a B&B and stay as long as we need to."

"We'll leave first thing tomorrow. Do we know how to destroy this phylactery?"

"What I've read seems to suggest fire is the best bet. Somewhere inside the enchanted circle."

"Do we think we'll know it when we find it? The phylactery, I mean?"

"I think it might be wise to do a bit more research when we get there. Check the local library or see if there are any book shops dealing with local mythology. It might fill in any gaps before we go to the woods."

Mark leaned back so he could look at Elizabeth's face. He traced the line of her jaw gently with his forefinger. "I'm sorry you have to go through this. I'm sorry there's nothing I can do to make you feel any better."

She smiled sadly. "Just your being here is helping. I'm sorry I can't be better company."

"Don't apologise for that."

"Just hold me tonight. Hold me until I can fall asleep. I might, eventually, knowing you're there."

Elizabeth lay back on the pillows and Mark settled in beside her, wrapping his arms around her. "I'll always be there for you, Elizabeth. I'm never letting you go." It was the first time he'd vocalised this thought, although it had been rolling around in his mind for weeks, and he felt a bit saddened it had taken a tragedy for him to find the nerve to say it.

Elizabeth switched out the light before settling back into Mark's embrace. "Be careful saying things like that," she said in the darkness. "I might well hold you to it."

Neither of them spoke after that. Mark listened to the noises of the night for a while – the distant traffic outside; the occasional cry of a fox; the tick of the clock on the wall. Eventually Elizabeth's breathing got deeper and more even, and he was satisfied she was sleeping. Not long after that, he fell asleep himself, still with his arms around the girl he now knew with certainty he was going to love forever more.

CHAPTER 35

Neither of them slept well that night, and they were both awake early. They were up and packed and on the road by the time dawn broke.

Elizabeth had insisted that they swing by the gun club before hitting the road for Gloucestershire. She told Mark to wait in the car while she went in, an empty sports bag slung over her shoulder. Fifteen minutes later she returned to the car, the sports bag appearing noticeably heavier. The unmistakable barrel of a shotgun poked out of it. As she approached the car, Elizabeth pointed to the boot. Mark got out and opened it for her. "We're taking guns?"

"Better safe than sorry." Elizabeth carefully packed away her armoury, hidden out of sight underneath the rest of their bags.

"I can't believe they let you take these off the premises."

"It's not easy, trust me. All kinds of forms to fill in. Even though these are my property. If anyone asks, the official reason I want them is that we're going shooting in the Forest of Dean. Which, technically, I suppose we are."

"I doubt that guns will have much of an effect on the lich. It's some kind of magical creature." Mark closed the boot securely and they both got back into the car.

"It wasn't the lich I was thinking of," Elizabeth said. "It's in case we meet any more zombie hordes."

Mark looked at her in surprise, his hand halfway to the ignition key. "You're really expecting to meet more zombies? We've seen nothing since that one batch, and that was weeks ago."

"So where have they gone? I don't think it's a coincidence they were reported after the lich returned from the dead. I think he's raising an undead army."

"Really?"

"It's always best to be prepared for the worst. If I'm wrong, we've lost nothing. If we meet trouble, at least we're prepared. Now let's hit the road. We've got a long drive."

It was still early when they reached the motorway, and they were way ahead of schedule by the time they hit the services at Reading. They stopped there for a break.

Elizabeth toted the laptop bag in with her. Once they were settled in the coffee shop with coffee and muffins, she booted it up and logged on to the Wi-Fi network. Mark munched on his blueberry muffin, musing on the fact that he felt like he had been plucked from his life and transported to some alternative existence, where everything was skewed and nothing was the way it should be. They were travelling across the country, just the two of them, with suitcases in the car. But it was hardly a romantic getaway. Helen, Linus and Chelsea were dead, they'd seen real zombies lurching through London, and his best friend had been possessed by some kind of undead creature.

He watched Elizabeth frowning over the laptop screen, tapping away at the keyboard, and eventually decided to ask, "What are you doing?"

Elizabeth continued to study the screen. "I'm looking up antiquarian and specialist second-hand book shops in Lynley. Thought it might help to save us a bit of time later."

"Oh. Found anything helpful?"

"Actually, I think I have. There are two or three that are looking promising. They all seem to be in the vicinity of the High Street, so we don't have to traipse around town to get to them all." She rummaged around in her bag and emerged with a notebook and pen.

"That's a really good idea," Mark declared. "And there I was thinking you'd brought the laptop in because you didn't want to leave it in the car. You are a very smart lady."

Elizabeth glanced at him and the shadow of a smile flitted across her face. "That's why you like me."

"I'm not denying it. Smart chicks are sexy."

"And don't you forget it." Elizabeth made a note of the names and addresses of the bookshops on her pad.

"I'm not likely to. So, I guess we now have a plan. We hit these places first?"

"We check in somewhere first, drop off the stuff, and then we hit these places." Elizabeth returned to tapping away on the keyboard. "Now that we know where we need to be based, we need to find a B&B in the area. This place looks like it might do. Pretty basic, but it's right at the bottom of the High Street and it's got guest parking." Elizabeth pulled out her mobile phone and tapped in a number.

"Sounds good." Mark rummaged in his pocket for his wallet and put his credit card on the table. "If you need to guarantee the reservation, use my card."

Elizabeth grinned. "Such a gentleman. Oh hello," she said into the phone. "Can you tell me if you have a double room available for tonight?"

As Elizabeth arranged the room booking, Mark reflected that maybe he was worrying about her for nothing. She might be struggling with this terrible trauma, but she was holding it together. No matter what happened, Elizabeth always seemed to manage to stay in control. Maybe that was the way she had to deal with things. It made him love her all the more. Some men liked women who needed protection – playing out the Knight in Shining Armour fantasy.

He supposed he could see the appeal of that fantasy, but real life rarely played out the way you wanted it to, and when it came down to it, he'd rather be in love with a woman who could take care of herself. He would worry a lot less about her knowing that.

As Elizabeth picked up his Mastercard and recited the number into the phone, Mark stared out the window, into the car park of the service area. The sky was no less grey than it had been when they set off early that morning.

They were making good time, and they should get there early enough to spend a couple of hours browsing the bookshops. He hoped they would find what they were looking for. He knew in his heart that they would not be heading back to London until they destroyed the lich. No matter how long it took.

Elizabeth rang off her call and handed his credit card back. "It's all sorted," she said.

"Excellent."

"If you're done, we should head off." Elizabeth gathered her things back into her bag and slung it over her shoulder.

Mark stood up and returned the credit card and wallet to his pocket. "So are we heading straight for this B&B?"

"Yes."

"You know where it is?"

"Of course," Elizabeth said, following Mark out of the coffee shop. "I'll direct you. Don't worry."

"Am I worried?" A blast of cold air hit Mark as he stepped outside, and he hunched his shoulders against the cold.

Elizabeth took his arm. "You're not doubting my navigational skills, are you?"

"I wouldn't dare do that."

"Good. Besides, my mobile's got GPS on it. Don't worry, I'll get us there."

"And I have every faith in you. Really. Let's go. It's cold out here." Mark took Elizabeth's hand and hurried back to the car.

CHAPTER 36

Elizabeth was true to her word and got them to the B&B without getting them lost. It was a large, two-storey white stucco house. It looked like it had originally been built as a large single dwelling, but at some point had been converted into a guest house.

The place was quiet as they headed for reception with their baggage. The desk was manned by an old white-haired man with a thick West Country accent. He was friendly and charming, and the confidence with which he moved around the building made Mark think he was probably the owner.

Once they'd checked in, the old man took them to their room. It was small, but clean and tidy. The double bed took up most of the space, but there was a large window with a view overlooking the bottom of the quaint high street. There was a small en-suite bathroom with a power shower over the old bath tub.

They took a few minutes to unpack, and then they decided they may as well get started. They hit the high street, armed with the list of book shops Elizabeth had pulled from the Internet.

The first two shops had looked promising, but turned out to be disappointing. The first dealt with second hand books, but mostly first edition fiction hardbacks. The shop didn't even have a section on mythology, and the only person working was a sullen teenage Goth who spent his time hunched over the computer and seemed unwilling to be dragged into a conversation.

The second shop did have a small section on mythology, but it covered the world; there was nothing specifically on even West Country legends, let alone local legends.

Discouraged, and still feeling tired and thirsty from the drive, they decided to stop at a tea shop on the high street.

Half an hour later, fortified by tea and homemade cake, they decided to hit the next shop.

"According to my list, there are two more places we can try," said Elizabeth. "The third one is at the very top of the High Street. The other one's tucked away down one of the side streets."

"Let's try the one down the side street," Mark suggested. "Maybe a place a bit more tucked away will be more what we're looking for."

Elizabeth got out her mobile phone and checked the address against the GPS map on it. "We have to back track a bit," she said. "Look for Star Street, down on the left, and head down there."

It took them about twenty minutes, but they eventually located the shop. It was a dusty little store front, nestled between a solicitor's office and a jewellery shop. The window looked like it needed a good wash and the interior was so dark that Mark thought for a moment that the shop was closed. But the faded sign hanging on the door read "open". Elizabeth pushed the door and it swung open with a faint jangling of wind chimes. They stepped inside.

The interior of the shop had the distinctive smell of musty old books, underlined by old wood. The place had clearly been around for several hundred years, and most of the beams supporting the ceiling looked original. There were books everywhere. Book cases lined every wall, and more books were piled on tables in the middle of the shop. Other books formed towering piles on the floor. Mark stared in wonder. "This place is a treasure trove."

"Where do we start?" said Elizabeth.

"Can you see a mythology section?"

Elizabeth pointed to a sign on the wall. "'Magic & Myth'. Over there." There was an arrow on the sign that indicated the back of the shop.

They stepped carefully past the mountains of books; past sections on language, philosophy, and world history. At the back of the shop, the 'local history' section sat next to 'mythology', followed by a row of shelves on 'magic'.

"This looks to be exactly what we want," Elizabeth said, indicating two shelves at the bottom of the local history section that had been titled 'local mythology'. She got to her knees to peer at the low-level shelves. Mark carefully moved a stack of books off a footstool and sat down on it.

Elizabeth pulled two books off the shelf, and handed them to Mark. "I think the quickest thing to do is to check separate books," she said. "Start with checking the index. Look for any reference to Ragnor. Then we might have a starting point."

They worked quickly – checking each book in turn, putting it back on the shelf when they were done, and then taking the next one. Mark developed a system. Check back index first for the name 'Ragnor' in some form. If it wasn't there, he went to the front of the book and scanned the table of contents for any reference to magic, wizards or liches. If nothing fit the bill, he put the book back and tried the next one.

They worked their way through the first shelf without finding anything useful. Mark had found chapters in a couple of books referring to magic, but it was mostly to do with healing magic. One book referred to a local midwife who'd been accused of witchcraft, but there was nothing shedding more light on Ragnor. Then Elizabeth said, "Hold on a minute."

"What have you found?"

Elizabeth was sitting cross-legged on the floor with a thick hardback in her lap. The cover was torn and shabby.

"There's a whole chapter on Ragnor in here." She held up the book so Mark could see the title: 'Dark Forest – a history of black magic in the Forest of Dean' was emblazoned in dramatic white letters against an image of dead black trees against a green sky. "

I think this is one of the reference books the creator of the website used for his research."

"Is there anything in there that we don't already know?"

Elizabeth peered at the book. "It's got a lot of detail about the ritual, including all the words. The instructions Ragnor left to his lackeys about how to bring him back from the dead. I think we should maybe buy this book, and study it back at the room."

They had a quick look at the rest of the shelf, but no other book seemed to be quite so helpful. So when they had put everything back on the shelf, they picked up the Dark Forest book and got to their feet.

When they had entered the shop, there had been no sign of any proprietor. But as they made their way to the front of the shop, where a cash register that looked like it hailed from the 1950s sat atop a table that was totally covered in books, they noticed a tiny old woman sat behind the table with her head bent over a fat hardback. Her thin grey hair was pulled back into a bun and she wore a powder blue cardigan over a floral dress. She looked just like a generic idea of someone's grandmother. But when Mark and Elizabeth approached she looked up, and Mark saw a pair of highly intelligent eyes behind the fragile spectacles.

"Good afternoon," Elizabeth said cheerfully. "We'd like to buy this book, please." She placed it atop the pile of books on the counter.

The old woman adjusted her glasses and peered at the book that Elizabeth had placed before her.

She frowned, and peered suspiciously at the younger woman. "I hope you're going to tell me that this is for your thesis or some such, and you're not planning on studying the Black Arts," she said sternly.

Elizabeth smiled. "I'm just interested in local legends."

The woman continued to frown. "It's no legend, young lady. Magic exists. Those that are arrogant enough to believe they can control its power almost always pay a high price."

"It sounds like you know something about this."

The old lady adjusted her glasses and stared at Elizabeth. "Let's just say I had a mis-spent youth. I was lucky enough to see the error of my ways early enough."

Elizabeth exchanged a glance with Mark. "I think you may be able to help us," she said.

CHAPTER 37

"I don't suppose you've ever heard of someone called Ragnor the Black?" Mark said. "Magic user? Used to live round here? Hundreds of years ago?"

The old woman blinked at him through her spectacles. "You don't want to be dabbling in that sort of magic. No, indeed."

"We're doing some research on him," Elizabeth said. "If you can tell us anything about him, it would be immensely helpful."

The old woman frowned, looking first Elizabeth and then Mark up and down. She had eyes the colour of cold steel, and there was an intensity about them that made Mark squirm. "I can tell you're not from these parts," she said. "And I also think there's something you're not telling me. Your aura is looking very distressed."

"My aura?" Mark said.

The old woman gazed at him. "Of course. You can tell everything about a person by their aura. Yours is looking very agitated. And you, my dear." She turned to Elizabeth. "You're grieving. You're also full of vengeance. And you come in here asking after Ragnor the Black. It makes me worried. That kind of power must not be taken lightly."

"We're not magic users," Elizabeth said.

"But you're planning on using it. And that is very dangerous, when you don't know what you're doing. Very dangerous indeed."

"Maybe you can help us."

"Perhaps we need to chat. Why don't you both come into the back and we'll have a nice cup of tea. My name is Ivy, by the way."

Mark took Elizabeth's hand. "I'm Mark. This is my girlfriend Elizabeth. That would be lovely, but who's going to watch the shop?"

Ivy gestured to the empty book shop. "I'm hardly inundated with customers now, am I? If someone comes in, the bell will ring." She moved back and parted a beaded curtain in the wall, gesturing for Mark and Elizabeth to follow before disappearing through it.

Mark looked at Elizabeth and shrugged, moving towards the beaded curtain. Elizabeth followed behind, with the Dark Forest book in her hands.

The area behind the curtain opened up into what looked like a small staff rest area. The only natural light came from a tiny window high up on one wall, therefore it was dim. Artificial light was provided by two standing lamps adorned with fringed fabric shades. A rattan sofa and two matching chairs, covered in colourful cushions, provided seating. Books were piled up everywhere, including on both of the chairs. In the corner of the room was a tiny kitchen area – larder fridge, a small counter with a kettle and a microwave, and a cupboard affixed to the wall.

Ivy scooped the pile of books off one of the chairs and balanced it on the floor. "Please, make yourselves at home. I'll make the tea."

"Thank you. Mark sat on the newly cleared chair while Elizabeth perched on the sofa. He found himself staring at a lovely picture that hung on the opposite wall. It was a woman with long hair, wearing a simple medieval-style dress and belt. Behind her was a winter woodland scene, while she focused her attention on a deer. It was beautiful, peaceful, and somehow strangely festive. Next to the picture was a wicker shelf unit. The first two shelves were jammed with crystals and rune stones. Two well-used packs of tarot cards perched on the end.

Mark noticed that Elizabeth was looking at the same items. "Are you a Wiccan, Ivy?" she asked.

The old lady chucked as she collected mugs from the little cupboard. "I suppose you could call me a lapsed Wiccan. I don't really practise any more. But in my youth, I was quite devout. Age makes one cynical."

"So you don't believe in this power anymore?" Mark asked.

Ivy frowned at him. "Being a lapsed Wiccan isn't like being a lapsed Catholic, young man. You don't stop believing in the power. How can you, when you have witnessed the force of it for yourself? It's more the fact that I don't feel I have the emotional energy – or the mental desire – to harness it any more. I sell books and I do the occasional tarot or aura reading."

Ivy brought over the tea in a charming china tea set with a floral design. The tray she had put it on had a picture of Tintagel Castle on it. She cleared books from the small coffee table and laid out the tray. "Now then, perhaps you want to tell me why nice young people like yourselves are asking questions about Ragnor the Black."

Elizabeth looked at Mark and he nodded, silently relaying his consent that she should lead this conversation. Elizabeth sighed. "We first came to these woods about four months ago, as part of a game. A role playing game. You know. Live action role playing."

Ivy nodded as she picked up the pot and poured out the tea. "A lot of such groups use these woods. They all seem to come down from London. I must admit I don't understand it myself, but it seems that those with high-powered jobs that spend all day cooped up in the city, feel that running about in the woods all weekend whacking people with foam swords is a good tension release."

"That about sums it up. Anyway," Elizabeth continued, "we came to play this game. The game involved performing a ritual. It was supposed to banish the fictional monster. Only, we found out later that the words of this ritual came from one that Ragnor created. After we got back to London, terrible things started happening. People died. The friends we went playing with. My brother." Elizabeth trailed off.

Mark continued the tale. "There were six of us performing that ritual. Three of those people are dead, ripped apart. There's only me and Elizabeth left, and our friend David. And we think David's involved, somehow. He's changed."

"And was it your friend David who uttered the words of this ritual?" Ivy asked.

"It was. We think maybe Ragnor's possessed him, somehow. He's different. Harsher. Colder. And he looks so old and haggard."

"Do you happen to know the words of this ritual? But please, don't say them aloud."

"We've got them written down." Elizabeth reached for her laptop case. All the notes she'd been making during her research were tucked into the side pocket. She extracted the words she'd printed off the internet and passed them over.

Ivy smoothed the piece of paper out on the table and pushed her glasses further up her nose while she studied it. She looked up sharply. "Oh my. This is the summoning ritual for Ragnor the Black."

Mark added milk and a generous helping of sugar to his tea. "We sort of figured as much."

Ivy gingerly passed the paper back to Elizabeth. "Where on Earth did you find this?"

"The Internet," Elizabeth said. "There was a whole site on Ragnor, and the words of the ritual were written out in full. David put the game together. We figured maybe he came across this and decided to use it in his plot."

"The accursed Internet, again." Ivy sighed. "People are completely ignorant of the power they are unleashing when they mess about there. An entire universe of knowledge; available to absolutely everyone. People are too stupid to realise how dangerous this is. Your friend has opened a door to terrible power. If he's stepped through it, it might be too late to bring him back."

CHAPTER 38

"But there must be a way to stop it," Elizabeth said. "We've been doing our own research. And we're about to buy this book from you." She waved *Dark Forest*. "It says something about a phylactery. Destroying the phylactery destroys Ragnor."

Ivy sighed, and poured out more tea. "To understand how to defeat Ragnor, you must first understand what you're dealing with. The ritual that released him was something he created himself. In life, he was harnessing terrible power. He called upon the favours of ancient evil beings to give him the power he had. He thought he had discovered the secret of life after death, and he left detailed instructions as to how he should be buried. Like all evil men, Ragnor was charismatic, and he had followers. He promised them everything they wanted. The human heart can be weak in the face of avarice and materialism. Ragnor promised he would grant every wish. Money, success in love, success in business – whatever you wished for, Ragnor would make it happen, as long as you became a loyal follower. What he was less inclined to document is that for every wish granted, there was a price to pay. The entities that granted Ragnor his powers demanded a blood sacrifice every time he called upon their powers."

"What sort of blood sacrifice?" Mark asked.

"Generally it would be the blood of an innocent," Ivy said. "I suspect that initially Ragnor used goats and sheep and such, but as he got a taste of the power, he wanted more. Therefore the sacrifices became greater. For such rituals, generally a child is bled to death. A child represents the ultimate innocence."

"There have been deaths," Elizabeth said.

"The others who were there that night. And they always come after something good happens to David. When he passed his exams, someone died. When he bought the house he wanted, his girlfriend was killed. Then he got the job he wanted. That's when my brother died." Her voice trailed off, into the silence broken only by the ticking of the clock on the wall.

"Has Ragnor possessed David?" Mark asked. "Is that what the ritual did?"

Ivy looked at him sternly over her spectacles. "The ritual brings Ragnor back from the dead. Literally."

"What, like resurrection?"

"Not quite. Even Ragnor cannot harness that kind of power. The magicks he invoked can re-animate the body. He became a walking corpse."

"A zombie, then," Mark said.

"Zombies, as they are depicted in common myth, are mindless creatures. The power that brought Ragnor back would allow him to retain his intelligence, and more importantly, his ability to use magic. But it cannot regenerate his body. Only re-animate his corpse."

"But he's been dead hundreds of years," Elizabeth said. "There can't be much left by now."

"That's why he left instructions that his body was to be preserved. He was very explicit that his instructions be followed to the letter." Ivy took the book from Elizabeth's hands and turned to the chapter on Ragnor the black. "It is detailed in here, see. His organs were to be removed, dried, pickled and kept in a jar. His body was to be dried out. He was effectively leaving instructions on how to be mummified."

"So we are talking about a lich after all?"

"If Ragnor has come back from the dead, he will be very powerful. He retains the ability to do magic, and the dark power he has harnessed will give him superhuman strength."

"So it's Ragnor that killed our friends," Mark said. "Not David."

"I think it more likely that your friend David is in the thrall of Ragnor," Ivy said. "I said he was a very charismatic individual. Even after death, he will retain that power. No doubt he has been promising your friend whatever he wants. You mentioned earlier passing exams, a dream job, a house. These are the sorts of things that Ragnor can promise. And the price is always a sacrifice. Ragnor demands blood and all he needs is permission to take it. His re-animated state requires a great deal of energy to sustain itself. He is probably taking this life energy from the people whose lives he takes."

"But that means David has been making a deal with this re-animated magic user," Mark said. "Allowing him to kill people."

"Don't underestimate the power that Ragnor has on people," Ivy said, blinking at him from behind her glasses. "The promise of your life's ambitions being fulfilled can be very seductive, especially for people driven to succeed."

"Okay," said Elizabeth. "We know what's going on. The question is, how do we stop it?"

"It may be too late to bring your friend David back. He may be too tightly gripped by Ragnor's power."

"But there's got to be a way of stopping Ragnor, right?" Mark said. "The research we've done said that the key is to destroy the phylactery. Once we do that, Ragnor is destroyed."

"You must be aware that if you destroy Ragnor, you may also kill your friend David. Ragnor's influence on him may be too strong at this stage to save him."

"We have to try," Mark said. "We can't let this power stay loose in the world. Too many people have died already."

Ivy sighed. "The phylactery is the key. You are correct."

"But what's a phylactery?"

"They were used in mummification, weren't they?" said Elizabeth. "The organs were taken out of the body and kept in a phylactery, then buried with the mummy so that the dead person could collect them before their journey to the underworld."

"Gross," said Mark.

"The ancient Egyptians were advanced enough to know that soft tissues decompose," Elizabeth explained. "So they knew they had to take them out of the body if they wanted to preserve it. But they also thought the body would rise again to travel to the afterlife and hence would need the organs, so they had to be preserved and kept close by."

"Ragnor's organs were also preserved," Ivy said. "He left instructions that they were to be buried in a safe place, within the enchanted circle in the forest, where he believed the power he was harnessing was strongest. The organs are the key to his continued survival. Destroying the phylactery will destroy Ragnor and mean he can no longer walk the earth. But the organs must be completely obliterated. Burning them would be best. Fire is always the most effective way to destroy magic. It's why witches were burned at the stake."

"The next question is," said Elizabeth, "where do we find the phylactery?"

CHAPTER 39

"There's another book I think you should see," Ivy said. She put her cup down on the crowded coffee table, and went through a small door at the back of the kitchen area that Elizabeth and Mark hadn't noticed earlier.

She was gone for a while, and when she came back she had a large square book in her hand. The cover was black, opaque and shiny, with a silver pentagram etched into it. She carried the book in a tea towel and cleared some space on the table to put it down. There was no title or author name. Elizabeth reached to pick it up. As she touched the cover, a feeling like a mild electrical charge coursed through her body. She snapped her hand back quickly. "What is this?"

"A very powerful book indeed," Ivy said.

"I can tell," Elizabeth said. "I can feel it."

Ivy wrapped her hand in the tea towel and began to turn the pages. "I would suggest wearing gloves to handle this book. It's not one I would recommend to anyone. I keep it hidden in the stores because in the wrong hands, this book is deadly." She opened the book up to a page with an intricately detailed map. "This map tells you exactly how to find Ragnor's phylactery. See the 'x'? It's buried in a lead box at that point."

Mark peered at the map, being careful not to touch it. "It says this is dated from the seventeenth century."

"We'd have to cross reference against a modern map," Elizabeth said. "But the forest hasn't changed that much."

"What's this circle marked out?" asked Mark.

"That's the focus of the power," Ivy said. "The ritual has to take place within it to work. It's a fairly large area, as you can see. Ragnor's body was also buried there. This other marked spot on the map. That's where the body was."

"So what are we going to find now? A big hole? Did he crawl out of his grave?"

"I don't imagine Ragnor had to stoop to such crude measures," Ivy said drily. "The sort of magic he was using, he could probably teleport straight out of his grave. The phylactery, however, will have to be dug up the old-fashioned way. And when you burn it, you must make sure that it is well within the circle of power."

"So all we have to do is dig up the phylactery and set fire to it?" Elizabeth said doubtfully. "It sounds a bit too easy."

"It will not be easy." Ivy gazed levelly at the younger woman. "Ragnor will try to stop you."

"So we have to be fast," Mark said.

Ivy slid her gaze to him. "Ragnor already knows what you're planning on doing. He will try to stop you before you get as far as digging."

"But no one knows what we're doing, apart from you. We made a spontaneous decision to come here yesterday."

"You are still not understanding the breadth of the power that Ragnor has access to," Ivy said sternly. "Time is not linear to a creature like Ragnor. He can see past, present and future simultaneously. He already knows you plan to destroy him. He will intervene at the point that he will be able to stop you. And if he fails the first time, he will try again. Ragnor will not let you succeed in your plan. You must be careful. He will also send minions after you. Ragnor always has minions."

"What kind of 'minions' are we talking about?" Mark asked.

"Given the nature of the power that Ragnor possesses, the fastest way for him to create minions is to raise the dead; since their will is much easier to manipulate than that of the living. He will re-animate the dead and command them to follow his bidding."

"What, so we're talking about zombie hordes? Great."

"That would explain some of the strange things that were going on at home over the last few weeks," Elizabeth said. "Ragnor's been raising himself an army."

"He will gather them, command them to congregate, and then send them after whoever or whatever threatens him," Ivy said. "Individually these creatures are fairly vulnerable and can be defeated, but they will attack in a large group to better their odds of victory. Ragnor, however, will not be as easy to defeat. He is protected by very powerful magic."

"How can we protect ourselves against Ragnor?" Elizabeth asked. "We've already seen what he's capable of."

Ivy picked up the tea towel and turned a few pages of the book, carefully. "There's a repelling ritual here, which might help. Though be aware it will probably only hold him off for a few minutes. I will also enchant an amulet for each of you with a protection spell, though I can't guarantee how effective it will be. The power I can harness is nowhere near as potent as that of Ragnor."

Elizabeth wrapped her scarf around her hand and pulled the book closer. "So we can take this with us?"

"You will need to do so, if you are to have any chance of succeeding." Ivy got up and began clearing away the tea things.

"It looks really old and valuable. We'll take good care of it," Mark said.

"I want you to destroy it," Ivy said.

"What?"

Ivy paused, carrying the tea tray, and looked at him. "When you destroy the phylactery, I also want you to destroy that book."

"But why? If it's the key to defeating Ragnor, it should be preserved," Mark said.

"Because it's also the key to releasing his power. The ritual you used is in that book, along with the detailed instructions Ragnor left on how to bring oneself back from the dead. It's too dangerous. If it falls into the wrong hands, someone else could do what Ragnor has done. That kind of power was never meant to be used by mere mortals."

"But this stuff is all over the Internet," Mark said. "It's already in the public domain."

"Without this book, there's a limit to how effective it can be," Ivy said. "The book has power. This young lady knows. She touched it."

"It's true," Elizabeth said. "It was like getting an electric shock. The book…is charged."

"That's why when you've destroyed Ragnor, you must destroy the book as well. This book is the original. All other copies of the ritual – including those on the Internet – channel power from this book. When the book is destroyed, the ritual no longer has any power, even if it is recited in the right place and at the right time.

"Why not destroy the book years ago, if it's that powerful?" Elizabeth asked.

"A potent question, young lady," Ivy said. "When this book first fell into my hands, years ago, I didn't understand its power. I was afraid of it, nonetheless, and I hid it away. Only now that you two have come to me with this tale do I understand its power. I was foolish and reckless in my youth. Fortunately for me, I retired from using magic before it was too late. However, if I had been a wiser soul back then, perhaps we would not be in this situation now.

Nevertheless, what's done is done. As the power to regenerate Ragnor comes from these pages, so does the power to destroy him and you must use it for that purpose. Once Ragnor is defeated, destroy the book so he can never rise again."

"But if we destroy Ragnor's phylactery, won't that stop him from ever being raised again anyway?" Mark asked.

Ivy looked at him sternly over her spectacles. "Do not underestimate the power of dark magic, young man.

"Evil finds a way. The safest thing to do is to destroy the book, so that its dark power can never escape again."

She disappeared into the kitchen area with the tea tray, returning a moment later with a tea towel. She wrapped the book carefully in the tea towel and handed it to Elizabeth. "I need a few minutes to make some protective amulets, as I promised. It won't take long, but I do need to concentrate. Why don't you go back into the shop and I'll be with you as soon as I'm done?"

Back in the shop, Elizabeth put both books - the Dark Forest book and the one wrapped in the tea towel - by the cash register. The shop was quiet - no customers had come in while they had been talking to Ivy. "You're very quiet," she said to Mark. "Are you alright?"

Mark looked around the dusty shelves of the shop. "I'm trying to take all this in. This is heavy-duty stuff. We have to go kill a lich before it kills us. This is hard-core D&D. I never imagined all this stuff was real."

"I know. But we have to deal with the fact that it is."

"It seems a real stroke of luck we found Ivy," Mark said. "We wouldn't have had a hope of stopping this thing if we hadn't met her."

"I don't think it was coincidence," Elizabeth said. "I think something brought us here."

Mark frowned. "Like what?"

Elizabeth shrugged. "If Ragnor's drawing on this super evil power, maybe there's something else out there counterbalancing it. A healing power. The kind of energy that Wiccans draw on for their good magic. The kind of positive energy my yoga teacher talks about."

"Up until a few weeks ago, I would have dismissed all that as rubbish."

"And now?"

"With all the weird stuff that's been going on, let's just say my mind has been broadened."

A moment later, there was a rustle of beads as Ivy came back into the shop. She carried a small cloth bag.

Elizabeth gasped involuntarily. Ivy looked unwell. Her skin was grey, her eyes were dull, and the lines on her face were more pronounced. As she rounded the counter, she staggered slightly and leant on the counter to steady herself. Mark hurried over to take her arm, and Elizabeth grabbed the chair from behind the counter.

"What's wrong, Ivy?" Elizabeth asked, as they helped the old lady to sit down.

Ivy sighed. "I have had to tap into a lot of power to make these for you." She handed the bag to Elizabeth. "There are two amulets, on chains. I suggest you put them around your necks before you head into the woods and don't take them off until Ragnor is destroyed."

"I thought this was good magic," Mark said. "Why is it damaging?"

Ivy peered at him over her glasses. "Good and evil are human concepts. Magic doesn't work that way. It's far more abstract. It's more to do with what the power is used for. The power that Ragnor is tapping into is highly destructive. The power I use is healing. But there's still a price to pay, even if you are trying to do good with it. Channelling power means that it taps into your life force. It can drain you of energy. Channel too much of it, too often, and it can drain so much life force that it will take all of it, and leave you a husk. This is why it all goes wrong for so many people.

They start off wanting to do good, but they get addicted to the power. I could have gone that way myself, when I was young and foolish, but fortunately for me I managed to stop before it was too late. But it has been a long time since I have had to tap into the amount of power I've used to make those amulets. And I'm not young anymore. I don't have that much life force left to use up. I have to rest."

"Are you sure you're alright?" Mark said. "Can we call someone?"

Ivy waved him away. "I shall be alright, young man. I just need to rest and get my strength back. I should probably shut the shop for the rest of the afternoon and get some sleep."

"We really appreciate all you've done for us," Elizabeth said.

"It's not just for you, young lady. When it's a matter of saving the world, one does what one must. Now go, leave me. Go and stop Ragnor. He must be destroyed, or none of us will live beyond next week."

CHAPTER 40

Mark and Elizabeth took the two books and the amulets back to the B&B. They bought a road map of the area from a nearby garage and laid it out on the bed, next to the old map of the woods from Ivy's forbidden book. Elizabeth tried to overlay the modern map with key landmarks from the old one, but she got frustrated.

"Nothing is the same as it was five hundred years ago," she said. "Even the trees aren't going to be the same. Where do we start?"

Mark lay on his stomach, poring over the book and chewing on the end of his pencil. "It says there's a cave," he said. "The phylactery is supposed to be buried in the cave. Maybe we should start with that. Chances are, that's still there."

"Even if it is, it's probably grown over by now. We could be hunting about for quite a long time. We don't want to be doing it in the dark."

"Let's start first thing tomorrow, after breakfast."

"We ought to get some supplies. A compass would be really helpful. And we need to pack ourselves some food and water. We could be out all day. We'll need weapons too. It'll be just like packing for a LARP overland – except we need real weapons."

"I don't think weapons are going to be much good against Ragnor."

"Ivy seemed to suggest we might be facing zombie hordes as well."

Mark groaned. "How the hell are we supposed to defeat zombie hordes?"

"Haven't you learned anything from *Resident Evil*? A well-aimed head shot will do the trick. That's why I brought the shotgun."

Mark tossed the pencil onto the book. "Why don't we head out now? I can't get my head around this map. There was a camping shop on the high street. We can go there for the gear we need, and then stop by the supermarket for picnic supplies."

Elizabeth fingered Ivy's talisman, which she had already put around her neck. "If Ragnor decides to come after us tonight, we're in trouble."

"I guess we have to take the chance. Hopefully, it'll take him a little while to catch up with us."

They left the room and went back down the high street. They arrived at the camping shop ten minutes before it closed, so they were swift in collecting the supplies they thought they would need. From there, they found a DIY superstore and bought an axe and a spade. Finally, they paid a visit to the mini supermarket for sandwich stuff, chocolate bars and bottles of water.

By the time they finished shopping it was dark. They returned to the B&B for long enough to dump the supplies in their room, and then departed again to find somewhere to have dinner.

Elizabeth was very quiet during the meal. Since she and Mark had started working together, conversation between the two of them had never been a problem. From the very start, they had spent hours discussing the books they'd both read, the TV shows they'd both watched, and the computer games they'd played. But things had changed since Linus's death. Mark no longer knew what to say to her. He wished there was something he could do to heal her pain. He wanted to enfold her in his arms and tell her everything would be alright, but he wasn't sure it would be. If they couldn't stop Ragnor, nothing would ever be alright again. Although he didn't want to think about it, he couldn't stop dwelling on the fact that if they failed in their task, Ragnor would kill them.

Even if they did succeed in stopping Ragnor, nothing would bring Linus back. And what of David? Ivy had suggested that they might not be able to bring back the person he had once been. What would happen to him if they succeeded in destroying Ragnor? Mark realised that he had been holding vainly onto the hope that one day the David he'd always known would come back. Now he had to face the possibility that he might have already lost his best friend. Mark thought about all the hours he'd spent with David around the kitchen table at his parents' place when they'd been teenagers, drinking Coke, discussing girls and films, LARPing, and all manner of other things that had been important to them back then.

Mark looked over at Elizabeth who was pushing the remains of her pasta around the bowl. She looked equally miserable. "We can't go back, can we?" he said.

She looked up at him as she picked up her wine glass. "What do you mean? Back to where?"

"Back to the way things were. Before the role playing game. Chelsea and Helen are dead. So is Linus. We've lost David, too. I see that now. Things will never be the same again."

"No. They won't be. But you and me are still here. And that isn't going to change."

"Do you mean it?"

Elizabeth put down her glass and covered Mark's hand on the table with her own. "I need time to come to terms with not having Linus around. He was my big brother; it's a shock not having him there anymore. But the one good thing – the only good thing – that came out of this is that it's made me realise how much I love you. Whatever we're about to face tomorrow, I want you to know that."

Mark stared at her. The light from the candle on the table cast flickering shadows on her face and dancing highlights in her hair. He thought she'd never looked more beautiful. "I love you, too. And I don't want to let you go."

"Whatever this thing throws at us tomorrow, it won't take you away from me. That I'm sure of." Elizabeth blinked at Mark and he saw tears in her eyes.

He squeezed her hand. "What's the matter? Why are you sad? Are you missing Linus?"

Elizabeth sighed. "Yes, I miss Linus, but that's not why I'm crying. I'm afraid we're not going to beat this thing. I just can't bear to imagine a future without you in it. Having to deal with a future without Linus is hard enough, but to imagine my future without you in it too – that's just too much to cope with. I don't want you to leave me."

"I won't ever leave you." Mark took her other hand, and held them both over the table. "I promise. Already I find myself missing you when you go to your own place."

"Then let's not ever say goodbye again," Elizabeth said. "When this thing is over, let's move in together."

Mark was momentarily taken aback. "My place will be cramped with two of us in it."

"So will mine. Let's look for a place together. If we have two salaries to pay rent, we can afford someplace a bit nicer. Some place with a bit more room."

"You've got a deal." Their faces moved closer together, and their lips met in a kiss over the table.

When Mark pulled away, he saw Elizabeth's face shining in the candlelight. A tear rolled down her cheek. He gently put his finger to her face and wiped it away. "Whatever faces us tomorrow, we'll face it together. When you're with me, I feel like there's nothing I can't do."

"Somehow, I feel that's going to be put to the test," she said gravely.

"We should probably pay up and go get some sleep," Mark said. "Tomorrow will be the day from Hell. Literally."

CHAPTER 41

The following morning, they packed their backpacks in silence with the compass, water, food, maps, and books. Elizabeth carefully packed the weapons. They made a point of enjoying the English breakfast the B&B provided, then headed to the car by 9am.

It was not a long drive to the woods. They found a car park on the outskirts, where they left Mark's car. There were no other cars parked there. It was a grey, cold morning, and rain threatened. It was not the sort of day for a leisurely walk through the woods. Just as well. If they were going to run into Ragnor, it was better there were no innocent bystanders around.

Elizabeth got out of the car and zipped up her waterproof jacket, before rummaging around in her backpack. Mark locked up the car and hefted his own pack onto his back. They'd shared out the water, the snack bars and the chocolate bars between them, but his pack held the sandwiches. Elizabeth had the book. She had removed it from her pack and turned to the page where the map was. Then she ripped the page out of the book.

"You can't do that!" Mark said, shocked. "That book's really rare and old."

Elizabeth looked at him. "And Ivy said she wants us to burn it. Your point?"

"OK, fair enough."

Elizabeth put the book back in her pack and pulled out some more pieces of paper. "The book is too heavy to carry around. I want to have the old map and the new one in front of me at all times, but I don't want to have the book out." She unfolded the new map and studied it.

"What about the repellent ritual?" Mark asked. "That's in the book. I know we spent time last night memorising it, but if Ragnor suddenly shows up I might panic and get the words wrong."

"That's why I copied it out." Elizabeth produced two sheets of A4 paper, and handed one to Mark. "Two copies. One for you, one for me. Keep it safe – zipped in your front pocket, maybe. Do you have Ivy's talisman?"

Mark's hand automatically reached for it. It was on a chain around his neck, with the talisman tucked into the front of his jacket. "Yes."

"OK, good. I don't quite know how this is going to work, but if the talismans aren't enough to keep Ragnor away, then start reciting the ritual."

"Do we know what happens with the ritual?"

"No," said Elizabeth. "We're really going into unknown territory here. I've got no idea what's going to happen. Right, I'll keep the map and do my best to work out where we're going. Can you keep the compass with you? That should hopefully make sure we don't go completely in the wrong direction."

Mark dug the compass out of his backpack. He folded up the bit of paper with the ritual on it, and stowed it into one of the zipped pockets of his hiking pants. He hefted his pack back onto his shoulders, as Elizabeth fed her arms through hers. "OK. Are we ready?"

"I think so." Elizabeth studied the map. "I think we're entering the forest here." She stabbed a gloved finger at the map. She overlaid the old map over the new. "I'm not quite sure where we are on the old map. This forest was much bigger in the sixteenth century, but I think the circle of power starts about three miles due north of here."

Mark checked the compass and pointed towards the trees in the distance. "North is that way."

"Let's go." Elizabeth moved off, her sturdy hiking boots leaving deep footprints in the muddy ground.

Mark followed. He normally enjoyed watching Elizabeth's back view, but most of her curves were hidden behind layers of hiking gear and the pack obscured most of her back. The shotgun – safety on – was securely tied into loops on the side. It wasn't exactly an alluring sight. Nevertheless, he found himself admiring her for being a girl who dressed appropriately for the occasion. He thought back to the ill-fated LARP game, when Chelsea had complained constantly about being cold and dirty. Her idea of 'practical shoes' had been a pair of ballet pumps, which had been ruined by the end of the first day. She'd complained about that, too. Elizabeth had tried to give Chelsea advice about wearing thermals underneath her costume, and wearing sturdy hiking boots regardless of what kind of character she was playing, but Chelsea just lacked common sense. Elizabeth had even treated her cloak with a waterproof spray, and she had worn waterproof hiking trousers underneath her cleric's robes.

It felt strange to be back here, in these woods. Generally when Mark was here he was wearing chain mail, carrying a foam sword, and on the lookout for people in monster masks who would jump out of the bushes and attack them. But the attacks were all part of the game – there was an emphasis on never hurting anyone. Now they were about to face real monsters, who might very well kill.

They trekked in silence; no noise except for the thud of their boots on the mud and the occasional cracking on a twig on the forest floor, or the rustle of clothing against stray branches as they moved them out the way to pass by. There was a rough trail in the forest, but it veered North West.

They were heading due North so after a while they had to leave the trail and traverse through virgin forest. It was hard going.

Not many people passed through this bit of the forest – it was one reason they liked using it for their games. It felt untainted by human influence.

There were no buildings or power cables or roads to remind you that you were in the twenty-first century. It was easy to imagine you were in a faraway land or a distant time. It was even easy to imagine you were in the sixteenth century.

It was cold. Mark shivered in his layers of hiking gear. August was never this cold; not even taking into consideration the UK's most rubbish summers. It felt more like November. The weather forecast had been going on for weeks about the unusual weather, using the excuse of an unpredicted cold front from the North veering off course and hanging over the UK. Everyone had been escaping to mainland Europe for the holidays, which had apparently escaped the weather front and was hot and sunny. Radical religious sites had been talking about the weather – along with the rise of mysterious, violent deaths and sightings of strange and unnatural creatures – as portents of the impending Armageddon. Most people didn't take these declarations too seriously. Armageddon had been predicted many times before in mankind's history, and the human race continued to populate the planet.

There had been an increase in zombie-related deaths. Mark had noticed that there was usually some reference to an unexplained violent death on the evening news. Some of them had been in broad daylight, in full view of witnesses, whose reports of the perpetrators varied from "scruffy looking gangs of youths high on drugs" to "homeless people". Some people had even declared on TV that they had been attacked by zombies. Generally these reports were dismissed: the witnesses viewed to be weirdos and crackpots. It was strange, Mark thought; the way that people were so ready to dismiss things that couldn't be explained.

Anything that threatened their view of reality and what was safe and normal, was quickly buried.

The majority of people could not entertain the notion that zombies might be real.

A few months ago, he would be among them. But now he knew the truth. He had seen it with his own eyes. In the meantime, various conspiracy theories to explain the increase in violent deaths were sweeping the country. One of the more popular theories was that some corrupt corporation had been tainting the water supply with mind-altering chemicals to control the population. Other people were convinced that a new designer drug had hit the streets and it was turning people into deranged killers. But no one had any evidence, and every time a new incident was reported, a new theory seemed to be born.

Up ahead of Mark, Elizabeth had been keeping a steady, determined pace, not even looking back at him to make sure he was following. In spite of his large breakfast, he was beginning to feel hungry. Forest trekking was hard work. He was considering calling out to Elizabeth to ask if they should take a break to eat their sandwiches when she slowed down, digging out both maps and studying them carefully.

The compass indicated they were still travelling in a Northerly direction. He stopped alongside Elizabeth. "Everything OK?"

She pointed ahead, to an enormous tree a short distance ahead of them. It looked like an oak tree, but it was long since dead; its hollowed-out trunk stuffed with leaves and mulch and its stark, bare branches stubby and truncated. "That tree," she said. "It looks really old."

"It's dead."

"Yeah. But I think it's on the map." Elizabeth smoothed out the old map, and turned it the other way around. "Look here. It talks about a cluster of oak trees. Right behind it, is the Circle of Power."

"We have no way of knowing if that oak tree's the one mentioned on that map," Mark pointed out.

"No, but we know that one's old enough to be on the map. And there's only one cluster of oak trees mentioned on this map. So I think maybe that's one of them. Besides, there's power nearby. Can't you feel it? The talisman's getting warm."

Now that she mentioned it, Mark noticed a slight vibration against his chest. He put his hand around the talisman. It was warm, the way a heat pad warms up when you activate it. With his hands around it he could feel the mild vibration – like an electrical charge. It felt the way a plug did when it was plugged into an electrical socket and power was coursing through it.

"I think it's channelling power from the circle," Elizabeth said. "Ivy said that was the source of Ragnor's power. It starts the other side of that tree."

"The place feels....wrong. I'm getting the creeps. I can't believe we came here in the dark last time and never noticed." Mark looked up at the sky, steel grey and ominous above the trees. There was a chill in the air that seemed to cut through the layers of Gore-Tex that he was wearing. It was hard to believe it was summer – it felt like the dead of winter. Now that they had stopped walking, the sound of their footsteps had ceased and the forest was silent. No birds singing. No crickets chirping. Not even the faint sound of traffic in the distance. Nothing.

"Something's wrong," Elizabeth said, her voice sounding unnaturally loud in the silence. "Can't you feel it?"

"What I'm feeling is the impulse to turn around and get as far away from here as possible."

"That's part of it." Elizabeth scanned the trees. "There's something old here. Something...evil. I think Ragnor's here."

"I can't hear anything."

"Yeah, that's part of it too. The forest isn't normally this quiet. Where's the wildlife?"

"So let's do what we need to do and get the hell out of here."

Elizabeth folded up her map and tucked it into the front pocket of her jacket. Her hand went unconsciously to the talisman around her neck. "Ragnor's power is strongest in that circle. But we have no choice – that's the way we need to go. We have to cross the circle of power."

CHAPTER 42

There was a clearing in the trees, just beyond the old oak tree. In appearance, it didn't look any different from the rest of the forest. But Mark had taken barely ten paces past the tree when things felt different. The air was noticeably warmer and he felt the hairs on the back of his neck stand on end. The talisman around his neck heated noticeably. It was getting so warm, it almost felt like it was going to burn his skin. And it was emitting an audible hum.

Elizabeth stepped close to him and he heard the same hum coming from her talisman too. Under normal circumstances, the noise would be so faint he wouldn't have noticed it. But in the absolute silence of the forest, it filled the air.

"We're inside the circle of power," Elizabeth said, her hand going to the talisman around her neck.

"Yeah, I figured that. What does this mean? Is Ragnor close?"

"I have a horrid feeling that he's not far away." Elizabeth peered at the two maps, old and new, comparing the two. "The cave is on the North side of the circle."

Mark looked at the compass. "North is straight ahead, that way."

"Right through the middle of the circle."

"Is it dangerous? Should we go around?"

"The circle's pretty big. And a lot more trees have grown in it in the five hundred years since this map was drawn. If we go around it, it'll take us ages. Even then, we still have no guarantee we'll avoid stepping in the circle. We may as well take the direct route."

With the two maps held up in front of her like a shield, she strode forward and kept a brisk pace. So brisk, in fact, Mark had to step up his pace to keep up.

"So, the phylactery's supposed to be buried in the cave?" he said.

"Allegedly."

"So presumably the cave is in the circle as well." Mark looked around as he followed Elizabeth. The ground was still rough here, strewn with dead leaves and branches, and he had to be careful not to stumble. A twisted ankle would be very bad news indeed. He knew they had to be close to where they had come, all those months ago, for the game. But he couldn't pinpoint exactly where. Everything had looked different in the dark. It felt like so long ago. So much had happened since then.

Still the talisman around his neck grew ever warmer. He could swear the humming noise was getting louder too. The only other sounds were the noise of their breathing and their boots on the soft earth. Occasionally the quiet was broken as one of them kicked aside a branch.

The forest got thicker again after only a few feet, and travelling true North was difficult. They had to step around trees and bushes and stumble over tree roots. The air became oppressive. It became thick and cloying, the way it does before a heavy thunderstorm.

They halted when their progress was blocked by a tangle of bracken and bushes. Elizabeth laid a hand on Mark's arm. "I can see some rocks over there, underneath the undergrowth," she said. "It might be our cave."

Mark stared at the thick brambles and overgrown branches that all but covered the rocks, leaving just a glimpse of grey if you looked hard enough. "If the cave is there, how the hell are we going to get to it?"

Elizabeth looked at him. "What do you think the spade and axe we bought are for? You didn't think we'd just be able to stroll into an open entranceway after five hundred years, did you?"

"I suppose I was being optimistic."

Mark sighed and pulled the pack off his back. The spade and axe were tied neatly to it with loops.

He began to work at the knots holding them in place. "We've been camping in this forest countless times, doing LARP games. I never gave it a second thought then. I'll never be able to come here again."

"One step at a time." Elizabeth pulled gardening gloves out of her pack.

"Here, let me do that," Mark said, taking the gloves from her. He put them on and hefted the axe, looking once more at the tangle of brambles that covered the rocks. This was going to be prickly work, in more ways than one.

Elizabeth set her pack on the floor and spread the two maps out carefully on the ground beside each other. "I'm positive we're in the right place. We just have to get into that cave."

"OK, here goes nothing." Mark pulled out a branch of prickly bramble and began to hack at its base, as low down as he could, with the axe. Even with hefty swings it took several hits to complete the job.

Finally he cut through the first branch and tossed it aside. Still a tangle of branches covered the cave. He sighed and reached to pull out another one, when suddenly he felt the talisman round his neck get red hot. "Ow!" he yelled as it burned the bare flesh of his chest. He pulled on the chain and yanked the metal away from his skin.

"Oh my god," Elizabeth said. Mark looked at her. She was fingering her talisman too, so he thought that the same thing was happening to her.

She was looked away to his left, a horrified expression on her face. Mark followed her gaze. A few feet away, a cloud of thick smoke was curling up from the ground, seeming to solidify. A strange noise emanated from the smoke – a high-pitched keening sound. Mark shivered.

The temperature in the circle of power, which had felt a few degrees warmer than the rest of the forest, had dropped dramatically. It was suddenly very cold. And there was an unpleasant smell, faint at first but getting stronger.

A smell of something long-dead and rotting.

"Has your talisman got hot?" Elizabeth said. He nodded, unable to take his eyes off the rapidly solidifying pillar of smoke.

It was vaguely man-shaped and about seven feet tall, and as Mark watched, frozen in terror, the form began to take shape. It was a horrible parody of a human in tattered robes. It had a grinning skull where its head should be with shreds of leathery skin clinging to it, and empty shadows where the eyes should be. The terrible smell got stronger as the shape solidified – the smell of the grave; of something that should no longer be walking the earth.

The talisman, now hanging down over Mark's jacket, had turned golden and was glowing with a brilliant fire. The hum had increased in pitch until it was almost a shriek, splitting the silence of the forest with an unearthly howl.

"Come on!" Mark yelled as the undead thing settled into solid form, the swirls of smoke around it dissipating. He grabbed his pack with one hand and Elizabeth's arm with the other. She scooped up her own pack and slung it over her shoulder, still clutching the two maps tightly in her hand.

Stumbling over roots and tree stumps, Mark pulled Elizabeth along and ran as far away from the thing as he could, running blindly through the forest. He ignored his screaming lungs, and the brambles and dead tree roots that caught on his clothes and tried to hold him back.

All he could think about was running – putting as much distance as possible between himself and the evil thing that had once been Ragnor.

CHAPTER 43

Lungs burning, they eventually stopped to catch their breath. Mark leaned against a tree. He could feel his heart hammering inside his chest and for a few minutes he couldn't speak. Elizabeth sat on a fallen stump, rummaging around in her pack.

When Mark's breathing began to calm, he pulled out the compass and checked it. They'd been running blindly, with no concept of where they were. Getting lost here would be a bad thing. "I guess now we know for sure that Ragnor's after us," he said eventually.

Elizabeth pulled the old book out of her pack and rested it on the log. "Ivy said as much. That was no surprise." She laid four plain white candles on top of the book.

"The question is, what do we do now?"

"We have to get into that cave. We're obviously on the right track, or Ragnor wouldn't have shown up like that." Elizabeth produced the box of matches from her pack. She'd sealed them into a ziplock bag, to protect them from the damp.

"It's going to take us ages. He'll rip us apart long before we get anywhere near that cave. I know the talismans must work to a certain degree – I felt mine heat up. But I'm not sure I want to test out how good they are."

Elizabeth picked up the four candles and stood up. "We don't have a lot of choice. If we don't get into that cave, we can't get hold of the phylactery. Ivy said Ragnor knows what we're doing, and he'll try to stop us." She took several purposeful paces forward and bent down to drive one of the candles down into the soggy floor of the forest, ramming it down hard into the soft mud until it stood upright.

"But he might succeed. Have you thought of that? Did you see that thing? It looked like something out of a horror movie. That's why I freaked out. What are you doing?"

Elizabeth took several paces forward from the first candle, squatted down and drove the second one into the ground. "The book says the repellent ritual can be cast in one of two ways." The second candle secure, she got to her feet, took a sharp left turn and then several more paces. "You can direct the ritual at Ragnor, for an instant effect." She crouched down again and drove the third candle into the ground. The three candles appeared to roughly mark the corners of a rectangular shape.

"So what happens then? Does he vanish, or something?"

"I have no idea. It just says it repels him." With the third candle in place, Elizabeth stood and took several more paces to mark the fourth corner. "But it also says if you mark out an area with candles, and cast the ritual inside that space, Ragnor can't enter it. Sort of like an enchanted circle. Or, in this case, an enchanted square." The fourth candle driven into place, Elizabeth got to her feet and brushed off her hands. Mark realised the tree he was leaning against and the fallen log were both within the square.

"We don't know if it's going to work," he said. "More to the point, we don't know why Ragnor didn't follow us."

Elizabeth returned to the log and opened the book, flipping through the pages. "He's probably biding his time. As long as we're nowhere near the cave, we're no immediate threat."

"He could have ripped us apart right then and there," Mark said. "He didn't. Why not?"

With the open book balanced on the log, Elizabeth shook out the book of matches and removed one. "I don't know. I don't really want to dwell on it. But I thought if we activate this area with the ritual, we can stay here long enough to regroup.

Get our breath back, have some water and some food maybe. While we're in here, Ragnor will leave us alone."

"We can't stay here forever. We need to go back."

"Maybe we can come up with a plan." Elizabeth studied the book. "I think I'm going to need your help with this."

"Sure." Mark pushed himself away from the tree. "What do you need me to do?"

Elizabeth handed him the matches. "The candles need to be lit at certain points of the ritual. If I read the ritual, can you light each candle at the right point?"

"How do I know the right point?"

"I'll nod at you whenever it's time to light a candle, and then we move to the next one."

"OK," said Mark uncertainly.

Elizabeth picked up the book and walked to the first candle. Mark followed with the matches. Elizabeth took a deep breath and began reciting the ritual. Mark lit a match and stood over the candle. The ritual seemed to be in Latin, not a language Mark was familiar with. He didn't know if Elizabeth could speak it either, but he was impressed with the smoothness with which she read the unfamiliar words. The flame burned down the match as he stood over the candle, sheltering the tiny light from the wind. Just as he thought the flame was about to start licking his skin, Elizabeth glanced at him and nodded. He quickly stooped to touch the flame to the wick, and the candle began to burn just as the match extinguished.

Elizabeth moved onto the next candle, still reciting the ritual. Mark shook another match out of the pack and struggled to light it as he followed her. His hands were shaking so badly it became an effort.

With three candles lit, Elizabeth kept on reciting the words in a steady voice, with Mark crouched over the fourth candle, lit match in his hand. Elizabeth raised her hand as the tone of her voice seemed to reach a crescendo. She glanced at Mark and nodded, bringing her hand down in a flourish. Mark touched the match to the final wick.

All four candle flames suddenly flared up, shooting up a foot in the air simultaneously. Mark stepped back, startled. But the synchronised flare lasted only a moment, and then the four candles continued to burn normally.

Elizabeth stopped speaking, looking down at the candles. "I think it worked," she said.

Mark looked in turn at each candle. The flames seemed tiny and fragile, blowing gently in the forest breeze. "What happens if the flames go out?"

"I don't think they will," Elizabeth said. "They're being magically sustained. Can't you feel it? It already feels warmer, just in this little bit."

Mark paused to consider. Underneath his jacket he did feel a bit warm; he could feel sweat starting to trickle down his back. But he thought perhaps the adrenaline-fuelled dash through the forest had attributed to that, too. "So what do we do now?"

Elizabeth closed the book and put it back in her pack. "Why don't we take this opportunity to eat some of those sandwiches? It might be a while before we get another chance for a breather. Whatever you do, though, don't step outside the barrier created by the candles."

"I think that's probably sound advice." Mark perched on the fallen log and pulled his pack towards him, rummaging for their plastic box of sandwiches and bottles of water.

Elizabeth took a sandwich and then paused with it halfway to her mouth. "Can you hear that?"

"Hear what?" Mark mumbled, mouth full of bread and cheese.

"That rustling sound."

"Probably just forest creatures."

"There were no forest creatures. It was absolutely silent earlier." Elizabeth stood up. "There's something out there. Can't you hear?"

Mark stopped, straining to listen. He could hear something now. The rustling of leaves as something brushed past. Another, strange sound. Like a shuffling. It sounded like something moving slowly and laboriously. And it was getting closer. And then came another sound. A low, guttural groan. And it was very close.

Elizabeth grabbed her pack and wrestled with the ties holding the shotgun to it.

"What the –" Mark began, but Elizabeth shushed him. Beyond the clearing, leaves quivered and branches parted, and the thing making the noise emerged. It was a man, or at least it had been once. The remains of the figure's clothing were tattered and filthy, and there was little left of the skin on its face. Its dislocated jaw hung at a skewed angle, and its dead eyes wept pus. One arm was rotten and damaged, and hung uselessly at its side; it shuffled along on legs that it seemed to have forgotten how to use properly. Behind the walking corpse, two similar figures emerged.

The sandwich Mark had been eating fell out of his fingers and his stomach churned. Elizabeth clutched the shotgun in one hand and thrust the axe towards him, her eyes wide and panicked. "Zombies," she hissed.

CHAPTER 44

For a long moment, Mark was frozen in fear, his mind resonating with an internal scream and his body incapable of obeying the simplest commands. One thought flooded his brain: *Holy fuck, they're zombies. Real zombies.*

Elizabeth poked him in the chest with the handle of the axe. "Mark, wake up! I mean it!"

Mark took the axe. "What the hell am I supposed to do with this?"

"Use it as a weapon, what do you think? You've got to take off the head. That's the only way to take them out.

"You expect me to get close enough to hack at them? That's suicide!"

"We've only got one gun, and I'm a better shot." Elizabeth hefted the shotgun with both hands and aimed at the closest zombie. She pulled back on the trigger, and the shot echoed through the forest, shattering the silence. Knocked back by the ricochet, Elizabeth staggered, struggling to stay on her feet. The head of the zombie she aimed at exploded in a mess of rotted brains and mucus. The body teetered for a couple of steps, and then pitched sideways, hitting a tree trunk on the way down.

"Holy shit," Mark said.

"You're going to have to help me out. There are more of them coming in." Elizabeth raised the shotgun.

There were now half a dozen lumbering zombies visible, and the groans and quivering leaves behind them suggested there were more on the way. Mark hefted the axe nervously.

A female zombie – identifiable by the long matted hair and the tattered remains of her dress, rather than by her face which was mostly rotted away, shuffled towards him. Her arms were outstretched and she was making that guttural moaning noise that seemed to be the only sound they could make.

She was perhaps fifteen feet away from Mark, and two other zombies flanked her, moving ever closer. Mark hefted the axe again, but his feet were rooted to the spot. The zombies moved slowly, so maybe his best chance was to charge whilst swinging the axe, then run away before they got a chance to get him.

"If one of them bites me, do I turn into a zombie?" he asked.

"How the hell do I know? That happens in fiction but these are real. I don't know what the rules are in real life." Elizabeth aimed the gun again, and it fired another roar of flames. The female zombie fell backwards, most of her face blown off. "At least we know shooting them in the head definitely works."

The two zombies behind her staggered as the body fell into them, and then they swivelled their dead gaze on the source of their peril – Elizabeth. The groans sounded angrier as they began to shuffle towards her.

But they both now had their back to Mark. He moved forward, quietly as he could. The stench coming off the zombies was by now overwhelming – but the smell was still not quite as bad as the lich.

The back of the nearest zombie was now less than five feet away from Mark. The thing was wearing the remnants of a tattered sweater, that might have once been blue but it was hard to tell. The flesh underneath was green and puffy, blotched with dead grey patches. Mark fixated on the bloated neck, visible beneath the straggly hair. He moved two feet closer and raised the axe, bringing it down as hard as he could.

He let out a yell – and missed the neck, burying the axe in the zombie's back. A spray of putrescent green goo arced from the entry wound and sprayed the front of Mark's jacket. The smell was awful. Trying not to gag, he let go of the axe and jumped back as the zombie, knocked off balance by the force of the blow, fell forwards and sprawled on the ground.

Mark stepped forward and put his foot on the zombie's back, trying to ignore the squelchy feel of the rotting flesh underneath his boot. He then grasped the axe in both hands in an attempt to pull it free. It was stuck fast. The zombie roared in rage, flailing its arms as it tried to grab Mark.

He put a foot on each of the zombie's shoulders, trying not to think about the squelch under his feet, and put both hands on the axe. He tugged again, trying to keep his legs and ankles out of range of the zombie's flailing arms – it was on its front, so it was not at the right angle to grab him. But then he was overwhelmed by the stench from behind him. There was a low growl in his ear, and a pair of skeletal hands landed on his shoulders.

Mark lashed out, trying to escape from the zombie, but he stumbled over the body of the one with the axe sticking out of its back, and fell to the ground. The zombie that had come up behind him fell on him, pinning him to the ground, its mouth open in a frenzied attack as it lunged to bite him in the neck.

The stench from its open mouth was just terrible. Mark was close enough to see the blackened gums and spongy, rotted tongue. He yelled and struggled, but the thing was surprisingly strong for something dead and rotting.

The blast of the shotgun rang out so close to Mark's ears that they began to ring, and for a moment he could hear nothing else but the echo of the blast singing in his head. The zombie's head dissolved in a spray of putrescent goo and rotted brain matter, much of which hit Mark in the face.

He looked up to see Elizabeth standing above him, the smoking shotgun in her hand. "I thought you needed some help," she said.

"Thanks." Mark struggled to his feet, his arms and hands slimy with zombie goo. He wiped his hands on the leaves of bushes growing from the forest floor, then stomped hard on the back of the struggling zombie, gripping the axe and pulling it from the zombie's back.

He swung the axe and brought it down as hard as he could on the neck of the zombie. This time his aim was true and the zombie's head came off with an unappealing squelch, followed by another spray of nauseating green festering goo. "That's 'coz your friend got gross zombie juice all over me," he muttered savagely, hefting the axe and stepping first over the decapitated zombie and then the one Elizabeth took out.

Another shotgun blast went by his ear, as he came face-to-face with another zombie with its arms outstretched. Elizabeth's shot took out the back of its head, and it was toppling over. Mark only just managed to dodge out of the way as it fell forwards, landing on the body of the decapitated one. He stood up on shaking legs, clutching the axe and staring wide-eyed at Elizabeth, and just managed to squeak, "Behind you!"

Elizabeth whirled around as another zombie reached out to grab her with bloated, rotting arms. She raised the shotgun and slammed the butt into the zombie's face. It roared and staggered backwards. Elizabeth bore down on it again, screaming as she bashed it repeatedly with the shotgun. Mark staggered over fallen branches made slippery with zombie goo. Another zombie appeared in front of him, thick black liquid oozing from its broken jaw; its arms making a grab for him. He swung with the axe, burying it in the zombie's shoulder.

Its half-rotted arm broke away as he pulled the axe free, but this did not deter the zombie.

Mark screamed and swung the axe again, burying it in the zombie's forehead with enough force to split its skull in two. Mark dodged out of the way as the zombie fell down, and rushed to help Elizabeth. She'd beaten her zombie into submission and had it on the ground. She rammed the butt of the shotgun into its head repeatedly until its skull broke and it lay still. She turned to look at Mark, wide eyed, her glasses smeared with zombie goo and her hair wild and frizzy.

He opened his mouth but before he could speak she said, "More over there." He turned around to see another three zombies emerging from the foliage. Elizabeth hefted the shotgun and fired off a shot, so close to Mark's ear that it nearly deafened him.

One of the three zombies fell, while the other two continued lumbering forward. Elizabeth got ready to fire another shot. As the two zombies focussed on her, Mark moved to the side. He crouched behind a tree and waited for the two zombies to pass. As the closest one went by him, he hacked at its kneecap with the axe. The zombie roared and struggled to stay upright as its shattered leg gave way beneath it. Mark gave the zombie a shove to help it on his way, then jumped on the fallen zombie and hacked its head off with the axe.

He heard the roar of the shotgun one more time as Elizabeth took out the remaining zombie. Mark stood up, his heard racing as he tried to catch his breath. As his breathing eased, he suddenly realised the forest had fallen silent. There were no more groans.

He looked up. There was no movement from the trees, and no sign of any more zombies. Elizabeth staggered through the undergrowth and clutched Mark. He dropped the axe and put his arms around her. She was shaking like a leaf, and as he held her she started sobbing. He stroked her hair and whispered comforting words. The battle was over and they were still standing – covered in dirt and goo and stinking to high heaven, but still alive.

The worst was yet to come.

CHAPTER 45

"You were awesome with that shotgun," Mark said as they headed back to the cave.

Elizabeth smiled weakly. "Maybe all those hours I spent playing *Resident Evil* weren't wasted after all."

"I mean it. You're an incredible shot. I thought I was history. Do you think we're going to encounter any more zombies?"

"I'm more worried about Ragnor. The shotgun's going to do no damage to him at all. He's the one we ought to be thinking about."

The day was wearing on, and they still had a lot of work to do to get into the cave. They were well aware of the fact it would be dark before they got through to the phylactery, and that was something they didn't want to think about.

Elizabeth sat cross-legged on the ground with the book open at the page that had the repellent ritual, while Mark used the axe to hack away at the branches obscuring the cave. This was the way they'd decided to work. The ground they were working on was too rough and uneven to mark out a clear area with the candles. So while Mark worked, Elizabeth was watching his back. If Ragnor showed any sign of making an appearance, Elizabeth would fire the ritual off at him. They had no idea how effective this would be – and Mark was trying not to think about it.

Mark's task was hard work. After only half an hour of hacking away, he was dripping with sweat.

He paused to peel off his jacket, tossing it on the ground with his backpack, where Elizabeth sat like a sentry, her eyes scanning the forest in every direction. "Still looking good, yes?" he asked.

She nodded, not taking her eyes off the horizon. "So far so good."

"Maybe he's gone."

Elizabeth cast a glance at Mark. "You don't really believe that, do you?"

Mark sighed. "Not really. I'm just an optimist." He turned back to the task at hand. He'd abandoned the gloves; they'd been shredded to ribbons by the thorns, and now his hands were full of scratches, sore and chapped. He felt like he was making barely any progress, despite the growing pile of branches on the ground.

He worked in a forward line, towards where he thought the entrance of the cave was. The branches on either side of him pulled at his clothes. He pulled another branch forward, and as he began to hack at it he thought he caught a glimpse of an opening in the rock face ahead.

Encouraged, he began hacking at the base of the next branch. He had shed all layers but a thin t-shirt and was sweating buckets. His skin was burning.

Then he realised the burning sensation came from a particular area of his chest. The talisman was getting hot again. He paused. Beneath the sound of his own laboured breathing, a determined humming noise, gradually increasing in volume, could be heard.

He looked back at Elizabeth. She was staring fixedly at a spot off to the right, where a thin column of smoke spiralled up from the ground, swirling around as it gained mass.

"Keep working, Mark." Elizabeth sprang to her feet still clutching the book. She stretched out her right hand, balancing the book in her left and began to recite the words of the ritual in a clear steady voice.

Mark forced himself to turn away and to keep on hacking. The quicker they got to the cave, the sooner they could get rid of Ragnor. He had to trust Elizabeth to do her part. She'd never let him down before.

A moment ago Mark had been reflecting on how hot he was feeling, but the temperature seemed to have dropped twenty degrees in a few seconds.

An icy chill permeated the air. The sweat was freezing on his skin and suddenly he felt chilled to the bone. One last chop at the branch had it loose in his hand and he tossed it to one side without a backward glance. Behind him he could hear Elizabeth reciting the ritual, her voice never wavering. He grabbed the next branch.

A feeling of panic began to creep in, starting in the pit of Mark's stomach and working its way up his body. His hands were shaking, and the branch in his hand trembled. Somewhere behind him a high-pitched keening started up, and Elizabeth's steady voice rose in pitch and volume. She spoke the words of the ritual with confidence, pronouncing each word clearly and calmly. She didn't falter this time over any of the unfamiliar words.

Run! Every fibre in Mark's being screamed. *Run far, far away! Run away now!* He clutched the branch in his hand so tightly his knuckles went white, and he could feel the rough bark digging into his palm. *Don't listen,* he told himself firmly. *It's a fear spell. You can't leave Elizabeth. We can win. It knows that, that's why it's doing this.*

The high-pitched keening noise rose in timbre, getting so loud that Mark thought his eardrums would shatter. A sudden gust of freezing wind battered him, nearly blowing him off his feet. The branches all around him waved and pummelled him, smacking him in the face.

He let go and crouched down, shielding his face with his hands. The urge to turn and run was overwhelming. *Don't do it,* he told himself firmly.

He willed himself not to move, imagining roots growing from his feet and down into the ground, wrapping themselves around ancient tree roots and holding him in place.

The wind blew him so hard he fell over, landing on his back, just as the keening got so loud he thought his ears would explode.

From his vantage point on the floor, he caught a glimpse of the undead thing Ragnor, less than ten feet away from Elizabeth. But as she uttered the last phrase of the ritual, a bolt of white light exploded from her outstretched right hand and enveloped the creature. It emitted a screech of rage, and suddenly disappeared in a cloud of black smoke.

In the sudden silence that descended, Elizabeth dropped the book and collapsed onto the floor. Mark tried to pull himself to his feet, but his legs were like jelly. He crawled over to Elizabeth and put his arms around her. She was shaking like a leaf.

"I guess it worked," she said in a small voice.

"You were amazing," Mark said. "I think it was casting some kind of fear spell. I was struggling to fight this urge to run away. But you were so calm, so together. Not scared at all."

"I was terrified. But I knew what it was trying to do, and convinced myself to stand firm."

Mark smiled "I guess you made your save roll."

"Advantage of a high wisdom," she said.

CHAPTER 46

Not too long after Elizabeth repelled Ragnor, Mark finally uncovered the cave entrance. The hole he'd cut in the bushes was only two feet high, but he could clearly see the dark hole that led down into the cave. Shrouded in moss, it emitted an unpleasant smell. A damp, mildewy smell.

Mark got on his hands and knees and peered in cautiously. The rocks were slimy beneath his hands and he could feel the wetness soaking through the knees of his hiking pants.

He could see nothing in the cave, so he retreated carefully. He climbed to his feet and returned to where Elizabeth was sitting. He grabbed his backpack and rummaged around in it for the head torch. "It's pitch black in there. I can't see a thing."

Elizabeth turned pages in the old book. "There's a section in here about the cave. It's a bit like the Tardis, apparently."

"What's that?"

"Bigger on the inside than it looks from the outside." She pointed to a map in the book. "These are directions to the phylactery. You have to look for a row of three stalactites shot through with pink rock. Near them is a circle of stalagmites. In the middle of that circle, the phylactery is buried six feet down."

"In the meantime, we're trapped in a cave at Ragnor's mercy," Mark said dubiously. "Not sure I like the idea of that. If he decides to make a move in the cave we're sitting ducks."

"I know, but there's no other way." Elizabeth picked up her pack and slung it over her shoulder, then picked up the shovel. "We just have to do it as fast as possible.

"Maybe you should stay out here?" Mark said. "Then at least if I get trapped, you can get away."

"Forget that idea right now. We stick together. If we find the spot, you dig and I'll read the ritual, like before."

She tucked the book under one arm, and with the shotgun in one hand and the shovel in the other, she stood in front of Mark with her face set in a determined expression. "Let's go."

They had to crawl on hands and knees to get through the foliage and into the entranceway. Pausing at the mouth of the cave with his head torch switched on, Mark surveyed the surroundings. "It's pretty narrow in here. We'll be crawling a good ten or fifteen feet. After that, it looks like it might open up a bit, but I can't really tell from here."

"Let's get going then." Elizabeth's voice sounded muffled. The crawl space had necessitated Elizabeth putting the book away and tying the shotgun to her backpack again. Mark knew she was worried about not being able to get to either item in a hurry.

Carefully, Mark began to move forward on his hands and knees. The rock beneath him was wet and slimy. The head torch illuminated the path a few feet ahead; the rock covered with moss and moisture. Some crystal substance in the rocks on the cave wall glittered as the torch caught them. Misshapen stalactites emerged from the cave roof. His knees and hands were cold and damp from the surface of the cave. His hiking pants were grimy with mud and cave slime already, and he was thankful he'd dressed in hard-wearing fabrics. The thick synthetic material had kept the worst of the thorns from scratching his legs too, although his hands were shredded. The pressure he kept on them to crawl along was making them hurt all the worse. He wondered what kind of nasty bacteria was going to infect his blood stream, gaining access through the cuts on his hands.

A steady drip, dripping noise was the only sound, apart from the increasingly laboured breathing of himself and Elizabeth as they made their arduous journey. The meagre light from the torch cast eerie shadows on the cave walls, and he tried not to think about all the rock above his head at this point. He'd never had a problem with claustrophobia before.

But then, he'd never been crawling along in such a small cave before. He was sure the air was getting thinner – he was starting to feel light-headed.

He only realised he'd stopped when Elizabeth bumped into him. "What's wrong?" she asked.

"It's getting hard to breathe. Are we sure there's enough air in here?"

"The entranceway is exposed. There's plenty of air getting in. Besides, look at the moss and lichen growing in here. Plants need air. They thrive on carbon dioxide, and they pump the air full of oxygen. That's good news for us."

"I just feel a bit dizzy."

"Are you feeling claustrophobic?"

"A bit, I guess."

"Take some slow deep breaths."

Mark sat on the cold rock floor and concentrated on his breathing. In. Out. Slowly and deliberately. "We haven't really got time for me to indulge in a panic attack."

"If you black out, that'll be worse." Elizabeth studied him, a frown creasing her face. "How are you feeling now?"

"Better, I think."

"OK. Ready to carry on?"

Mark sighed and got on his hands and knees again. "I think so."

"I think the cave opens out just up there. It might be better then."

"Let's go then." Mark crawled forward.

CHAPTER 47

The cave began to open up. The meagre light from Mark's head torch revealed that the roof curved upwards, widening the passageway. When there was enough room for head clearance, he climbed to his feet. It was no easier to walk – the ground was very wet and slippery. He took hold of Elizabeth's hand and used his other hand to steady himself against the wall. In this way, they made slow and careful progress.

They had seen no sign of Ragnor inside the cave, and this fact alone was making Mark feel antsy. The path they were travelling curved gently downwards, taking them deeper underground. Without the torches they would be stranded, in complete darkness, far underground. He didn't know how far down they were. They could be a mile under the surface, for all he knew.

Don't think about it, he told himself sternly; feeling the initial fluttering of panic starting up in the pit of his stomach.

The path in front of them curved sharply to the left. Cautiously Mark picked his way along the passageway, still holding Elizabeth's hand.

As they rounded the corner, the passageway finished abruptly, opening up into a great underground cavern. They stopped dead, stunned by the beauty of this hidden grotto. There was light here, glowing from some phosphorous material in the walls and bathing the area in an unearthly glow. Stalactites and stalagmites adorned the cave, glittering like diamonds when they caught the torch light. The place was like some secret fairyland.

"Beautiful," Mark said quietly.

"And to think – we're probably the first people to lay eyes on this in hundreds of years," Elizabeth said.

"So where do we have to go now?"

Elizabeth pulled the map of the cave out of her pocket, holding it in the light of Mark's head torch so that they could see. "This is the map from the book, explaining the cave. We have to look for three pink-tinged stalactites in a row."

"There are loads of stalactites. How do we know which ones to look for? And the features of the cave have probably changed in five hundred years."

"Possibly not as much as you would think. Features in a cave take thousands of years to develop." Elizabeth studied the map. "The ones we are looking for are to the north west."

Mark checked the compass. "That's in that direction." He pointed.

"Let's go then."

Using rock protrusions to steady themselves, they carefully picked their way across the knobbly cave floor. It was slow going, and the cave went back further than it appeared. Every time they rounded a crest of stalagmites, there were more.

It was chilly in the cave. A cool breeze was blowing in from somewhere – no doubt from the passage that they had just followed in. Mark focused on that, and the notion that the breeze meant fresh air was getting in. They were not trapped in the cave. There was a way out and there was plenty of air.

After a while, Elizabeth paused to check the map again. It had a crude drawing of the cave, with the hiding place for the phylactery carefully marked. "According to this, we need to be going over there." Elizabeth pointed.

The immediate feature in the area to which Elizabeth was pointing was a stalagmite and stalactite that had fused together, forming a column of calcified rock that stretched from cave floor to ceiling. Beyond it, there looked to be some open space. Three stalactites clung to the roof of the cave, forming a row of jagged teeth. "Might those be the three we're after?" Mark said. "They look sort of pinkish. Kind of hard to tell, in this light."

"There should be a circle of stalagmites by them. Let's go check it out."

They moved closer. Once they were past the column of cave rock they could clearly see a circle of stalagmites underneath the row of stalactites. The circle bordered a pool of black water. It was hard to see into its murky depths due to the dimness of the cave.

"This is what we want." Elizabeth propped her backpack at the base of one of the stalagmites and began rummaging in it."

Mark stared into the pool of water, seeing nothing but his own distorted reflection gazing back at him. He looked a bit of a state, he thought suddenly, with his face smeared with mud, his blond hair sticking out in all directions and his clothes rumpled, dirty and reeking of zombie goo. "So where is the phylactery buried?"

"At the bottom of the pool." Elizabeth pulled the candles out of her backpack.

"So I have to get in it and start digging?"

"Sorry, sweetie."

"Do I have to?"

"One of us has to. I was going to try and get the protective circle set up again. I can position the candles around the pool of water. Seems to make more sense for me to do that, and you to dig."

Mark sighed. "You're right, of course. It does. I don't suppose we know how deep this is."

"Only one way to find out." Elizabeth took the first candle and looked at the rocky cave floor. She lit a match, running the flame over the candle base until the wax started to melt. Then she rammed the soft wax onto the rock, pressing down until the candle held steady.

Mark set his pack down by the edge of the pool, took off his shoes and socks and rolled his trouser legs up to his knees. He picked up the shovel and cautiously stepped into the pool of water.

The water was cold and felt slightly gritty. His feet hit reassuring rock early on. The water was only a foot deep. "Whereabouts do I dig?" he asked.

Elizabeth paused in her candle placing to shine the hand torch onto the map. "Five paces south east of the largest stalagmite," she said.

Mark looked back at the circle of stalagmites. "How big is a pace?"

Elizabeth shrugged. "Assuming the map was created by an adult male, probably about the same size as yours. Though the average male would have been a bit shorter than you back then. Measure out five fairly small paces."

Mark waded out of the pool to the base of the largest stalagmite in the circle. "Okay, here we go. One." He took one step toward the pool. "Two." The second pace brought him ankle deep into the water. "Three". With a splash, he was fully knee-deep in the pool. "Four. Five. Hey, wait. I can feel sand underneath my feet now."

Elizabeth had placed three of the four candles. "Sounds promising."

Mark took the torch off his head and crouched down, shining the light directly down into the water. It wasn't the dirtiness of the water that was making it murky, he realised – it was lack of light.

The torch illuminated the water down to the bottom of the pool. His feet, looking unnaturally white in the cold water, were resting on a circle of sand about half a metre in diameter. "Okay," he said. "Time to start digging."

CHAPTER 48

The digging was hard work, requiring Mark to plunge his arms up to the elbows into the freezing water. He got into a rhythm: drive the shovel into the soft wet stand; stamp on it with his foot; pull a shovel full of sand out of the water; toss it onto the growing pile on the shore. After twenty minutes, the pile had grown quite large and it was no longer possible for Mark to dig without putting his face into the water to see what he was doing. Fortunately for him, Elizabeth had even thought to bring goggles. When he'd queried this, marvelling at her resourcefulness, she'd smiled and said she'd studied the map. "It had mentioned the pool of water. It didn't seem so surprising to me that the phylactery would be buried in it. If I was going to stash something and I wanted it to be hard to get at, I think I'd bury it under water too." She'd got the goggles from the sports and outdoor shop where they'd bought the rest of the equipment.

The goggles helped Mark to see where he was digging, but they didn't particularly make the task any easier. He was now thoroughly drenched, and feeling the chill of the icy water. Even with the exertion of digging raising his core body temperature, he was shivering uncontrollably. His feet had been planted in the water now for nearly half an hour and they were so cold they had gone numb. The water contained salt deposits from the rocks too, which stung the cuts on his arms.

Elizabeth had set up the candles to form a protective circle around the pool. She sat at the edge of the circle, her back to Mark, staring fixedly out into the cave with the book on her lap. She had the hand torch propped up on its edge. It cast eerie shadows across the cave.

Mark had the head torch, which shone down into the water, illuminating the area in which he was digging.

It was impossible to see into the hole; for as fast as he could remove the sand, more fell into the hole to replace it. He felt like he'd been digging for ages and made nothing more than a small indentation. But then he drove the spade once more into the hole, and felt it hit something. A scraping sound – metal hitting ceramic – confirmed this. The sound echoed in the silence of the cave, and Elizabeth turned her head. "Have you found something?"

"I'm not sure." Mark put down the spade. He plunged his hands into the soft sand on the cave floor. Something hard and unyielding met his exploring fingers. He traced a circle. "There's something here." He tugged. The circle gave a little, but not much. "I might need your help to pull it out."

Elizabeth put down the book, and took off her hiking boots and socks. She rolled her combat pants up to above her knees and splashed into the water to join him. With each of them gripping the object with both hands, they pulled upwards at the same time. Initially the object was stuck fast, but then there was a sudden sucking sound and it was released with such momentum that Mark lost his balance and fell backwards, landing in the water with a splash. He sat in the pool, spluttering, while Elizabeth looked down in wide-eyed surprise. She was clutching a ceramic pot with a cracked glaze coating. It could have been a small cooking pot.

"Guess we found it," he said as he clambered to his feet.

"There'll be another three." Elizabeth carefully laid the pot down by the edge of the water, making sure it was well within the protective circle.

"What do you mean, there's another three?"

Elizabeth looked at him. "A phylactery consists of four jars. One for the brain, one for the heart, one for the kidneys, one for the liver. The idea was to preserve these items.

It was thought they'd be needed in the afterlife, so they were buried with the corpse.

This was so that when the dead person rose again, they could collect them before they found their way to the afterlife. Ragnor was working on the same premise – that's why destroying them will destroy him."

"Oh, great. And while we're struggling with this, he's going to come after us."

"I'm surprised we haven't seen him already. But the circle will hold long enough to retrieve the phylactery. We're going to have to leave the cave to set the fire, and I bet that's when the fun will begin."

Mark staggered to his feet. Every inch of him was now soaked through. Drenched underwear was definitely an unpleasant feeling. He picked up the spade and squelched over to the hole in the sand. Peering down, he just caught the glimpse of what looked like a ceramic circle. "It looks like you're right. I can see what looks like another lid. Looks like these jars were stacked on top of each other. I'll need your help again."

Between the two of them, and with a great deal of effort, they managed to extract the remaining three jars from the sand. Mark cast worried glances around the cave. "I still can't believe Ragnor's not shown up."

"He almost certainly will when we open the jars."

"Should we open them now? Shouldn't we make sure they are what we want?"

"They are. Can't you feel the power?" Elizabeth held up one of the jars. "When I touch them, there's a tingling sensation. Like there's an electric charge in them. Besides, listen." She shook the jar gently. Something wet and squelchy sloshed around inside. "That sounds like a brain to me."

"Then I guess we need to get out of here. If we're going to set a fire, we need to be in the open." Mark opened his backpack. "I think I can fit two of the jars in my pack, just about, if you can take two in yours."

Their packs were roomy for hiking, but with the jars in them there wasn't much room for anything else.

Elizabeth packed up the candles. "We ought to set the circle up again when we burn the phylactery. I feel really vulnerable without it activated."

"Let's get a move on then, and get this over with," said Mark. Laden down with their heavy packs, and drenched with cave water, the two of them made their way out of the cave.

CHAPTER 49

Darkness had fallen while they had been in the cave. Outside, the woods were eerily silent and everything was swathed in shadows. The light from Mark's head torch cast creepy shadows on the swaying forms of the trees at the edge of the clearing.

He emerged from the cave behind Elizabeth, the torch light focusing on the seat of her hiking pants as she picked herself up from the crawling position. Her rear was scuffed with muddy marks and still damp from the cave. Even so, he caught himself admiring the view and had to remind himself sternly that this was not the time to get distracted.

Elizabeth hefted her backpack into position as she stood and headed back to the clearing. Mark had to increase his pace to keep up with her, his soggy clothing squelching uncomfortably with each step. He bit back a sneeze. He was cold, wet and scared, and wanted to get the hell out of this place. Elizabeth paused and glanced back at him. "Could you grab some of those branches you cut away from the cave? We're going to need firewood."

"Good thinking." Mark picked up an armful of dried branches, and hurried after Elizabeth.

He knew even without looking when he'd stepped into the circle of power. The ground was tingling. The vibration left an uncomfortable feeling; starting in the soles of his feet and moving all the way up his body. It was the same kind of feeling he got in his tongue when he used to put it, as a dare, on the contact point of a D-cell battery as a kid. Only this feeling was running through his whole body.

Elizabeth crouched on the ground, pulling the two phylactery jars out of her backpack. "Put the firewood down here," she said.

Mark put the branches down and dumped his backpack, relieved to have it off his back. The jars had made it really heavy. He unzipped the pack to pull the jars out. The hairs on the back of his neck stood on end and he felt decidedly uneasy, as if something was watching them. He scanned the treeline but could see nothing moving in the darkness.

"Can I have your pen knife?" Elizabeth asked. Mark dug it out the pack and handed it to her. She unfolded the largest knife, and slid the blade under the seal on the lid of one of the jars, prising it open. Mark looked out in the direction of the dark forest again. He could have sworn he'd seen a flicker of movement on the periphery of his vision. He could see nothing there, but the torch light did not go far, and it was impossible to see anything beyond it.

An overwhelming vinegary smell permeated the air as the lid popped off the jar. Elizabeth shone the hand torch into the interior. "I can confirm we've found the right jars," she said.

"What's in there?"

"Stand back." Elizabeth tipped the jar over, ensuring it was facing away from the pile of firewood. The vinegary smell grew stronger as a thick brown liquid – clearly some kind of pickling substance – splashed over the earth. It was followed by a grey jelly-like mass that plopped out of the jar and lay quivering on the scrubby grass. It was the right size and shape for a human brain.

"Gross," Mark said as Elizabeth shone the torch on the brain. She picked up the spade and cautiously shovelled up the organ, transferring the quivering mass to the pile of firewood. "Is something so gooey going to burn?"

"We have lighter fluid. It'll burn. But we've got to hurry up." Elizabeth picked up the pen knife and began to work the lid off the second jar.

The back of Mark's neck was still tingling. He just couldn't shake the feeling that someone was watching him.

He turned around again, and the head torch illuminated a cadaverous face, no more than ten feet away from him. He yelped and dropped his backpack.

"Hello Mark," David said. Only when he spoke, did Mark recognise him. He looked terrible. His face was grey, the skin parchment-thin and stretched tightly across his skull. His eyes looked bulbous in his too-thin face; his dark hair receding away from his forehead and streaked with grey. He looked about fifty. He was dressed entirely in black with only his face visible in the darkness. He looked weirdly like a disembodied head.

Elizabeth let out a small whimper and Mark felt her hand clutch his arm. With a growing sense of dread he tore his eyes away from David's dreadful face and followed down. David's hands were clad in black gloves, making them hard to see, but he clutched a pistol. And it was pointing directly at Mark.

Mark found his voice. "You don't want to do this, David."

"Don't I?" David's voice was flat, monotone.

"You know what this thing is, what it can do. How many more people have to die?"

"You're planning to destroy him. I have to stop you."

"David, it will kill you. Look at yourself. It's possessing you."

David stared at Mark. His face reminded Mark of the photos of anorexic young women in their last days of life. A face so shrivelled the eyes were too big for it. A face that was nothing more than a thin layer of skin stretched over a skull. He looked again at the gun in David's hand. It was pointing directly at his chest, but David's grip was unsteady. His hands were shaking.

"Don't you see what this thing has done to you, David? Let us do this, and release you." He took a step forward, aware that Elizabeth had released her hand on his arm and had moved backwards. Perhaps, if he could distract David, she could finish.

"All of my dreams could come true," David said, and laughed abruptly; a sudden short, harsh sound. "That's what it promised. But there was always a price. It wasn't as if I didn't know that."

"Put the gun down, David."

David raised it higher. "Don't come any closer. Put your hands up where I can see them."

"OK, take it easy." Mark spread his hands out slowly, and extended them open-palmed. "I haven't got anything." He took a cautious step forward. David's hand shook as he refocused the weapon on Mark's chest.

"I thought it was all going so well," David said, his voice wavering. "I wanted money. I wanted to pass my exams. I wanted a big house in Hampstead. And I got it all. I didn't care what the price was."

"Then let's end it all. We can release you." Mark took a slow, cautious step to the right, and then another. David's gaze was still fixed on him and the gun followed his movements, still clutched in David's shaking hand. But while David was on him, he wasn't looking at Elizabeth. Mark could hear the rustling behind him and knew she was grappling with the lid of the second jar.

David shook his head sadly. "It's too late for that. There's still one more wish I want."

"What's that?" Mark heard a distinct popping suck as the lid popped off the second jar, accompanied by the vinegary aroma. He fervently hoped David was too distracted to notice.

"You can't take it all with you," David said. He seemed to be staring at Mark, but his eyes were unfocused, as if he was seeing something else. "See, Ragnor's five hundred years old. He can show me how to be immortal. And that's my final wish."

Mark was aware of a sudden buzzing noise and an intense heat at a spot on his chest.

The talisman was heating up. Behind David, a column of smoke materialised and swirled, building into a solidified form that Mark was all too familiar with.

He became aware of several things simultaneously. A wet plopping noise behind him, followed by the sharp tang of lighter fluid. David's gaze shifted from Mark to Elizabeth, behind him, and he swivelled the gun around to point in her direction. The moment David was no longer looking at him, Mark moved. He threw himself at David and tackled him to the ground.

He was aware of Ragnor solidifying behind him and that high-pitched keening noise loud enough to hurt his eardrums. David struggled madly and howled; for all his fragile appearance, he was still surprisingly strong. A wave of light and heat made Mark look up. Elizabeth had ignited the fire. But Ragnor was advancing, David still had the gun, and there were still two jars of the phylactery in Mark's backpack.

Just as these thoughts were whirling around in Mark's head, David pulled the trigger and the gun fired.

CHAPTER 50

Elizabeth wasn't surprised to see David. Ivy had warned them that Ragnor would be able to see the future, and it seemed entirely predictable he would send David after them. But he was clearly unbalanced and waving a gun around like that made him an additional danger. While he was fixated on Mark, and seemed unfocused and unsure, she decided to make the most of the distraction.

The second jar contained the heart. As she threw it onto the pile of firewood, Ragnor started to materialise. There were still two jars in Mark's backpack. Elizabeth squirted lighter fluid on the pyre and with shaking fingers she lit a match; stepping back and hoping for the best as she tossed the meagre flame onto the pile. It caught, and a wall of flame shot up. But only two of the organs were on the fire and it wasn't enough to stop the lich. If anything, it just made him angry. The figure emerging from the smoke seemed to get taller, and opened his skeletal mouth in a roar.

The gun shot sounded unnaturally loud in the silence of the dark forest. Elizabeth saw Mark collapse to the ground and her heart leapt into her mouth. Ragnor was moving closer. Elizabeth felt the first tremblings of fear in her stomach. *Run!* A primal voice was screaming at her. *Run far away!*

"You have no power over me," she muttered angrily, scrabbling in her jacket pocket for the page containing the repellent ritual. "You have no power over me, you bastard. You have no power over me!" This last phrase was screamed, directed towards Ragnor.

She forced herself to concentrate on the alien words on the page that were somehow becoming familiar to her, reading each word loudly and clearly, fighting the fear as Ragnor began to move closer, floating across the ground on a cloud of smoke.

She forced her thoughts away from worrying about Mark, who was lying still on the ground. Forced herself not to look at David, who was climbing to his feet, still clutching the gun. She focused on the words of the ritual, and a mantra in her head. *I am not afraid. I am not afraid.*

From the corner of her eye she could see the lich moving closer, that high-pitched keening noise getting ever louder. The talisman around her neck got so hot it was burning her throat. A blast of freezing air emanated from the lich and enveloped her in a breath-taking coldness. But still she kept on. David was limping towards her too, focusing his gun in her direction.

I am not afraid. I am not afraid. As she reached the last two lines of the incantation, she had to struggle to keep her voice steady. The lich kept coming closer, skirting round the fire where his heart and brains burned, emitting a terrible smell of rancid burning meat.

Then Elizabeth saw Mark move. He rolled over onto his side and stuck out an arm, grabbing David's ankle and pulling hard. David stumbled, the gun falling out of his hand. As he fell, Elizabeth uttered the last word of the incantation, a cone of hot power shooting from her outstretched right arm and hitting the lich in the torso. The lich screamed and erupted in a puff of smoke, the dissonant screech of his rage fading away as the smoke dissipated.

Elizabeth knew it wouldn't hold him off for long and David was still a threat, but at least Mark was still alive and conscious. She grabbed Mark's backpack and yanked the jars out. For five hundred years the thick clay had protected Ragnor's power, buried under sand and water. The clay was too thick to shatter. With the pen knife, she worked on breaking the seals of the two remaining jars. She was just going to have to do it the hard way.

* * * *

The bullet grazed Mark's side. The pain was intense and left him unable to breathe. When he realised he wasn't dead, he waited for the dizziness to subside. David was getting to his feet and scrambling for the gun. Out of the corner of his eye, Mark saw Ragnor manifesting into solid force, and knew he was going after Elizabeth. To have David and his gun on her, too – no way could Mark let that happen.

David was already on his feet, and Mark didn't have time to go after him. Desperately he rolled over and reached out, lunging for David's ankle, hoping to slow him down. He pulled hard and David stumbled and fell. A sharp pain coursed through Mark's injured side and he had to let go, instinctively clutching his hand to his side. His t-shirt was already drenched in blood, and moving was painful. His intervention had been enough to knock David off balance, but already he was getting up and scrambling for the gun again. It was lying less than two feet away from Mark's left foot. Desperately he reached out his leg, kicking the gun away from David's grasp. David howled and threw himself over Mark, squeezing both hands around Mark's neck. Mark kicked and thrashed on the ground as he struggled to draw breath. David wore the expression of a mad thing, screaming and howling as he tried to strangle the man who had once been his best friend.

Mark couldn't see where the lich was, or whether Elizabeth was still in danger. His vision was going red at the edges and he was starting to see double. He focused all of his strength into his right leg and drew it up hard, kneeing David in the groin as hard as he could.

David squealed and let go, rolling off him as he drew into a foetal position with his hands clutching his crotch.

Mark sat up, shaking his head to try and clear it.

The head torch had been knocked off his head and lay in the grass. But the fire that Elizabeth had started bloomed, casting a red glow and dancing shadows around the clearing.

Mark struggled to climb to his feet, looking around for Elizabeth as he did so. He saw her by the fire, desperately trying to wrench the lids off the two remaining jars as two of Ragnor's vital organs cooked in the fuel-enhanced fire. He guessed she'd read out the repelling ritual again, as Ragnor was nowhere in sight. But already a column of smoke was forming again, heralding Ragnor was once again about to make an appearance. Perhaps the ritual lessened in potency the more it was read out, or maybe it was just that Ragnor was desperate to stop them. Mark shouted out, desperate to warn Elizabeth about the lich's imminent return. She glanced his way and he pointed at the column of smoke. She nodded once and made a quick gesture at Mark, a worried expression on her face, before returning to the task of prising off the lid of the phylactery jar.

Mark glanced behind him, and realised Elizabeth's warning to him was that David was on his feet again. He was staggering, looking around wild-eyed, probably trying to find the gun. Mark didn't want to give him a chance to find it again. The next shot might not be a glancing blow. He staggered towards David, but the enraged man saw him coming and grabbed his arms, twisting them round painfully. Mark yelled and kicked back, catching David in the shin.

David exploded with fury, launching a right hook that caught Mark right in the nose. There was a crunch, an explosion of blood, and an excruciating pain that blossomed out from Mark's nose.

He put a hand to his face and it came away covered in blood. David stood in front of him.

He looked like some kind of nightmare creature, emaciated and bloodied with a mad grin on his face.

He began to cackle wildly. "It's too late. He comes back. Ragnor returns. There's nothing to stop him now."

Even without turning around, the high-pitched keening and the sudden drop in temperature that always accompanied Ragnor's presence were enough to let Mark know he had taken on solid form again. He was going after Elizabeth, who had the phylactery and posed the greatest threat. And Elizabeth had to face him alone. Mark couldn't help her until he'd dealt with David, who seemed to be intent on killing him. Or whatever this thing that David had become was. Mark remembered riding around the neighbourhood with David on mountain bikes, aged about eleven. He remembered the two of them playing video games late into the night. He remembered the night he stayed over at David's, and David snuck into his dad's desk and stole the whiskey; they had both got extremely sick after drinking it, and that was the last time Mark was allowed to sleep at David's house. He remembered when David had sat behind Becky Shaw in Year Eight English, on whom he'd had a hopeless crush. He'd spent the whole year staring hopelessly at the back of her head, and she never once looked back to acknowledge his existence.

But the David of Mark's memory had gone. The creature in front of him was a parody of David, something that wore his face but had changed it into something grotesque and unrecognisable. It was too late to save the David he had once known. But he had to do something, before it became too late to save Elizabeth.

The David-thing was coming at him again, screaming and flailing limbs. Mark edged backwards, nearly tripping over something. He glanced down and realised that it was the spade.

As David bore down on him he stooped to grab the spade, gripping it with both hands. He put as much strength as he could behind the swing, and the edge of the spade smacked firmly into the side of David's face.

He teetered for a moment, a look of surprise registering on his face, and for just a moment he looked like the old David.

Then he collapsed like a marionette with its strings cut. There was a horrible crack as his head made contact with a rock on the ground.

Mark began to turn around, with the intention of going to help Elizabeth, but suddenly the strength evaporated from his legs and he collapsed on the ground. The fear burst out of his throat without warning and suddenly he was crying, tears and snot mingling with the blood running down his face from his broken nose.

CHAPTER 51

The perpetual cold emanating from the lich did not dissipate when Elizabeth repelled him, and a combination of fear, cold and adrenaline made her hands shake as she tried to prise open the lids of the remaining two jars. Already she could see the smoke swirling – the lich was wasting no time returning, and she feared the creature was becoming resistant to the repellent ritual.

The knife slipped and sank into her hand, drawing a deep cut across her palm. With tears of frustration forming in her eyes, she renewed her grip on the blade and forced it into the seal that was holding the lid onto the jar she was clutching. Mark and David were having a punch up at the edge of her range of vision. She heard Mark scream and automatically glanced in his direction – he was still standing, but he had a hand covering his bleeding nose. She wished she could help him, but it was up to her to deal with the lich.

The lid came off, and the foul aroma of the pickling liquid intermingled with old, old meat rose up from the jar. She tipped it up until the organ slopped out – the liver, apparently. She stabbed it with the pen knife and tossed it onto the fire, where it began to cook and crackle, adding to the black, foul-smelling smoke that was rising up from the fire.

Beyond the fire, the malicious form of Ragnor had materialised, floating closer on a cloud of smoke; skeletal mouth open, with his claw-like fingers extended towards her. A wave of fear swept over Elizabeth and she tried hard to remember her mantra. *I am not afraid. You have no power over me.* But still her fingers shook as she fumbled for the fourth and final jar.

The creature was a horror to behold, and she'd never seen it this close up. Scraps of leathery flesh clung to the skeletal body.

The ancient robes were mouldy and tattered, and exuded a terrible stench of death and decay. The air around it was frigid. Elizabeth's teeth were chattering, and she was shivering so much it was getting hard to hold the blade steady in her hand, let alone force it into the seal securing the lid to the jar.

She tried not to look at the creature, but it was so close now, and she was so afraid, it was hard to concentrate on what she was doing. "It's a fear spell," she chanted to herself. "I am not afraid. It has no power over me. I am not afraid." But her body betrayed her. Every fibre of her being was screaming at her to get up and run. It took all of her will to not move, to concentrate on the job at hand, to continue breaking the seal.

She looked up. The thing was less than ten feet away, its skeletal claws reaching out towards her. "Fear me," it rasped, from the depths of what had once been its throat.

Elizabeth looked up at the creature as the lid of the final jar came loose. "I do not fear you. You have no power over me!" she screamed, and dumped the contents of the jar onto the fire.

The pickling juice landed on it as well as two pickled brown kidneys, and the fire smoked and smouldered under the liquid. The creature hissed and raised its arms in the air, letting out a terrible screech. Elizabeth grabbed the lighter fluid and squirted some more on the fire, then squirted a good amount in the lich's direction as well, just for good measure. The high pitched keening noise got louder and louder.

Elizabeth grasped the matches and tried to strike one, but her hands were shaking so badly it took three attempts. When she did light it, she tossed it in the lich's direction, and the thing shrieked at an ear-shattering volume as a plume of flame shot up the length of its tattered clothing. The fire in the circle flared up in synchronisation.

Elizabeth staggered backwards, feeling the heat from the fire on her face.

The horrible shrieks from the lich were deafening, but its form was shrinking as the fire raged, and suddenly it exploded in a cacophony of sparks and smoke.

And then everything was silent. Elizabeth could hear only the sound of her own laboured breathing and the gentle crackle of the fire, which had died down into something that was no more menacing than a camp fire. And then she heard quiet sobbing, from Mark, collapsed over David's inert body.

On shaking legs, she made her way over to Mark, wrapping her arms around him and burying her head in his chest. His face was a mess – streaked with blood and dirt; his nose skewed at a crazy angle. And there they stayed, huddled together, for quite a long time, in the dying embers of the fire.

CHAPTER 52

In the aftermath that followed, Mark and Elizabeth's trip to Gloucester was unexpectedly extended. The police had to be called, of course – David's body could not be easily explained. Naturally the two of them were questioned. In the end, their story about being concerned about David's state of mind for some time, and having to defend themselves when he attacked them was accepted – David's fingerprints were all over the gun.

There was nothing left of Ragnor. The phylactery was nothing more than a pile of ashes, left over from what could just as easily have been a camp fire.

Mark was taken to hospital, but the wound in his side turned out not to be too serious. The bullet had taken a chunk of flesh out of his side, but it had not hit any muscles or organs, and there was no permanent damage.

They extended their stay in the B&B, and when all the questioning was done and they were told they could go home, they went to pay Ivy a visit.

The shop was as deserted as it was the first time they came. Not a customer was in sight. The bell above the door jangled as they entered. A moment later, Ivy appeared from behind the book shelves, a stack of ancient tomes in her arms. When she noticed them, her face creased into a delighted smile. "Well hello, young friends. I'm so pleased to see you again. I hope your quest was successful."

"It's kind of a long story," Elizabeth said wearily.

"Well, why don't you come into the back and tell me all about it. I'll make tea."

Mark and Elizabeth followed the old lady behind the beaded screen once more and, sitting in the same chairs as they had done before, they told her the story. About finding the phylactery; about their battle with Ragnor; and about David.

Ivy looked at them sadly. "I did fear it might be too late for your friend."

"I still don't understand how he found us," Mark said. "Was he following us?"

"I did tell you that time is irrelevant for Ragnor," Ivy said. "He would have known about your plan to destroy him. All he had to do was tell your friend David when he had to be at the forest. He may well have got to the area before you did."

"When he died, he looked so…old," Elizabeth said. "David was no older than us, but he looked like he'd aged about forty years."

"Ragnor's power is both seductive and highly destructive," Ivy said sadly. "That's why I wanted you to destroy the book. You did, I hope?"

Mark nodded. "We burned it on the fire, after the lich had been destroyed. There's nothing left but ashes."

"That repellent ritual saved our lives more than once," Elizabeth said. "We owe you a lot of thanks."

"The biggest threat from Ragnor is his fear curse," Ivy said. "He had the ability to command people to fear him. Most people run away, screaming. There's nothing that can be done to fight that, other than sheer force of willpower. That you did on your own, and without your own strength of mind you would not have been able to defeat him."

"Elizabeth was amazing," Mark said. "She didn't falter once. I succumbed to the fear a couple of times, but she never did."

Ivy cast a glance at Elizabeth. "This young lady of yours is quite a force to be reckoned with. A keeper, I think is what they say nowadays. I hope you appreciate what you have in her."

"I do," Mark said, and exchanged a shy smile with Elizabeth.

"We want to thank you for the talismans, as well."

Elizabeth laid the two talismans on the table. "They really helped. Apart from everything else, they were an early warning system."

"You may keep them, if you wish," Ivy said. "I'm not sure if you want a memento of such a traumatic battle, however."

"I only wish we could have saved David," Mark said. "We'd lost so many friends to Ragnor already. Then we lost him too."

"The friend you knew was gone once Ragnor took hold of him," Ivy said. "There was no coming back from that. At least you have destroyed Ragnor, so he cannot take any more lives."

"I just feel so sad, and it seems there's no one left to mourn David other than us. His parents are both dead, and he's got no siblings. Over the last few months, he was pushing everyone away. The police have released his body for burial, but who's going to sort things out?"

"We can do it," Elizabeth said. "If there's no one else around to care, then we need to prove that we do. We should have a memorial service somewhere in London. Maybe his colleagues and the people he went to medical school with will come."

"A cremation might be best. We could scatter the ashes in the Forest of Dean," Mark said.

"Are we sure that's such a good idea?" Elizabeth said doubtfully. "We don't want another lich on our hands."

"Ragnor's power was unique, and it's been destroyed," Ivy said. "There's no more threat. But if I were you, I would avoid scattering ashes anywhere near the Circle of Power. Just in case."

"Some of my happiest memories are role playing with David in the forest," Mark said. "I like to think they were for him, too. Maybe he can find peace there." He picked up the talismans from the table.

"If you don't mind, Ivy, I think I would like to keep these after all. It's a way to remember David. The way he was before all this happened. He used to be on the lookout for things like this all the time. As props for the game."

Afternoon was creeping into dusk by the time Mark and Elizabeth left the shop. They headed back to their B&B in silence, hand in hand, Mark walking at a slower pace than usual because of his injury.

"I guess it's all over," Elizabeth said. "We can go home."

Mark watched the sun sinking over the roof tops in the distance. "It's getting late now. Let's have one more night here, and head off first thing in the morning."

"We've got a lot to do when we get home," Elizabeth said. "Sorting out the funeral arrangements, for both Linus and David. Catching up on all the work we missed while we were away."

"There's the house to sort out, too."

Elizabeth frowned at Mark. "What house?"

"Remember that conversation we had? It feels like it was ages ago now, but it was just a few days. About maybe getting a place together?"

"Oh, that. I thought that was just idle talk. You were getting twitchy about making a commitment, as I recall."

"Yes, well, when you're staring death in the face it tends to change your perspective," Mark said.

"I love you, Elizabeth. I can't stand the thought of not having you in my life, and I want to go to bed with you every night and wake up with you in the morning. Let's get a place together."

Elizabeth squeezed his hand. "Sounds good to me. What did you have in mind?"

"I think we should buy a place. If we pool the money we've both put aside, and save a bit more, we'll probably have enough for a deposit in a few months."

"Wow, a mortgage. That's a serious commitment, you know. Twenty-five years' worth. Longer than some marriages last."

"I'm not proposing to you. Not yet, anyway."

With the setting sun casting long shadows on the ground, the two of them wrapped their arms around each other and headed for their room in the B&B to enjoy one last night of peace, together, before heading back to the bustle of ordinary life. After the ordeal they had just been through, Mark was confident that whatever life held in store for them, they could face it together.

END

ABOUT THE AUTHOR

Sara Jayne Townsend was born in Hyde, UK in 1969 and spent the first ten years of her life in the North of England before emigrating to Canada with her family in 1980.

She returned to England after high school ended in 1988, and now lives in Surrey with her guitarist husband Chris and their two cats.

She writes horror and crime fiction – either way in her stories, someone dies a horrible death.

She is co-founder and chair person the T Party Writers' Group, which at its inception in 1994 was the first genre-focused writing group in London.

Sara was welcomed aboard as part of the Kensington Gore publishing family in May 2015. Her first horror story "The Whispering Death" is the first of many we hope.

Sara's website can be found at:

Http://sarajaynetownsend.weebly.com

Made in the USA
Charleston, SC
26 August 2015